PRAISE FOR JIM VAN PELT'S
THE EXPERIENCE ARCADE

"James Van Pelt's stories are the kind that make you lose track of time when you sit down to read. His characters never fail to charm, and his stories—sometimes deceptively simple—invariably seem to matter. From a story of elderly lovers to one about genius kids, from a tale of middle-aged suburban combatants to that of an AI who can cry, this volume will delight readers. It will also leave them wondering, which is what science fiction and fantasy stories should do. If you're not a Van Pelt fan yet, you will be after you read this delectable collection."
—Louise Marley, author of *The Child Goddess*

"James Van Pelt's stories capture the essential joy and boundless optimism of Golden Age science fiction better than any writer alive. *The Experience Arcade and Other Stories* contains tales of weaponized ghosts, warring lawn fairies, a poet who investigates a murder on a starship, a young Tom Corbett's secret initiation into the Solar Guard, a couple who exchange gifts after death, ghost ships, and even more wonderous things. If you love SF in all its strange wonder and constant surprises, this book is your ticket."
—John O'Neill, *Black Gate Magazine*

"Prolific, masterful, and stunningly original, James Van Pelt is a modern virtuoso of science fiction. This collection of short stories both defines the genre, and pushes it forward into newly charted territory."
—Ted Kosmatka, author of *The Flicker Men*

"When I was trying to learn enough craft to break into print, I remember looking to James Van Pelt and his crisp, powerful short fiction. Nearly two decades later and the master craftsman is still producing brilliant, beautiful work that captivates and compels. In *The Experience Acrade and Other Stories*, we get a broad view of Van Pelt's range as a speculative fantasist. If you love short fiction, it belongs on your shelf."
—Ken Scholes, author of *Lamentation*

THE
EXPERIENCE
ARCADE

AND OTHER STORIES

THE
EXPERIENCE
ARCADE
AND OTHER STORIES

JAMES
VAN PELT

FAIRWOOD PRESS
Bonney Lake, WA

THE EXPERIENCE ARCADE AND OTHER STORIES
A Fairwood Press Book
November 2017
Copyright © 2017 James Van Pelt

Fairwood Press
21528 104th Street Court East
Bonney Lake, WA 98391
www.fairwoodpress.com

Cover by Max Mitenkov
Book Design by Patrick Swenson

ISBN: 978-1-933846-69-9
First Fairwood Press Edition: November 2017
Printed in the United States of America

To Tammy who gives me space to write,
who reads the roughest of rough drafts,
and then helps me celebrate a story sale by going out to dinner.
Thank you for everything. You are my foundation.

CONTENTS

THE
EXPERIENCE
ARCADE

AND OTHER STORIES

INTRODUCTION

PATRICK SWENSON

I KNOW JAMES VAN PELT A LITTLE. OKAY, MAYBE A LOT. I knew him early on from the short stories he'd sent to me for the magazine I edited, *Talebones*. I received a story from him called "Miss Hathaway's Spider." I don't remember if it was the *first* story he sent me, but it *might* have been. He'd submitted it to a ton of markets and couldn't sell it, but he believed in the story. It just goes to show you that sometimes you need to put the right story in front of the right editor at the right time. Jim is a teacher. Whaddya know? So am I! I instantly understood what he was doing in the story, including its clever structure around Bloom's Taxonomy of the Cognitive Domain. I bought it for the Spring 1998 issue. Nine more Van Pelt stories followed, on up until 2008, a year before the magazine closed.

In 2001, I knew him well enough to know I wanted a short story collection from him. *Strangers and Beggars* came out the next year and was an ALA Best Book. My good luck is that James Van Pelt keeps coming back to Fairwood Press. Also, he is a prolific short story writer, with over 150 published stories to date. Including this new book, I've now done five collections with him. I also published two of his novels. His first, *Summer of the Apocalypse*, is my bestselling title to date. It *still* sells well, over ten years later.

In 2007, I started a writers retreat called The Rainforest Writers Village, which I host at Lake Quinault, WA, every February and March. (There are three different sessions over three weeks.) Jim has been to one of the sessions every year except the first one. While the primary activity at the retreat is *writing*, I schedule a few one-hour talks by professional writers on topics that might be of interest to the attendees. Jim has taught a lot of them over the years, and they're always well attended. (Remember I said he was a *teacher*?)

A couple years ago he said he was planning to write a story a week for a year: a challenge that Ray Bradbury had once suggested writers do if they wanted to improve their writing skills. (You'll read more about this in Jim's afterword.) He asked if he could do a talk about the entire process and the results, knowing that when the 2016 retreat started, he would have just finished his year of writing. Naturally, I said of course.

He sold a lot of those stories he wrote during that year. Thirty-five of them. That means he sold 67% of the 52 stories he wrote in one year. It's an impressive feat, to say the least. This collection includes twenty-four of those published stories. That's close to *half* of the stories he wrote in a year.

My point is: James Van Pelt can write a short story. He'll confess he learned quite a bit during that year, but he's one of our best speculative storytellers. Certainly, a writer can learn to do better. (We can *all* learn to do better at *any*thing, if we practice a lot.) He presented the talk a second time this past February, but to a different session and to a different set of writers. He talked about the process and what he learned. During this long trek, he traveled into weird country, saw peculiar dead ends, discovered hidden cities, and blazed new trails (for him). So it seemed natural that he should share what he learned during his travels into the writing process and persistent invention.

Jim and I would have done another collection, regardless of his story-a-week challenge, but now we had something unique: here was a chance to publish a collection that contained only the published stories from this year-long journey into the writing wilderness. Jim also had the idea that he should make this collection of interest to readers and writers alike. He decided to write a story note *before* the story that would be of interest to *readers* (which is pretty much all of us, isn't it?), and to write a story note at the *end* of the story that would be of interest to *writers*. (I'm also one of those, so *bonus!*)

Many years ago, Jim and I talked about putting together a writing book about plot. We would get permission to reprint some classic SF stories, and then Jim would deconstruct them and explain why they succeeded on the plot level. Stories included Robert Silverberg's "Caught in the Organ Draft," Bob Shaw's "The Light of Other Days," and many others. He would talk about plot being a metaphor. (We thought *Plot is a Metaphor* might be a great title for it. Jim mentions this idea in a story note for writers after his story "No One is So Fierce.") While this project never quite coalesced, I hope to some day talk him into bringing it to fruition. In the meantime, we have something even better: James Van Pelt's newest short stories and his fascinating insights about them.

I chose not to single out stories in this introduction. Seriously, if you've bought this book, you'll read them (in whatever order and in whatever manner you like) without me having to convince you that they're fabulous. I've read them and loved them, as I have read and loved most of his stories. I've read and published, in five collections, 98 of his 152 published stories. (If you go to his website, you'll see all of them listed there in his bibliography.) This pretty much makes me an expert on his short stories.

I know him well, so take my word for it and read a Van Pelt story—or twenty-four. Experience *The Experience Arcade*. Immerse yourself into the fireworks show, the fantastic carnival, and try your luck. But keep your pocket change handy. You'll be back for more.

A comfortable walking distance from the Rain Forest Resort Village on Lake Quinault in Washington rests a beautiful cemetery, surrounded by stately trees and lush underbrush. All cemeteries are evocative. Wandering among the stones can't help but make one thoughtful, and rural cemeteries that take on the community's personality magnify the effect. This story arose from a leisurely hike in the rain and the unexpected discovery of a Mylar balloon clinging to an old grave marker.

IN MEMORIAM

THE PINK GRANITE STONE STANDS OUT AMONG SO MANY gray markers in their long rows, catching afternoon sun and shining from the recent rain, two names carved on its face, Thomas Bramwell, 1930 – 1998, and Esther Bramwell, 1932, but no death date for her. Underneath Thomas's name, "Husband" is inscribed, and underneath Esther reads "Wife." Jammed into the ground on Thomas's side of the stone, a black iron plant holder, its solemn "J" at the top to hold a flower basket, sported a Mylar balloon instead with just enough helium in it to keep it floating, but not enough to pull the narrow ribbon that held it to its place taut. "I Love You," said the jaunty script on the pink balloon.

Cemeteries hold stories like butterflies alight on your palm. Every stone a revelation. Every flower laid on the ground, some with nothing left but stems, some as fresh as yesterday, every framed picture faded in the sun, leaning on the stone, or stuffed bear, fur weather-beaten and one eye out, tells a story, but mostly the cemetery is empty. One could sit on the solitary bench for hours on a week day and see no one. Just traffic noise from the highway over the hill, the staccato bark from a semi's air brake and the soothing hiss of wheels rolling on asphalt. Some birds too, chattering away, no doubt thankful for the rain.

The balloon twists back and forth. Thomas died seventeen years ago at 68. Esther, if the stone was to be believed, still lives and would now be 83. Maybe a son or daughter visited the grave and tied the balloon to the plant holder, but that's not the story the balloon tells. A bereaved, old woman bought the balloon at the supermarket maybe, choosing it over the superhero balloons and the happy birthday ones and the anniversary ones. She stood at the grave, alone in her thoughts, and then fastened it to her dead husband's memorial.

Graveside tokens appear as if by magic. Today, nothing. To-morrow, a huge flower arrangement. Many graves are visited, but the mourners come and leave unseen.

A Mylar balloon might float for a month. Did she come once a month? Did she live far away and made the long drive as a pilgrim-age, the balloon bouncing against the ceiling behind her?

Thomas saw Esther sitting on the Denver Public Library front lawn. Poe images had been filling his thoughts, and a morning deep in the library's stacks, pulling books on Poe scholarship had attuned his eyes to darkness and old wood cuts, beautiful black and white illustrations from "The Pit and the Pendulum" and "The Black Cat," but mostly he saw the fat king from "Hop-Frog," holding his beer mug, and the two leering cabinet ministers behind him, laughing at the belled dwarf-fool who was Hop-Frog. How Hop-Frog loved! How Hop-Frog suffered from their derision, but he stayed pure to himself and to his love for Trippetta, who like him was society's outcast.

It's a dark revenge story that ends with lovers united that swamped his vision as he made his way across the library's marble floors and the blinding June light. Thomas blinked away tears and shook his head as if struggling from Poe's embrace. Hop-Frog's world contained no flower gardens, to hear Poe tell it, and no automobiles, no shining, state capital's golden dome, and no girl, sitting on the lawn in a summer dress, leaning against a suitcase, reading a slim book.

Thomas almost staggered. He was six months from finishing his undergraduate work, and he'd already applied for graduate school. For months, he'd only thought of Poe and Ambrose Bierce and Nathaniel Hawthorne, "the dark musketeers," as he'd called them in class. He was twenty-three, but he already identified himself as a confirmed bachelor, a lone scholar, and a man of letters. He would write treatises some day. He would lecture to earnest students, perhaps at Oxford, which he imagined as filled with dark-oak studies and leather-bound tomes.

He shifted his note-heavy briefcase to his other hand as he approached the girl, delirious, lost as to why he was doing it. His shadow crossed the book, but she didn't look up. She wore scuffed saddle shoes, short, white socks. The dress, now that his eyes had cleared, sported large blue circles on white, and her light-brown hair, curled at the ends, almost touched her shoulders.

"What are you reading?" he said, at a loss for anything else. His voice sounded harsh to him, as dry and dusty as old bookshelves.

She looked up. For the first time he saw her face, and whenever he saw it again for the next fifty-five years, when he saw it on his deathbed, this was the face he saw, a smiling, June-filled complexion whose eyes shone the deep, dark blue of raven wings sheening in the sun.

"It's Tamerlane," she said.

"Edgar Allan Poe?"

She smiled anew, and so he was wed at that moment.

Cemeteries look empty, but they have visitors, quiet people who check the register for a name, like Ziegler, block C, row 3, site 5, or returnees who come on a schedule every weekend or once a month or once a year who know their way around. Some people like to walk the cemetery, and occasionally a jogger will bounce through, all life and motion and beating heart. But there's evidence of others too who must slip over the wrought-iron fence after the gates are locked. Beer cans strewn across the graves, or empty liquor bottles. Sometimes hypodermics. Candles. Condoms. Once a glow-in-the-dark Frisbee. A jacket. Fast food wrappers. A paperback book.

The cemetery has an equipment shed. It used to house a backhoe, but that work is contracted out to Bill Wynn, who supplements his farm income by digging graves. The shed holds cement grave liners, lowering straps, plywood grave covers, shovels, two jackhammers for the frequent rocks that stop the digging, an air compressor, pry bars, coffin rollers, folding chairs, two podiums, a riding lawnmower, a small tractor, grass trimmers, fertilizer bags and grass seed, flower seed, and Astroturf blankets to throw over the excavated dirt.

The shed is a comfortable place in the summer with the double doors open. Shady, cool, smelling of motor oil and dirt.

From here, mourners are visible, walking onto the grounds, real or artificial floral arrangements in hand. Families trekking solemnly to their departed. Little ones, too young to stay still, running across the graves. Mothers yelling at them to be respectable.

Part of the grounds keeper's job is to tidy up. When the plastic flowers have faded from exposure. When the toy car has rusted. When the stuffed animal has rotted out, they are gathered into trash bags. The policy is that "temporary memorials" or "memory tokens" can stay for up to six weeks, then into the bag they go.

Thomas carried the blanket. A picnic basket dangled from Esther's hand.

"Poe didn't love death," said Thomas. He waved at the tombstones, which cast long shapes in the setting sun. "He hated it. His mother died too young. His wife died too young. He lived in the 1800s, where death often came too soon."

Esther nodded. She'd become used to Thomas's impromptu lectures since they met a year earlier. "He seemed fascinated with it, though."

Thomas grunted. They'd reached their favorite tree at the back of the cemetery. Here the ground rose, the stones like small boats floating on a swelling, grass wave hill. Beyond the crest, the cemetery ended in a bluff overlooking the river. Graves lined the hilltop. The two lovers stood among them and looked out on the river.

"What a lovely place to rest," Esther said. "A grave with a view."

They spread the blanket. Esther unpacked the sandwiches and wine. Sitting as they were, the nearby stones hid them from sight, as private as a bedroom. The Grouchers, the Clays, the Fisks, and the Van Houts. Travis Groucher, the family patriarch, had the largest stone, a mammoth, black slab with the somber verse on the back,

> Remember me as you pass by,
> As you are now, so once was I,
> As I am now, so you will be,
> Prepare for death and follow me.

Thomas uncorked the wine. "There was this apocryphal story about Poe's youth that a young woman died and was buried. A week later, they had to exhume the body—I don't know why—but when they did, they found the fabric in the casket had been shredded. The woman's fingernails were torn off. She'd stuffed her fingers into her throat. Clearly, she had been buried alive. They say Poe's obsession with being buried alive came from that incident. The story might not be true, but in the early 1800s people became fascinated with premature burial. Companies offered a 'safety casket' with a rope in it attached to a bell on the tombstone. That way if you woke after being buried, you could pull the rope. People would hear and then save you."

"Ask not for whom the bell tolls," said Esther.

"It's a great idea, the message from below."

After they ate and drank most of the wine, the wind came up off the river, swept between the stones, chilling them. She gave him his birthday present, cufflinks shaped like ravens. Laughing, they lay on the blanket. Thomas grabbed an edge, then rolled over Esther. They rolled two more times until they were bound in the blanket, face to face, as tight as a pair of bundled babies. They kissed, the heat building between them, until they didn't care about the breeze anymore, or the grave markers. Esther slid her hand around his hip until she held him, sweat on her brow, her breath tight in her throat.

"I can't . . . move," gasped Thomas. He unrolled them as they both laughed and panted, unclothed each other beneath the blanket, but there were gaps and holes, and now the cooling evening breeze could reach them, but they didn't care.

They didn't care.

They didn't care.

People talk about ghosts and hauntings. "Don't you ever get the creeps out there," they ask, "when you are alone at night?"

"I couldn't do it," say others. "Not even on a bet. I'm not superstitious . . ." they always say, ". . . but still."

At night the cemetery is just a quiet park. The riding lawnmower's lights paint the grounds with sharp shadows. The mower roars irreverently, throwing grass into the catcher. The evening smells sweet from the distant river and the fresh cuttings. In the silence when the clippings are put into the composter, crickets chirp. A frog croaks somewhere. Bats squeak as they circle the one light post, snatching up bugs.

It's peaceful, not spooky. If there are ghosts, they walk secretly. They bother no one.

When there is noise, it's almost always something human. Someone trespassing. The shed holds flashlights too, big ones, so that it's safe to search for intruders.

A bear, once, came through. The flashlight caught him first, a great shape behind the stones. A grunt. A huff, like a furry demon. At first, the flashlight shook. Was this the supernatural ascending? Had hell opened up and brought a creature forth? It shambled a few feet, then stood still, an unrecognizable shape in the darkness. A gleam might have been an eye, but indescribable, not familiar. For a moment, all the fears others voiced about a night in the cemetery arose. "What if the dead can walk?" they'd say. "Surely the weight of so much death must have an incarnation, a coming into flesh. Surely, centuries of stories about spirits and hauntings must have a truthful thread within them. All séances could not be faked. All mediums could not be charlatans. Not all."

And for a moment, rationality fled. The world became much stranger, much broader, and way, way more interesting, until, at last, the bear stood, and in standing, reduced in stature. It was just an ordinary black bear. A single yell, and the bear fled the grounds. Peace reigned. Steady hands locked the shed that night, not quivering ones.

A cemetery's silence is of the mundane sort. Nothing seeps from a crypt. No rattling chains. No moans that are not the wind. No bones clattering against bones. What lies below stays below.

An ailing Thomas said to his aging wife, "I never got to Oxford."

They sat on a blanket beneath the tree at the top of the cemetery's hill as they had every Sunday for forty-four years. He looked much older than her. His dark hair grown gray and thin, deep lines in his face, skin sagging from his neck. He thought she still glowed, and when he turned to look at her, she surprised him as she always did with her presence, and that she was with him.

"England's a humid, foggy place. You wouldn't have liked it," she said.

He laughed, which turned into an extended coughing bout. When he stopped, it took a minute to get his breath. "I could have taught 'The Fall of the House of Usher.' I could have connected it for them, the premature burials, Virginia Poe, undying love, 'Annabel Lee,' and 'The Tell-Tale Heart.' I would have talked about the dark romantics. I always wanted to visit Oxford. I can see it. The spires, the halls, nine-hundred years of scholarship."

They held hands on the blanket. The late afternoon sun warmed their faces.

"Poe died when he was forty, two years after his wife. I've contemplated those two years. What was he thinking? He visited her grave often. Poe had a friend who reported Poe would even come to her grave during winter nights and stay with her until he nearly froze. When he stood there, did he leave flowers? Did he hope to see a sign from her?" Thomas closed his eyes against the sun. His chest felt heavy, but he loved sitting on the lawn. He loved Esther's hand beneath his own.

Esther's breath caught in her throat. Thomas asked questions. That was his life: asking questions and trying to answer them. Eternally curious. Always peeling back the mysteries.

Esther said, "They had so little time together. They were so young."

A cloud moving across the horizon, darkened the cemetery, cooled their faces. Esther shivered.

"I couldn't do it," said Thomas. "I couldn't live without you."

His breath rattled. His hand trembled on hers. Was it the cold? Was it fear?

Esther said, "You won't have to. We'll be forever."

They ordered the pink granite tombstone on Monday.

Work at the cemetery is rhythmic. After eleven years, the repetitions feel ingrained. In late April, after the last, deep frost, sprinkler heads need inspection. Broken ones require repair or replacement. Roses want early spring pruning. Soon, there is fertilizing. Summer has its chores. So does fall and winter. Monthly chores exist too, as do weekly ones. Every day, the gates open, the grounds are inspected. Who is to be buried this week? Which plot needs to be prepared? What setup will the grave-side service require?

Tending a cemetery demands discipline, a devotion to quality, and a reverent sense. Every stone reminds that lives end. Dates bind them. Epitaphs describe them. "No pain, no grief, no anxious fear can reach our loved one sleeping here," or "Dust thou art, to dust returnest, was not spoken of the soul."

There is no epitaph on Thomas Bramwell's marker, no brave little verse. His stone contains no hint of the man, but the twisting balloon, the partially inflated Mylar with its "I Love You" speaks eloquently. It's easy to stop work in the cemetery, holding a black trash bag filled with dead flowers and rain-soaked cards, their messages lost in moldy paper. The ribbon detaches easily from the iron bar, and the balloon deflates with almost no pressure. It joins the other memory tokens in the bag.

"Thank you for leaving it up so long," says the voice behind.

She's surprisingly slim and upright for an eighty-three year old. Hair that's gone white. A summer dress. Saddle shoes. She holds an empty wine bottle. "I finished this last night, thinking about him," she said. "I thought I would leave it. Flowers are so clichéd, don't you think?"

It's embarrassing to be caught graveside, throwing away another person's expression of grief. There's nothing to be said.

She crouches, leans the bottle against the stone, then runs her hands over the grass as if searching. "We always leave each other something," she says. "Until I join him, it's what we have, these little exchanges."

She sighs. "Ahh," and stands. She turns, holds what she found on her palm. "It was his birthday present," she says. Two silver cufflinks, crusted with dirt, catch the sunlight. They are shaped like ravens.

The question is hard to force; it's so ridiculous, but she said "exchanges." What did that mean?

"Was he buried with them?"

She nodds. "Last month he gave me his watch. I wish I had buried him with notecards and a pen. He could write."

She laughs. "That's silly though, isn't it? It would be asking too much."

The woman puts the cufflinks in a pocket, then lays her hand atop the stone. "Until next month, Thomas. We are forever."

There are chores to be done. The grounds are huge. Maintaining them requires constant movement, but time stops in the enormity. She left remembrances for him in death, but he . . . but he . . . it is too hard to grasp, leaves tokens to her *from* death. The old woman raises her face, eyes closed so the sun is full upon it. "I thought to put an epitaph on the stone. I liked, 'If there is another world, he lives in bliss If not another, he made the most of this,' but we have no need for final words, Thomas and I, no need at all."

She walks away, steady in her stride. A taxi waits at the iron gate. Across the cemetery are other communiqués: flowers, balloons, photographs, more than one liquor bottle like the one leaning against Thomas's stone, toys. Someone left a putter and sleeve of Titleist balls on the grass two graves down.

Eventually they will go into the trash bag, the gifts in memoriam. But each tells a story. Each speaks in a voice of the living and dead. Each talks, and the conversation goes on.

Who is to say the story ever ends?

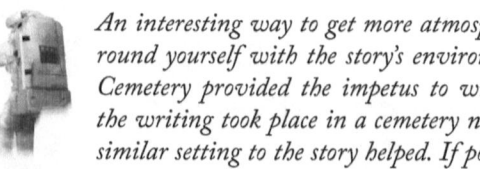 *An interesting way to get more atmosphere into a story is to surround yourself with the story's environment. The Lake Quinault Cemetery provided the impetus to write this piece, but most of the writing took place in a cemetery near my house. Writing in a similar setting to the story helped. If possible, try finding a setting similar to the story you are working on, then go there to write. See if it makes a difference.*

The nine Tom Corbett books appeared from 1952 to 1956. Like the Bobbsey Twins, the Hardy Boys, and Nancy Drew, they were written under a pen name by a variety of authors. For an adult reader, the plots are clunky and uneven, the prose is forgettable, and the characters are stereotypes. The Tom Corbett books never measured up to their much stronger progenitor, Robert Heinlein's Space Cadet, *but a ten-year-old doesn't read like an adult. The young readers who discovered science fiction through Tom Corbett and grew to love it probably still wish they could join the Space Academy and become members of the Solar Guard.*

THE CONTINUING SAGA
OF TOM CORBETT:
SPACE CADET

T OM'S NAME WAS HER CURSE. SHE STARTED WITH Tomiko, but by the time she was four, everyone in her family called her Tom, and once that stuck, her grandfather made a joke: "Tom Corbett, eh? How's the Space Academy? Are you going to be in the Solar Guard this year?" Or "Have they let you drive Polaris yet? How's your buddies, Astro and Roger Manning doing?" He was relentless.

It was irritating until she turned ten, found out who this "Tom Corbett" person was, and then took her birthday money to the used bookstore where she found copies of *Stand by for Mars* and *Treachery in Outer Space*. From there, she discovered Tom Corbett videos on the Internet, Tom Corbett comics, and Tom Corbett View-Master discs, which meant that she had to buy a View-Master in the toy store. For the sixth grade Halloween party, she made her own Solar Guard uniform and wore it every day until Christmas.

Of course, the other kids started calling her "Space Cadet," which they didn't mean in a good way at all.

By the time she was a freshman in high school last year, "Space

Cadet" was a label. She put the Tom Corbett books away. She took the "Space Academy" badge off her shirts, but it didn't matter. The nickname stuck. Some of the kids called her SC, which rhymed with "Jesse" without the "J." Some of the teachers too, who didn't even know where the name came from, called her that, even though she carefully printed her full name, Tomiko Corbett, on every piece of homework. For most people, she was Tom, Tom Corbett: space cadet.

She had taken the Solar Guard medallions off her shirts, but she couldn't take them out of her heart. Tom sat at her desk that faced her bedroom window. Her house topped a hill with open country on all sides. Her parents bought here when they thought a subdivision was going to spring up around them, but so far they were the only house. Outside, in the dark, with no trees or obstructing buildings, she had an unencumbered night view, straight east. Leo Minor nearly touched the horizon. The bright light by its mouth was Jupiter. She knew star names: Regulus, Algieba, Procyon, Pollux, and Alhena. She wondered what it would be like to be an astrogator, or to sit in the pilot's seat on the control deck. She'd toggle the intercom. "All stations report," she'd say. "All clear on the radar deck," a voice would answer, and then another, "All clear on the power deck."

She'd be in command, the control panels displayed in front of her, the power to take off to the stars underneath her hands. Tom looked at her own hands, resting on the keyboard at her desk. If only she could press the right buttons. Her bedroom window could be the control deck view panel. The stars would rush toward her. She would look up slightly, chin thrust forward, a picture of confidence and adventure for all who could see.

Tomika got up from her desk, cracked the bedroom door open. The hallway and living room were dark. Her parents had gone to bed. Good. Their room was on the other end of the house. They slept with their door shut and a fan going. When they were asleep, she could be as loud as she wanted. She shut the door, snapped off her lights, turned up the sound on the computer's speakers, and then clicked the icon on the screen. The rumble started in the background very low, almost subliminal. Tom leaned back in her chair, looking out the window, trying not to see the drapes hanging on each side. She just wanted stars as the rumble sound grew and grew. It was rocket engine noise, building, and there were electronic sounds in the background. Doors irising open or closed maybe? Blasters? Emergency klaxons? And then the engines cut out, and were replaced by footsteps on metal decks. Distant orders being shouted out. The ping from ranging equipment.

Tom strained to hear, but the voices were always indistinct. Occasionally, she'd make out a word, "Asteroid," "Orbit," "Translunar," but never an entire sentence. She'd set the sound clip to replay. The entire audio was almost ninety-minutes long. Most nights, she'd fall asleep with it playing before the engine noise started again, but tonight, it replayed five times. The sun rose directly in her window as she watched.

She turned the sound off. The rising sun filled the room with warmth. She thought, if I close my eyes now, I can get a half hour of sleep before Mom tells me to get ready for school.

At breakfast, Mom, a slight, slender woman with long black hair, and Dad, whose hair was brown and curly, talked about real-estate values. They'd been looking at houses on the north side of town that they could buy, refurbish cheaply, and then sell for a huge profit. Dad thumbed through the obituaries in the newspaper.

"Here's one," he said. "The guy was ninety-four. It says his family lives in Chicago."

Mom nodded, a coffee cup in one hand and her tablet in the other. She swiped at her screen methodically. Tom wasn't sure what Mom was looking at. She said, "We could give 'em a lowball offer. Out-of-towners won't know the market, and they'd probably be glad to unload the house. I'll drive by this morning and put a flyer in their mailbox."

While Tom finished her cereal, her parents talked about discount carpets and how a cheap, new carpet in an old home could return the purchase price by one hundred and fifty percent. "Fresh paint and new carpet covers a multitude of sins," said Dad.

They left together for work before Tom had to start her walk to the bus stop. She realized as she headed out the door that neither one had spoken a single word to her, but that was pretty normal.

At every stop, more elementary and junior high kids crowded onto the bus. Most high schoolers drove themselves or went with their friends. In high school, only losers took the bus, but Tom didn't mind. She gave up her seat to two fourth-grade girls who liked to sit together, and then walked down the aisle looking for an empty place. The only spot was next to Jacob Rose, another sophomore, who everyone called "Jacob the Hut," because he was huge, the biggest kid Tom had ever seen. If it weren't for Jacob, Tom would be the best mathematician in the tenth grade, but it didn't earn Jacob any friends. Jacob covered much of the seat. He scrunched next to the window to give Tom more room.

"Sorry," said Jacob in his deep voice. He held a book on his stomach, his finger marking a spot.

"What 'cha reading?"

"You'll think it's boring."

Tom settled into the seat. She braced her knees on the chair in front of her. "Try me."

Jacob shrugged. "Ok. It's *Atoms to Andromeda : Selected Lectures on Theoretical Physics, High-Energy Nuclear and Cosmic Ray Research, Plasma and Thermonuclear Physics, Astronomy, Astrophysics and Electronic Computing.'"

When Jacob opened the book to continue reading, Tom could see pages filled with tiny print and math formulas. "Is there a graphic novel version?" she said.

Jacob glanced up, surprised, as if he'd already forgot she was there. The bus lurched into motion. Kids yelled back and forth. A ball of paper flew past them. It was a typical day. "Do you play *Destination Ceres?*" he asked.

Tom knew the game, a third-person PC shooter set on fantasti-
cal versions of Mars, Venus and Ceres. The science in it was terrible.

"Do you?" she said.

"No, not really. But I like to wander around in the game. The
worlds are beautiful." He looked at the kids on the bus. "I don't
think I belong here."

Tom nodded. "I know just what you mean."

When they got to the school, Tom watched Jacob walking de-
liberately down the middle of the sidewalk. Kids ran around him as
if he were a moving island.

She thought he had a kind of dignity in his steady pace.

Tom dreaded English. Last year, in the junior high, she'd turned
in a book report on *Stand by for Mars*, the first book in the Space
Cadet series. The assignment had been, "Choose an influential book
that you read in elementary school, and explain its impact on you."
Tom wrote how the book made her check out astronomy texts and
encouraged her interest in rockets. Ms. Schneider, a second-year
teacher, scheduled a private meeting with Tom after she turned it
in.

"I'm concerned about your choice of reading. I don't think a
young, twenty-first century woman should be interested in this sort
of book," said Schneider to open their conversation. "It's terribly
sexist. You could select much more appropriate literature."

Tom didn't have a chance to reply.

"Look at this quote," said Schneider. She had a faded copy
marked with several sticky notes between the pages. "Here, Corbett
and his friends, Astro and Roger Manning have gone to Crystal
City. They are trying to book a room at the hotel, and Manning
treats the clerk, who is a woman, of course, like a prize. He even
says, 'What's the matter with beautiful girls? They're official equipment, like a radar scanner. You can't get along without them!' What
sort of universe is this? Women are always 'cute' or 'pretty' or they
get whistled at. Where are the women who are cadets or command-
ers?"

Schneider snorted derisively. "Terrible. Here, I think you should read this." She handed Tom a copy of *Girls Who Looked Under Rocks: The Lives of Six Pioneering Naturalists*. "I think this has much better role models for you."

Tom took the book. "Does it have rocket ships?"

"Phallic tripe," muttered Schneider.

Tom was pretty sure that the comment wasn't directed at her, but if Ms. Schneider didn't think that Tom knew what "phallic" meant, then she was underestimating her.

Tom read the book. It wasn't terrible, but the next book she read was *The Rocket Robot*, which was the third time for that title. She paid closer attention to Tom Corbett's world. Schneider was right about the story being all about the men, but that wasn't how Tom read it. In her mind, the characters weren't about being boys or girls. They were about having adventures, and anyone could have those. She wanted to read about going to space, and if she had to do it with male pronouns, so be it. When she read, she boarded the ship. She gave the commands. She looked out the port to see the curve of a new planet.

Today Ms. Schneider gave the class a fill-in-the-blank quiz. The first sentence was, "If a doctor gives you advice, you should listen to what _____ says." The second question was "If a kindergarten teacher is speaking, the class should pay attention to _____."

Most of the class filled in the first blank with "he" and the second blank with "her," which Schneider used to springboard into the unconscious sexist assumptions in the society. Tom's answers were "the professional" and "the alien in the corner." She didn't share that with Schneider.

After school, Tom didn't ride the bus. The land behind the school was undeveloped. It rose to a treeless, flat-topped hill, littered with nearly-white limestone on dark soil. Almost no vegetation. For the last month, Tom had been climbing the hill to work on her project. She dropped her backpack, picked up a pair of melon-sized stones, and then added them to the thirty-foot tall letters she had been forming. The perspective was wrong for her to get a proper look at what she was writing, but if her plans were right, from directly above, the message read "TAKE ME WITH YOU."

Mom and Dad were at the kitchen table arguing about landscaping when Tom walked in the front door. Open Chinese takeout boxes surrounded their briefcases. Dad said, "Fewer plants and *newer* plants show better from the street. I say we rip out the hedges, lay down a nice, colored gravel, and plant a couple of roses. It cleans up the look, and the buyers will see possibilities."

Mom shook her head. "Too expensive and too much work. We get a gardening service to tidy up the bushes, and the house says 'I'm already beautiful' to buyers. No one gets into a house so they can spend their weekends putting in plants. Not in that neighborhood."

Tom put her backpack on the counter behind them, poured a glass of milk and grabbed a handful of cookies. "I'm home," she said.

Dad said, "A little extra investment at the beginning pays off big later. Curb appeal is everything."

"Lookiloos don't sign contracts. They don't even go inside the home. Mature landscaping is the right answer for this house."

"I'm thinking of starting a terrorist cell," said Tom. "We'll call ourselves The High School Freedom Front. I might get a tattoo."

Dad glanced her direction, nodded curtly, then turned to Mom. "Newness generates interest. Old bushes say worn out property. We've had this discussion before."

"Yes, we have. When you come to your senses, I'll be in the office faxing today's documents to the bank." Mom snapped her briefcase closed and stomped out of the kitchen.

Dad said, "Have you been home long?"

"Hours."

"There's some Moo Goo Gai Pan and rice in the fridge if you'd like some."

She held up the cookies. "I'm good," but he'd already turned away to study a thick sheaf of papers.

Back in her room, Tom opened her notebook that she'd titled "Ways to Get Off the Planet." She'd labeled sections: Rocket Engines, Ramjets, Ground-based Laser/Microwave, Space Elevator, Project Orion (nuclear bombs), Alcubierre Drive (warp drive), Piggyback Jets, Rocket Sled Launch, High Altitude Blimp Launch, Verne Gun, Launch Loop, and Cavorite.

She'd also designed capsules using empty gas station storage tanks, train tanker cars, heavy culverts with end caps welded on, and a host of others. Based on her figuring, there was no practical way she could make a capsule capable of maintaining an atmosphere when there was a vacuum on the outside from wood, ceramic, plastic or concrete. Lately, she'd been collecting articles on 3D printers. If she had a large enough printer, she should be able to make a spaceship!

And, of course, nothing she'd put into her notebook could be built in the back yard.

She added the title of Jacob's book to her "To be Read" list. It was too long to remember, but she found it online from just the first three words: Atoms to Andromeda.

Tom opened her webpage that she'd been building for the last year. It was basic HTML (she did the coding herself in a plain text program). The page's title was SOLAR GUARD APPLICATION. Under that, she'd created what looked like a job application form. She modeled it on the college application forms they kept in the counselors' office. In it, she'd entered all her grades since 3rd grade (straight A), and included descriptions of what she'd learned in math and science. She had a section with the books she'd read, and her thoughts on them, several personal essays about what service in the Solar Guard would mean to her and why she should be chosen.

At the bottom, was an e-mail address that she'd set up just for the website. Although she'd never linked to the site anywhere, she received occasional e-mails. Some were fun, like "Is this for real?

Can I join?" Some were mean. "Get a life," or "This is stupid." And some were creepy, like "Are you really a girl? Show me your boobies."

But how else was she going to contact the Solar Guard? She'd sent Morse code messages out her window with a huge flashlight, and tried the same trick with a home-built laser. She'd taken apart an old DVD burner for the laser diode and followed instructions from the Internet. The beam was surprisingly powerful. It could burn a hole in dark paper. The most expensive part of the project were the safety goggles. She'd also sent signals through a walkie-talkie she'd found in the garage, which only managed to piss off a nearby construction crew who were using the same wave length, and then she'd built her own radio transmitter and receiver. She picked up static, distant stations in foreign languages, police and fire calls, and at certain wavelengths, the beeps, pings and pulses from satellites. She liked those best.

She scrolled to her web page e-mail. Three new messages. One read, "I thought this site was about solar panels. LOL." The second one said, "I'd rather be an officer on the *Enterprise* in the United Federation of Planets." And the third said, "We are looking for a recruit. Watch the skies."

If only, she thought. But she stayed up until the horizon lightened in the east, watching the skies.

At breakfast, Mom said, "Your dad and I will be attending a week-long realtors convention in Atlanta, starting this afternoon. I've left $40 on the mantle, when you need to buy anything, and you can call us if there's a problem. If we don't answer, it's because we're listening to one of the presentations, so leave a message."

Dad was coming down the stairs with two huge suitcases when Tom left through the front door.

She rode the bus with her eyes closed, next to a third grader with a SpongeBob Square Pants lunch box. Kids shouting blended into a white noise background. The swaying and bumps lulled her into near sleep. She wasn't dreaming, but her imagination ran free.

She stood before an entrance committee for the Solar Patrol, four officers with serious expressions. They argued among themselves. The one on the far left said, "Why take an Earthling, especially an American one? They've abandoned their manned space program. A few robot probes don't show a national commitment. We should be looking at Chinese recruits."

"Just because the country doesn't seem space-bound doesn't mean that we can't find a qualified candidate among them. Look at what this one has accomplished."

The first officer to speak said, "That's true. She has shown both aptitude and desire."

"We should test her further," said the officer on the other end.

"Yes, let's."

Something in the tenor of the background noise changed, and Tom realized she was still riding to school. Reluctantly, she watched the admissions committee fade away, and she was back in the bus, surrounded by noise.

She opened her eyes. A dozen kids sitting in front of her were looking over the backs of their seats. Tom thought at first they were looking at her, but a deep voice shouting incoherently behind her made her look back too.

Four boys were out of their seats, two in the aisle, two kneeling on a seat so they faced the bench behind them. Their open hands rose and fell, and the boys were laughing. Jacob cringed under their blows, his arms up, covering his face.

"Take it!" yelled one of the boys as his hand came down on the top of Jacob's unprotected head.

Smack. Smack. Smack. It was the laughing that infuriated Tom most. They weren't just hurting Jacob, they were mocking him. Some kids in the back of the bus chanted, "Fight! Fight! Fight!" but no one tried to stop the beating.

Tom looked to her right. The third grade girl was watching like everyone else. Tom grabbed her metal SpongeBob Square Pants lunchbox. It had a nice heft to it. Probably a thermos of milk inside beside a sandwich.

She slung it overhand at the nearest boy.

It was a lucky shot, but the results were spectacular. The box whacked solidly into the back of the head of one of the kneeling boys, popping open in an explosion of potato chips. At the same time, the bus suddenly slowed, throwing everyone forward.

"Hey!" yelled the bus driver, "what is going on back there? You kids get into your seats."

Three of the boys, still laughing, sat in nearby benches. One said, "That was a real bitch slapping. Did you video it?"

"No, doofus. How am I going to shoot it if I'm bitch slapping too?"

"Did you call me a doofus? A doofus? How old are you?" and they both laughed even louder.

The boy Tom had hit wasn't laughing. He had laced his fingers together over the back of his head, while eyeing the front of the bus balefully. Tom made sure not to catch his gaze. She was sure if he saw her grinning, he'd know that she'd thrown it.

Jacob sat with his head down. He rubbed a coat sleeve under his eyes. Tom picked up her books and sat next to him.

"Go away," he said.

Tom didn't move. "Are you all right?"

"Go away."

"No."

The bus made the turn toward the school after picking up the last kids. They were a mile from the building.

"They're just stupid bastards, you know," said Tom.

The boy sitting in front of them who'd been hit with the lunchbox, said to no one in particular, "I think I have a concussion or an infarction."

Someone nearby said, "Infarction isn't even a word. You're brain scrambled."

Jacob looked up, his cheeks bright red. At least a couple of the slaps had got through his arms. "We're surrounded by idiots."

"I'll grant you that," said Tom.

"And what kind of idiot lets idiots beat him up?" Jacob said bitterly.

"The kind of idiot who understands abstract algebra and differential equations in the 10th grade. You'll be buying and selling the likes of them before you're twenty-five. They're going to be sweeping the hallway outside your office so they can earn enough money to buy the inventions you're going to come up with."

Tom looked at him, his eyes bloodshot, his cheeks wet. "If I live that long. This is a bad place. I don't belong." He turned to the window and didn't speak for the rest of the drive. Tom wanted to do something, but even putting her hand on his shoulder felt patronizing. He was right. What kind of world did she live in where people could be so . . . horrible? If she could get away, she would, to a place where nobility was recognized, where the brave succeeded, and medals were earned. She needed to be in the Space Academy. She thought for a moment that she didn't have to go to school. Her parents were gone. She could walk home. For the rest of the day, she could reread the Tom Corbett books, do research on space flight, think about Mars and Venus and the places in deep space that had yet to be discovered. She could stay home all week if she wanted. The temptation was intense.

But when they got to the school, Tom shuffled down the aisle with the handful of high schoolers. She was taller than most.

As Tom stepped through the door, the third grader she'd been sitting beside exclaimed, "Someone stole my lunch!"

That night, Tom opened her bedroom window, turned her rocket noise clip as loud as the speakers could go without distortion. The night was particularly warm and clear, so clouds didn't reflect city lights. Every star shone like a diamond point. She pushed the desk out of the way so she could sit right at the window and see the most sky. But Tom hadn't slept much the last two nights, so she put her head back against her chair, closed her eyes, and let the ship sounds sweep over her. A subsonic rumble filled the background. She imagined the mighty engines throwing them forward, ever faster through space.

A life on a ship is one filled with purpose. Everyone has a job, and the destination is clear. Not like her life where she didn't know where she was going, where she didn't know her job. On a ship in the Solar Patrol, everyone belonged to the team. Each had a responsibility and purpose. She longed for clarity, for a mission.

Footsteps went by her on a metal corridor floor. A conversation rose and fell. Metal locks clinked open. Pneumatic pistons released pressure. Pumps engaged. She loved being on the ship. Gradually, she slipped into a dreamlike state. The Solar Guard committee sat before her again. "Tomika," said the first officer, "after much discussion, we have approved your application for admission into Space Academy. We can only take one from your planet, and you have been chosen."

Tom tried to contain her joy, but a smile spread through her anyway. "I'll do my best," she said.

The second officer said, "We know that. Your passion, your strength in math and science, and your drive to succeed won us over. We don't think you belong here. There's a place for you, if you earn it, among the stars."

She nearly leapt from her seat—she pictured herself throwing a handful of clothes in a bag, writing her parents a quick note, and then leaving, really leaving—but a thought stopped her. "You can only take one?"

"We don't have to take even that," said the first officer. "Sadly there are many years when we don't find a suitable candidate at all."

Tom swallowed hard. "I . . . shouldn't be the one, then. I know a better person. He's way stronger in math. A genius I think. His name is Jacob Rose. You should take him."

The first officer frowned, turned to the second one. The other two leaned in to the discussion. They murmured for several minutes.

The second officer addressed her. "We have Jacob Rose on our short list. His qualifications are known to us. You would give up your place and have him attend the academy instead? We won't offer this opportunity again."

She could see the stars glittering like a million promises behind them. What would it be like to be in the academy, studying with purpose, a future filled with service and adventure in front of her? What would it be like to climb the stairs to her own starship for the first time? "Up ship," she'd bark into the intercom. Deep in the ship's bowels, her power deck officer would reply, "Aye, aye," and the metal around her would come alive, quivering with the power that would send them out and out.

Tom felt the control buttons beneath her fingers. She smelled ship air. Everything, all of it, so real and only a breath away.

"Yes, you should take Jacob. He is better qualified."

The first officer shrugged with resignation. "We will consider your suggestion."

The committee faded, and when Tom opened her eyes, the rising sun sat on the horizon through her open window. She shivered in the morning breeze, and she realized her cheeks were wet.

She moved through her Tuesday listlessly. It was only a dream, she thought, but loss still weighed on her, like a real opportunity had passed. On Wednesday, a note from administration called her from her first hour class. She sat outside the vice principal's office with three other students. One by one they were called in. Tom went last. A stranger in a business suit and tie sat next to the vice principal. "This is Detective Tasker. He has some questions for you . . ." he glanced at a list on his desk, "Tomika."

The detective, a young man with a skinny, black moustache, asked her about Jacob. When did she see him last? Did he seem depressed? Had he said anything odd to her lately?

She told him about the slapping incident on the bus Monday. She didn't tell him about the lunchbox. The detective frowned as he wrote the information down. "This doesn't sound good," he said.

The vice principal looked concerned. "You should have reported this to us immediately, young lady. You know we have zero tolerance for bullying. We have other students to interview, but I will talk to you about your responsibility when the current situation blows over."

"What's the current situation?" asked Tom.

"Oh . . . I thought you knew. Jacob Rose is missing. He's been gone since sometime Monday night."

The detective gave her a card. "Call me if he contacts you, or you think of anything that might help us find him."

Some kids talked about Jacob during the day, but his absence didn't seem to affect anyone else. Tom, though, felt lighter. The dullness from yesterday faded some. She put her hand up in class more often. She chatted with the kids around her. Where was Jacob? The vice-principal seemed to think that he had run away, or maybe hurt himself, but Tom dared to hope differently. Jacob had said, "I don't think I belong here."

She imagined Jacob waking in the middle of the night. "We have an opportunity for you," the first officer might say. And Jacob, as smart as he was, would go with them. They would take him into space because he was the best candidate.

The thought made her happy. If it was true, that is, if Jacob was gone and safe.

That night, she sat at her window again, her room silent. The stars flickered just as bright, but they seemed impossibly remote now. She thought about Santa Claus and the Easter Bunny and the Tooth Fairy, the fantasies of her childhood, and she knew that Tom Corbett and the Space Cadets would fade into her past too. For now, the thought that Jacob had joined the impossible Solar Guard buoyed her, but what if it was true? She'd never know. If it was true, she'd given away her one chance.

Maybe she would sell real-estate, like her parents. She flinched just thinking about it.

Still, for the moment, the stars were beautiful. The impossibly remote night sky spread out like myths made real, a visible reminder of possibility. No world could remain mundane when every night the universe could unfold like this before her.

And high in the sky above the Pleiades, a star unhooked itself from the background. She thought at first that it might be a satellite, but it grew brighter and brighter, until it was no longer a star. It was a flame descending, and then she could hear it like a hum at first, but soon a roaring that shook the house and vibrated in her chest.

The ship landed, a needle balanced on end. A door opened in its side. A ramp extended from it to the ground. A tall figure emerged. Illuminated from the light within the ship, Tom recognized the first officer's uniform, and soon the officer stood outside her window. "Are you coming?" the officer asked.

"You said you could only take one. Didn't Jacob go with you?"

Standing on the lawn, only a few feet from her, the officer nodded. "The committee talked about you, Tomika. We decided that a candidate who would sacrifice her dream to save someone else is exactly the kind of person the Solar Guard should recruit."

"Yes, of course." Tomika could hardly breathe.

A meteor streaked across the blackness. Tomika saw it as she ran toward the ship. The light left a trail that glowed like a sign, an arrow, like a long invitation. She dashed up the ramp, glad beyond hope, her heart throbbing like a rocket engine's pulse.

Inspiration comes from so many sources. A bit of overheard dialogue in a cafe, a poorly recalled memory of an old movie, or the fading images of a dream. Inspiration comes from anywhere. Of all the sources of inspiration, though, the easiest to access is autobiography. Some people call autobiography the low-hanging fruit of inspiration. That doesn't make it easy to write from, though. Unless the writer is writing autobiography directly, the source material will be transformed and repurposed. Somehow it has to take on its own sense beyond simple reminiscence. A story might start with the writer fondly thinking about a series of books he read as a child, but by the end a very different child climbs aboard a spaceship, her hopes come true.

Google "ceramic lawn fairies." Are you back? Isn't that a strange and wonderful world for people who want their gardens to be more whimsical than prosaic? One of humanity's great joys is that people can pursue their obsessions. One or our greatest challenges is when our obsessions conflict with someone else's.

THE LAWN FAIRY WAR

RACE LILY WHITE PARTED THE CURTAIN TO PEER through her kitchen window into Ashley Tombley's yard. She squinted. Are those gargoyles? Yes, they are! It was bad enough that Ashley moved in, pulled up the grass, replaced it with black and gray gravel, and then tore down the nice, white picket fence so that she could erect a black, cast iron one, but now, gargoyles?

When Ashley repainted the house, Grace said nothing, although the house didn't need new paint. The Dearborns had freshened the property when they decided to sell. It had been a beautiful robin-egg blue with slightly darker trim, but Ashley painted it a stark, yellowed white with black trim. It looked like a daguerreotype of the house that used to stand there. Cast-iron furniture appeared on the porch. Two cast-iron benches faced each other in the black-graveled back yard. Cast iron meant a lot to Ashley, Grace decided.

No plants in Ashley's yard, just gravel, boulders and twisted hunks of driftwood. It looked like a nuclear wasteland as far as

Grace was concerned.

Grace loved, collected, and displayed lawn fairies. She also sought ceramic gnomes, leprechauns, elves, fairy bridges, fairy doors, and the occasional mobile if fairies dangled from it. Starting in February, when the snow cleared, she bundled out to her yard, digging, scraping, and rearranging the landscaping. By early spring, she planted seeds and bulbs, spread the new groundcover, and waited for when it was warm enough to relax in a lawn chair with a book, surrounded by her collection.

Grace opened a lawn ornament catalog on her kitchen table. She'd dog-eared the pages with new figurines, but she couldn't stop herself from returning her attention to Ashley's yard. It was lurid, desolate and terrible.

During the winter, she longed for summer smells, a good book's heft in her hand, the sun's caress on her shoulders, and the company of her lawn friends, peeking from under the lilacs, hidden among the daffodils, and frolicking in the periwinkle. Even now, she saw the fairy jamboree she'd arranged near the fence. Fairies danced through the Snow-in-Summer. A tiny tea party convened around a table in the purple Sedum.

For years, she added to the collection, never minding that the neighbors thought her a little batty. Once she overheard Beatrice Angelo talking to Wanda Lewis in the supermarket after Grace passed: "It could be worse; she could keep cats," said Beatrice. Of course, Grace would never keep cats, nasty things that dug into the sandy areas in her yard, hunting the little winged creatures who came to her fairyland bird bath.

The talk didn't bother her. What bothered her were little kids who'd sometimes steal her figurines, and the occasional hailstorm that broke them.

I'm fifty years old, Grace thought. I deserve to be happy.

She put on a shawl, went out her front door, down the rainbow-speckled steppingstones that lead to her fairy-green with yellow shooting stars mailbox, and down the sidewalk to Ashley's front gate. She paused as she unlatched the cold metal clasp. Ashley had added a pair of stone wolves just inside the gate. They stood hip-high, made of dark granite, posed viciously with snarling expressions and shiny, black teeth.

She'd never been inside the gate since Ashley moved in. Now she saw an iron snake coiled in a waist-high rock's shadow. Against the house leaned a very convincing tombstone. In front of it, a pewter hand, buried at the wrist, reached out as if a corpse was trying to claw from the grave. Figures hid everywhere behind the boulders, invisible from the street: scorpions, spiders, a weird half-bear half-man the size of a puppy, trolls, and by the porch, a pair of pale stone lions. Ashley had even painted the sidewalk black. Grace pulled her shawl a little tighter, mounted stairs to the door, grimaced, and then seized the skull knocker.

Ashley answered, cigarette dangling from her black lipstick painted lips. She was taller than Grace, the same age, broader in the shoulders, henna-red hair that hung to the middle of her back. Her maroon Victorian riding jacket sported dull silver buttons, but ordinary blue jeans and white sneakers spoiled the effect.

"You have gargoyles in your back yard," said Grace, primly, realizing that she had nothing else to say beyond that.

Ashley flicked her cigarette into a bucket by the door. "Do you like them?"

Grace couldn't tell if the woman was being sarcastic.

"They're facing my kitchen." She could picture their stone eyes now, contemplating her house. "They're inappropriate for the neighborhood."

Ashley laughed. "Your yard looks like a unicorn threw up on it. Who is inappropriate?"

Grace suddenly felt ridiculous. The conversation had turned improper and confrontational. "Could you display them so I won't see them? I like the view out my kitchen window."

"They're seventeenth-century stonework. Genuine articles off Irish Catholic monasteries. They're art. Get used to them. Have you heard of a gargoyle garden? I'm making one."

Grace swallowed weakly. "More gargoyles?"

Ashley nodded. "It's taken me twenty-five years to afford my own house. It's going to look the way I like."

"I'm sorry, Ms. White," said City Planner Filcher. "The area you live in is not covered by restrictive covenants. Ms. Tombley's obligations as a homeowner are to keep her yard clear of weeds and the house in good repair. She's not running a business out of the home is she?"

Standing in the kitchen, Grace gripped the phone tight to her ear. Ashley, in her back yard, unpacked a set of three, dishwasher-sized boxes. Two young men helped her cut the cardboard away. Their truck sat in the alley at Ashley's back gate. "No! I told you that she's putting repellent statuary in her yard. Did you get that she's using *black* landscaping stone? It looks like the House of Usher over there."

"Let me see what else is a possibility." Grace heard paper shuffling. "Is she noisy between the hours of 10:00 p.m. and 6:00 a.m., or are there large groups of people coming and going from the property?"

"No." The cardboard had come off the first box, but bubble wrap and strapping tape hid the contents. Ashley gestured to the corner next to Grace's yard. The two men levered the wrapped mystery onto a dolly.

"Are there noxious odors, trash fires, automobiles in disrepair, abandoned appliances, piles of used tires, industrial equipment or barrels of toxic chemicals?"

"No, of course not. I told you the problem."

"I'm just reading from the city standards for home owners, ma'am."

"Come out here and look!" said Grace desperately. "Or I can send you pictures."

"Wait a minute," said the city planner. "Are you Grace *Lily* White?"

"Yes, why?"

Papers rustled. Faintly, a computer keyboard's clackety clack came through. "You live in the fairy house, don't you? I thought your address was familiar. You're in the system. Theft and vandalism complaints. Oh, and the 'she's the mistress of darkness' call from last year."

Grace felt herself blushing. "That was a misunderstanding. Selma Wall is a religious nut. She said my yard ornaments were idolatrous and not right for a Christian community. They're fairies, not the devil!"

"I believe the city backed you up on that issue. Am I right?"

The memory stung to think about. In Ashley's yard the workman peeled the bubble wrap in a long strip off the delivery, revealing a black-stone winged figure crouched on a pedestal. Under Ashley's direction, the men turned the heavy piece so that it looked right into her window.

Grace stepped back, as if it could see her. "I have another option," she said, and ended the call.

Grace knew Selma Wall from grade school. They'd both lived in the neighborhood their entire lives, but never been friends. In elementary school, Selma carried a Bible everywhere she quoted from with a particularly grating precision. Then, in high school, she went through a brief slutty period, marked mostly by sleeping with each of the three boys Grace had a crush on. She returned to the Bible years later when her marriage fell apart. Grace wouldn't have any contact with her at all except that Selma put in the complaint with the city about Grace's yard.

They had sat on opposite sides of a conference table in the mayor's office. The mayor, a retired telephone executive who ran for office on a can't-we-just-get-along platform, mediated.

"Miss Wall. Could you explain your objections to Miss White's decorating choices?"

If Grace thought that the misunderstanding could be settled amicably, Selma's opening put that hope to rest.

Selma put a manila folder filled with papers on the table. "I've been investigating. Most people think of Walt Disney and Tinkerbell when they picture fairies, but it's not well known that faeries," (she spelled it out) "or the 'fae' as some practitioners refer to them, are minions of the devil. This woman's display is an affront to our community's Christian values."

Two weeks later, after four more increasingly acrimonious meetings, where Selma accused Grace of witchcraft, and Grace called Selma a "sanctimonious twit," the mayor dismissed the complaint on religious freedom principles.

Grace said to him later, "But I don't worship fairies. This isn't religion. They're not real. I just like them. They're pretty."

The mayor said, "I know, but she can't see it any other way. Take your victory and run."

Selma lived in a tidy bungalow tucked behind a much larger house that faced the street. Grace walked up Selma's gravel driveway, staying as far away from a huge dog that followed her on the other side of the big house's fence. It didn't bark, but Grace had never heard more threatening breathing in her life.

If Selma thought Grace's yard was bad, what would she make of Ashley's? Certainly the two of them had an angry history, but she hoped to convince Selma that the enemy of her enemy was her friend. Grace imagined Selma galvanizing her church behind her. Selma wouldn't make the mistake of going to the city this time. She'd organize protest rallies in front of Ashley's house, because, after all, fairies were innocent, while gargoyles were clearly demonic. She wondered what Selma would make of Ashley's black lipstick.

Smiling, Grace knocked on Selma's door.

A wave of incense washed over her when Selma greeted her. She wore a long, orange robe with gold tassels hanging from the hems and a loose yellow sash across her chest. Selma faced her hands palm to palm, fingers up, and bowed slightly as a welcome.

"Selma?" said Grace. The last time she'd seen her, Selma dressed like an Amish matriarch.

They shared tea. The incense burned so thickly that Grace's eyes watered. Grace knew long before Selma announced somewhat redundantly, "I've become a Buddhist," that she wasn't going to find an ally here in her battle with Ashley.

When Grace left, Selma said, "Namaste."

"Whatever," said Grace.

Late that night, a spring wind came out of the north. The weather station predicted a freeze, so Grace covered her roses and the more delicate flowers. She apologized to the fairy figures that she covered also. "I know you like the outdoors," she said, "but the plants need protection."

Wind whistled through her old home's eaves, and the oak tree in back that she'd been meaning to prune brushed the siding with creepy scratching and thumping. She pulled a quilted throw off the couch to wrap herself, sat in her favorite chair with a new book, and read by the light of her Tiffany lamp. On the table beside her sat a warmed scone under a napkin and a small glass of wine.

The book had come in the mail the day before, *Reflections of the Cottingley Fairies: Frances Griffiths - in Her Own Words: With Additional Material by Her Daughter Christine.* The Cottingley fairies had been a sensation around 1920. Two sisters claimed to have photographed fairies in their garden. Sir Arthur Conan Doyle, the author of the Sherlock Holmes books, became very interested and championed their experiences.

Grace ran her fingers over the black and white photographs of the two young girls who appeared to be within inches of the delicate creatures, but even to her uncritical eye, the pictures screamed fake. How could anyone have thought them genuine? Decades later, the girls admitted the images were false, but still maintained they'd seen fairies in their garden.

Grace sighed. She didn't believe that fairies were real, but she liked the idea that she lived in a world where she could imagine them.

Still, she did her own fairy photography. A digital camera and digital editing created convincingly interesting pictures. She'd covered the walls in her library with them, and now, by the Tiffany lamp's light, they looked over her benignly.

Something whapped hard against the side of the house, rattling the photographs. Grace jumped, straining her ears. The wind had picked up, but she didn't believe it could carry anything large enough to cause what she'd heard. It was if someone had smacked her siding with a shovel.

She grabbed a flashlight and a coat, slipped the deadbolt on the back door, then cracked it open. A cold breeze pushed in. She shut the door behind her. From the back stoop, the yard became a dark symphony of movement, illuminated only by a streetlight through the wind tossed tree. Shadows danced, branches creaked, and the fairy mobiles clattered like skeleton teeth.

Her flashlight cut through the night. Torn leaves and dust dashed through the beam, peppering her face. She swept the light to her left and right, but she didn't see anything that would account for the noise. Holding her coat tight around her neck, Grace moved to the corner next to the driveway away from Ashley's house. She didn't like the idea of looking at the gargoyles in the middle of the night quite yet. But nothing seemed out of place there either. Among the tossing flowers, her fairies and gnomes seemed content. The wind had pushed over one of the larger pieces. It could wait for the wind to settle down before she would put it upright.

A shape moved just beyond the light. A dog? Grace scanned

her neighbor's bushes. Other than the branches pitching left and right, nothing. Occasionally she'd seen a fox in the yards. Maybe that was the movement.

The front of the house was clear too. Her glider with canopy strained against the wind. The canvas awning snapped sharply, but she'd anchored the chair solidly against the possibility of wind (or thieves). It hadn't made the noise either.

With dread, she turned the corner toward Ashley's house. She directed the light at Ashley's yard. The new gargoyle, the huge one who'd been staring at her kitchen window, was gone. Had the wind pushed it over? She couldn't imagine the wind had been that strong, although now it plucked at her coat and blew hair across her face. A glittering in the flower bed before her caught the flashlight's beam. She had arranged a tableau of wood nymphs beside a two-foot tall fairy castle in the center of the bed. Grace's breath froze in her throat. A castle parapet hung loose, dangling from the ribbons that decorated the building. Below the drawbridge, fairy wing fragments and sparkling, ceramic remnants were all that remained of her display. At her feet, a delicate leg and a whole wing, like the remains of a tiny massacre, stood out in a scattering of unidentifiable ceramic shards. No wind could have done this. Grace swept the flashlight down her garden, revealing unbroken fairies, but not where she'd placed them, a busted gnome, and a fairy mobile, jangling crazily. She picked up a whole fairy, a delicate beauty in lavenders and pink, as long as her hand. It dropped into her pocket.

A torrent whirled around her filled with twigs and sand. She shielded her face against it and turned her back.

The light revealed a dent in her siding. On the ground next to the house, black marble pieces mixed among her white stones. Most were no bigger than jagged, ugly marbles, but one piece, as large as a softball stood out. With her foot, she rolled it toward her. The pointed ears and leering mouth revealed themselves. It was from the gargoyle Ashley had installed earlier in the day.

The wind wasn't even blowing from Ashley's direction.

A mass swept by her head, tugged at her shoulder. She jerked the flash up, but whatever it was vanished. From the bed of Virginia Bluebells, though, a faint globe of light rose, and from the geraniums, another. Dust swirled, stinging her eyes, but she could have sworn that within the light's auras, fairy wings fluttered, steady in the wind. More appeared out of the black-eyed Susans and the golden rod until a dozen lights floated above her head, like an umbrella or shield. Were they protecting her?

In the storm's roar, something howled. Panicked, Grace pawed through the lenten rose and coneflowers for unbroken figurines. She couldn't leave them outside, but the howl called again, and two of the globes winked out. A shadow against the roiling clouds swept above.

Her pockets full of fairies, and others cradled in her arms, Grace closed her back door against the wind and the unnerving noise. She gasped heavily.

Carefully, she put the fairies on a shelf, only a handful of her collection, and it wasn't until she took her coat off that she discovered a long cut in the shoulder, like a razor or a talon, and a corresponding rent in her blouse. Her skin was untouched.

Grace stood at the gate, waiting for the owner of Chōzō Gardens and Lawn Art to open. A tree limb had come down across the street, blocking the sidewalk. A city crew with chainsaws and a wood chipper closed a lane of traffic.

"Ah, Miss White. Glad to see you again," said Eiji Kagome. He held a large bundle of keys in one had, and a coffee in the other. "Your regular business pays my girl's tuition."

"No time for chit chat," said Grace. "I'm on a mission." She pushed by Eiji as he opened the gate and headed for statuary at the back of the lot.

Ashley rested her forearms on her cast iron fence. "Quite a storm last night."

Grace surveyed her yard. Besides the shredded flowers and several small oak limbs, the damage wasn't terrible, as long as she ignored destroyed figurines. Dozens more had shattered. Some were ones she'd owned for years and had sentimental value. She moved with determination, picking up trash and dropping it into a heavy garbage bag.

"I see you lost a gargoyle." Grace tried to keep calm. She had thought about going into Ashley's yard at dawn with a hammer, smash for ten minutes, and her losses would be avenged, but she ate a breakfast of toast and oatmeal instead while waiting for Chōzō Gardens to open. Did Ashley know what happened last night? Was she responsible?

"Yeah, darnedest thing. They must have installed it poorly for wind to knock it off the pedestal."

Grace didn't think Ashley knew. She bent and straightened, bent and straightened. It would take the rest of the afternoon to get the yard where she wanted it.

A delivery truck parked in front of Grace's house. She smiled, took off her work gloves, and went to meet it.

"I'd like them at the corners," she said. The college-aged workman with a thick neck and impressive biceps, wearing a T-shirt that said, OLD GARDNERS NEVER DIE. THEY JUST THROW IN THE TROWEL, grunted as he hefted a box onto a dolly.

"Back yard too?"

"I've cleared spots for them."

A half hour later, the last box had been removed and the statues leveled. Ashley watched through the process.

"Dragons?" Ashley said. "Not really your motif."

Grace wiped down the jade-colored beauty that faced Ashley's yard. The wings, partially extended, reached three-feet across, and the long head tilted slightly to the side, as if studying them. Each well-muscled, powerful creature looked poised to leap or fly. Strong faces. Unflinching eyes. Razor sharp claws and teeth.

"I think of them as heavy artillery," said Grace. The smallest dragon was half again as large as the remaining gargoyles in Ashley's yard. Much more imposing than Ashley's wolves. Dragons topped the mythological food chain, Grace thought. Nothing stronger. Nothing more intimidating, and nothing more territorial.

On the kitchen table, she spread her catalogs. The broken fairies could never be replaced. She mourned, but new ones could appear. Grace would grow to love them too. She imagined the tiny cottages nestled in the Marigolds, the fairy rings among the sunflowers, under the dragons' watchful gaze.

They'd dance, the fairies would, maybe only when the wind blew hard, but now that Grace knew, she'd come out at night with her camera. Maybe if she waited all night, perfectly still, full of the purest thoughts, they would dance for her like they had at Cottingley. Last night they protected her, and now she protected them. She'd told the mayor that she didn't believe fairies were real, just as she'd told herself that they were only pretty figurines.

What a relief to know she was wrong.

One way to look at how stories are structured is to focus on conflict. If you think of conflict in the terms your high school teacher presented it, though, you think that conflicts are identifiable into broad categories, like man vs. man, or man vs nature, etc. For writers, a better way to think of conflict is that a conflict has three parts: someone wants something, something stands in the way, and something of value is at stake. A fun way to build a story is to make what one character wants to be what stands in the way of what the other character wants. Once that structure is set up, just write and let the sparks (or fairy wings) fly.

If you haven't read Ray Bradbury, you ought to. I started with The Martian Chronicles. *It was the first book that made me look for other books by the
same author. Over my lifetime, I've bought a half dozen copies. A couple wore
out. A couple were borrowed and never returned, and a couple came home from
the bookstore with me because I went looking for a new book but decided that
rereading* The Martian Chronicles *in a brand new cover would be better than
any other book I could buy. Of course, Bradbury wrote much more than that
book. He had his subjects: Mars, Ireland, Mexico and fairs. Nobody has evoked
the strangeness of the traveling circus or carnival like Bradbury did. You can't
write about a carnival without acknowledging the shadow Bradbury casts.*

EXPERIENCE ARCADE

T HE JAPANESE DO THE COOL STUFF AND WORST STUFF
FIRST. They're the fad makers: video games, reality
TV, bizarre game shows, weirdness in fashion, hentai, must-own
electronics—they do it first. So, Experience Arcades came from
them.

They're perverse.

People walk like the undead along the boulevard of experience
booths, like cows bumping into each other. I'll bet some of them
just cycle from one end of the block to the other, never going in.
Many suck up novelty drinks from plastic containers shaped like
skulls or coffins or inverted crucifixes. There's a booth that sells the
container and fills it with frozen margarita: Grave Grape, Killer
Cactus, Lurid Lime, that sort of thing. It's a walking party. The
crowd's dead inside but moving. A guy in a silk vest over a Milwau-
kee Brewers T-shirt coming toward me waves his hand in my face.
"They're here already! You're next! You're next." So, I guess he's been
to the Invasion of the Body Snatchers Experience. Give them your
twenty bucks, and you get to be body snatched. A bit of drug, a lot
of virtual reality, and you're a pod person for a while.

Very convincing I'm told.

A huge LED display reaches above the booth to my right over the crowd, where a black-bladed pendulum swings slowly back and forth on a red background. Go in. They strap you to a table. The straps are real. Drugs again. Virtual reality goggles. The blade comes down in long, slow arcs. You get to see it. Hear the lazy swish. Feel the tug on your shirt when the razor edge first brushes you. Oh, the agony as it cuts deeper and deeper. It's the drugs, and the virtual goggles, and willing participation.

They'll sell you a video later. Part genuine. Part special effects. You show it to your friends. "This is how I died," you can say to them. "Does anyone need me to freshen up their drink?"

How real. How real.

Music blares nearby, and voices as if from a bar. A woman dressed as a Victorian prostitute beckons. "Come in, Deary. We got a bit of the Ripper if you like. Welcome to The Whitechapel Experience." Her British accent isn't convincing. She shows a lot of leg, but when I don't slow, she turns her attention to a woman walking behind me. "Fear for your life, Luv. Our Mad Jack will show no mercy." The woman holds an empty skull. She's twenty. Long hair. Big, jangly bracelets. How many times has she refilled the skull tonight? She sways while she considers.

"How long?" she says.

"The rest of your life," says the hooker.

The woman follows her into the Ten Bells Pub.

"For an extra fifty bucks, I got to keep my face-hugger," says a drunk middle-aged man to his buddy. They could be on the same bowling team. Identical green polyester shirts. He holds up a plastic bag with a gelatinous, bloody mess inside. "I was cocooned," he says, "hanging in the Nostromo. I could feel it growing inside me." He rubs his chest and grimaces. "Got to get the wife here."

Three girls run into the crowd out from under what looks like a summer camp sign: WELCOME TO CRYSTAL LAKE. A guy in a hockey mask, ragged coat, and cleaver leans against the wooden support. His blade drips onto the pavement. He says something to Freddy Krueger, who stands at the edge of a streetlight's illumination. The Elm Street sign hangs crookedly from the light post. Freddy's popular. There's a line at his door.

Popcorn smells. Hotdogs. Cologne. Sweat. Drunken breath. Flashing lights. Animated displays. Recorded screams and genuine ones.

RAVAGE OR RAVAGED? reads the sign over The Embrace of the Vampire Experience. A young woman staggers from the attraction, stumbles against me. I help her steady herself. She's flushed. Breathing hard. On her neck, a pair of puncture wounds, both bleeding, bruised. "If you really want to get into it, I mean REALLY into it, a hundred bucks into it, you can." She rubs her fingers across her wounds. Looks at the blood and then at me. "It's about wanting what you know you shouldn't have."

What do you want? Possession? Regan will take you to your priest now. The Overlook Hotel? You don't have to say "redrum" twice to us. A little chainsaw action? Leatherface awaits.

You've been there in your nightmares. Why not go for real?

I'm not kidding. For a hundred they'll up the ante. Not just virtual mayhem, but the real thing. The woman in room 237 will strangle you. No safe word. Hannibal Lector will carve a slice, even eat it. You can take a shower at the Bates Motel. You know you want to. You know he's watching. "Mother! Oh God, mother! Blood! Blood!"

For an extra hundred, the playacting is more real. Commercial self destruction. Why cut on yourself when you can go to an Experience Arcade? Being a depressed fourteen-year-old girl, or a middle-school Goth guy who can't shut out the voices, doesn't go away when you turn twenty, or forty or sixty, even. The place in the brain that loves the razor simpers in the background. The urge to rehearse death lingers.

I rub my forearm. Under the long sleeve, the scars feel like fine corduroy from wrist to elbow.

For a hundred bucks, they'll take it up a notch. For a thousand ...

The Invasion of the Body Snatchers Experience looks like a clinic. Dr. Bennel's name is painted on the door. Welcome to Santa Mira. I stop, hand on the doorknob. It's not the fear I need. I've known fear. It's not catharsis and resurfacing into the mundane, cleansed like these zombies around me. I have a thousand dollars. They have my pod. I will sleep, perchance to let my humanity drain away. No pain. No need for love or desire or ambition.

Give them the thousand bucks, and tomorrow I'll be one of them.

Life will be so simple.

Writing flash fiction can cleanse the palate. First, it's possible to do one in a single sitting. The entire rush of writing an opening sentence, of crafting the middle, and then crashing to the conclusion can happen in one day. A story writer who works more slowly, or a novelist, can find the rush of diving in and ending in one fell swoop to be invigorating. She can return to the longer project once again convinced that she can begin and end a piece. Second, a flash piece has so little time invested in it (comparatively), that it encourages experimentation. It's not such a big deal to throw one away. And lastly, when they work, they're awesome, like little firecrackers exploding just behind your forehead.

Stan Schmidt, the long-time editor of Analog Science Fiction, *once challenged a couple of writers over a lunch to write a story in a world where science has solved everyone's problems. No one had to work to earn the money to live. Technology would have freed everyone to pursue their passions. He suggested that it would be interesting to take society into a utopia to see what human stories there would still be to tell. I imagine that in such a world, there would be way more poets.*

DEATH OF A STARSHIP POET

T HEY FOUND MEWLANA'S BODY IN THE MEDITATION room, stabbed in the back with the chef's best knife. The chef, of course, was furious. It's not like he could walk to the chef store and buy a new one. At this point, The *Vita-More* was more than halfway to the star, Zeta Reticuli, and the settlement on Zeta Earth, although a performance mathematician told me that the concept of "halfway" wasn't valid in folded space. "Distance isn't a functional concept," he said rather snootily when I asked him how many of the thirty-nine light years we had covered. We'd left seven months ago and we'd arrive in six more. That seemed like more than half the distance to me, but what do I know? I'm a memoirist, not a physicist.

At any rate, the horrified chef dropped the knife to the floor when he heard what the blade had carved last, and headed for the sculptors foundry to have a new one made, although, as he said, "This was an heirloom! German manufacture. A limited edition, Wusthof Santoku. My mentor gifted it to me upon my graduation. His family had it for generations."

Mewlana was gregarious. Tall, brunette. She smiled often,

wrote funny limericks for each of the pilgrims, favored flower-scented colognes, enjoyed meals made from foods that rhymed, most often slept alone, and sometimes shared with me her progress on her epic of mankind's journey into the transhuman. She'd finished 83 cantos. It was beautiful, but I hadn't talked to her in a couple of months.

Why anyone would kill her escaped me.

Reinhold, our oldest philosopher, approached me in my chambers. His hair had grayed prematurely, and he liked it that way. We'd spent a great deal of time together in the first month, but he kept asking me things like, "Why is there consciousness?" and "What is sensation?" which I thought was charming at first, but he often stopped to ask in the middle of making love, which just annoyed me. He also put his hand on my shoulder when we were in public and steered me around like I didn't know where I was going. Very possessive. Very clingy. I don't know any paramour who would put up with that, and, sure enough, word got around, and now, unless he had a secret lover, his only company at night was one of the courtesans. I'm sure she only did it to expand her repertoire. Everyone enjoys a challenge.

But as the elder philosopher and the Committee chair, he was tasked with the Mewlana situation.

"Jayla, the Committee thinks you would be the best person to investigate this. You were not, however, *my* first choice." He stroked his chin as if he had a beard. Reinhold displayed many affectations beside the invisible beard and the poor conversational timing, but within his field he was respected. "Your art is in studying human interactions. You understand motivation. I hate to take you away from your work, but could you spare the time?"

I really hadn't been working on anything. I told people I was "between projects," but the truth was I had stalled. What topic would be worthy? So, his proposal tickled me. "Memoir of a Murder, is that what you are thinking? Why not ask an oracle?"

"They are often . . . vague about specifics. Good on the big picture: 'Your future prospects look bright if you cut that negative person out of your life,' and other such, but that's not helpful. We actually need to know who did this. It would be awkward, you know, if it were to happen again. We are claustrophobic here on the ship."

That was true. At first I thought the *Vita-More* felt spacious with its apartments, studios, performance center, restaurants and lounges, but with 400 people and nothing but time on our hands, within a few weeks, there were no more surprises. Lush carpet, brightly-colored murals, rich curtains, well-placed ambient light, and handcrafted furniture could only disguise the tightness of our quarters for so long. No room held us all. We even had to make dinner reservations to be assured of a table. And now, after seven months together, it seemed I always ran into people who tired me out.

"What about backups?"

Reinhold stroked the side of his face, going for the imaginary sideburns, I guessed. "You'd be lucky to get an imaging now. One extant dies unexpectedly and everyone wants to update their virtual. You'd be surprised how many people miss appointments."

I'd skipped my last three, I realized. "Intimations of immortality?"

"Yes, exactly. So you'll take this on?"

I nodded. It would be exactly like research, except instead of trying to create an entire portrait of a significant moment, I would be looking for the answers to just a couple of questions: who killed Mewlana, and why would they do it?

As I walked back to my apartment, down a hallway rich with paintings in their heavy frames, I considered avenues for investigation. Who had she been working with lately, or did she have enemies? That sort of thing.

I like writing on paper, which is something Mewlana and I had in common. It's archaic; most of our peers preferred composing mentally, but I'd never been able to keep my stream of consciousness that focused. In the middle of a discursive paragraph on a sub-ject's influences, consciousness, for example, I might insert erotic musings on who I'd been with the night before, or randomly toss in a gossipy thought I had about the subject. Paper's slower, but I can feel the thought to word connection with my hand. A paper-making artisan on the ship kept me supplied with notebooks, each a work of art. She grew ecstatic about fiber content and acidity. I just wanted it to take the ink well. My pen was lovely, formed from a single quartz crystal from a jeweler on a lower deck.

Alone in my apartment, I opened a notebook, then interfaced with the Directory. Mewlana formed in the space by my table. She wore a standard imaging robe for her backup. The memory room is chilly.

"Jayla!" she said.

"Hello, Mewlana. Sorry to disturb you. You're virtual."

She smiled, then looked at her own arm. "Thanks for saying so. I can never tell at first. You changed your hair."

"Yes, weeks ago. So, I've got some bad news. You're dead."

Mewlana frowned. "How much have I lost?"

The date for the backup showed above her display. "One-hun-dred and fourteen days."

"Damn, I really liked that body." Then she brightened. "Could we go to my apartment? I'd like to see what I've written in the last four months."

"Fine. Meet you there." I turned off the display.

Virtual life is disorienting. People turning you off, for example. You're sitting in one place, just chatting away, and then the room changes, and maybe different people are there. It's startling if you've been stored for several hundred years. Catching up on the news is terrible. What they need to do is to give you a display from your side of the interaction so you can see what time it is and where you are. It's disconcerting to always have to ask the time. I'd bet my performance mathematician would tell me "Time isn't a functional concept," and he'd be right, when you're virtual.

I called Aphra, a short woman with round cheeks, one of Mewlana's friends and an outstanding poet in her own right, to meet me at Mewlana's apartment. She might be able to tell me what had been going on in Mewlana's life during the missing time. Aphra was inside when I got there, going through Mewlana's closet. "I kept some clothes here," she said. Her hands shook as she folded an outfit on the bed. "They won't decant her for at least a couple of years once we get to Zeta Earth. This is tragic. You have to be extant for the competitions, and nobody goes to a virtual reading anymore. She won't be able to defend her title. What a loss."

"Ah," I said, while figuring out how to access the Directory in Mewlana's apartment. "The Akhmatova Festival is next week. You're competing too?" Mewlana had decorated her apartment with beaded and sculpted wall hangings that shifted color or moved depending on where you stood in the room. It was like standing in a particularly vivid and surreal dream.

Aphra said, "Yes, but it wouldn't matter. Have you read her cantos? Brilliant. Utterly brilliant. No one else would have even bothered reading after she performed."

I found the interface. Mewlana appeared. "It's like teleporting. I'd forgotten how abrupt virtual life is. You miss the transitions."

Aphra sobbed, "Mewlana, I'm sorry this has happened to you. It was so unnecessary."

Mewlana laughed, and took a step toward Aphra as if to embrace her before remembering they could not touch. "It's not so bad. If Jayla wouldn't keep activating me, the next time I open my eyes, I'll be extant and on Zeta Earth."

"True," I said. "In the meantime, Reinhold asked me to investigate your death." I called up an image of her corpse. Aphra gasped, but Mewlana leaned in for a closer look.

"I'm glad I don't have to remember that!" she said. "One wound in the back. Very efficient. Why would someone kill me?"

"I was hoping you could tell me."

"Last I remember, everything was fine. I read a piece of the cantos to a breakfast group, then I went to the backup session. I had an idea about the next section I was going to work on that evening. I keep the poem in the desk. I was on cantos 79."

I said, "I've read it up to 83. Exquisite work, Mewlana."

Aphra stood at the desk. "It's not here." She pulled the drawer all the way out. It was empty. "She always kept it here."

It turned out that Mewlana did not make copies of poems while she worked on them. She'd been writing this piece for four years and made no copies! Some of her readings from the poem had been archived, but much of the work only existed on those pages, and whatever she'd written since her last backup would be gone altogether if we couldn't find it.

Mewluana cried, "I never took the poem from the room! I only composed here!"

I talked her down from hysteria before I turned her off. I mean, time wouldn't pass for her, and it would be no fun for the next person who accessed her to deal with the emotional mess. Hopefully, when I talked to her again, I would have the poem.

Aphra wasn't helpful either. Between sobs, she said she hadn't visited Mewlana for several weeks.

I thought about her clothes in Mewlana's closet. "Weren't you sleeping here?"

Her face darkened. "She said she couldn't concentrate when I was with her. I wanted to share my drafts, but she said my voice was 'infectious,' so I moved on."

Aphra left, but I stayed in Mewlana's apartment, taking notes. The beaded hangings shifted colors around me. Writing memoir is about making sense from the chaos that is life. Nothing has meaning, really, not on its own until we start making the connections. One of my favorite techniques is to sit in someone else's space and to try to absorb something of their personality from how they inhabited it. How they live is one of the threads of their life. Whether I was instructing them on their own memoir, or if I was ghosting it, their objects became meaningful. I'm pretty good at paying attention to objects.

Nothing in the apartment seemed immediately helpful, though. Mewlana was a tidy person. She'd straightened her bedding before she'd left the apartment on the day she'd died. There was no evidence that she'd entertained anyone.

Either someone she knew killed her, and then my goal was to identify the criminal and figure out why, or the attack had been random. I shivered thinking about that possibility. How could I investigate a random murder? What if Mewlana had been in the meditation room contemplating her poem, and someone whom she had no connection with decided to end her?

Not only could I not solve the crime, but what could be more frightening than a homicidal person on board a starship? Anyone could be next.

Aphra had left the desk drawer open. The missing poem settled my nerves. If Mewlana was just in the wrong place when the killer came along, the poem should still be in the apartment. Unless something else was going on, her death and the poem were related.

Gathering all the poets into the same room was nearly impossible. They were an uncooperative lot. Some didn't like each other. Some were massively eccentric, and some might agree to come to a meeting, but then get lost in a composition and miss. I put high priority naggers on their invitations that couldn't be turned off. They were a sour-looking lot when I walked into the upper deck conference room. I suppose I would be angry too if for every ten minutes for the last two hours, a voice piped in my ear, "You have an important meeting at three o'clock. Please be on time."

Almost everyone on the ship self-identified as a poet, regardless of where they spent most of their time. Poet-ballerinas. Poet-musicians. Poet-synchronized gymnasts. Poet-origamists. Sometimes I even wrote poetry. So I limited the call to entrants in the Akhmatova Festival, which cut the meeting down to thirty-six, but it didn't start well.

A slender poet named Octavio who was stripped to the waist, the better to display the poems he wrote on himself, said, "Is it true that someone is targeting bards?"

"You're not a bard, you underdressed poser," snapped someone from the back of the room.

"Why are we worried about this?" said Lanying, who wore what looked like pajamas. "It would be a crisis if she were *erased*, but what's the problem?"

I wondered if Lanying thought she had a chance at the festival prize. "I don't believe anyone else is in danger . . ." although it suddenly occurred to me to wonder who was the next favorite for the festival now that Mewluna was out ". . . but you can help me to figure out what happened if any of you had contact with her in the last week."

The meeting went downhill after that. There were numerous angry versions of "We will not spy on each other," and "Our private lives must remain private."

Prickly bunch, the poets. I gained thirty-six suspects that split the crowd roughly into quarters: the Jealous, the Dismissive, the I-don't-cares, and the Falsely Sad.

The other topic concentrated on Mewlana's cantos. Where was the poem? Except for the Dismissives, there seemed to be universal agreement that the real loss was the missing epic effort. They'd all heard at least a part of it.

Near the end of the meeting, Rheinhold stepped into the back of the room. He stood next to Aphra; put his hand on her shoulder while saying something in her ear. Probably checking on my progress. I don't know what he made of the ruckus.

I went to the meditation room to clear my head. No evidence that Mewlana had died here existed. Bots sanitized the surfaces. The view window sported no smudges. In folded space, the window revealed nothing. The performance mathematician would tell me "Perception isn't a functional concept," and the blackness I perceived out the view window neither was nor wasn't there, but I found the black purity soothing.

Crime isn't exactly unknown—some people study historical novels—but it's rare. In a society where people live indefinitely, it doesn't take long to figure out who should spend their time as virtual personalities where they can't harm anyone. Many of the people in the Directory are flagged, and no one activates them.

While researching, I accessed more information about the bad old days than I wanted. Humanity hated itself for a long time, as far as I could tell. Just the stuff about prisons was disturbing enough. Murders, theft, rape, terrorism. The litany hurt to read. Crime investigators, though, they looked like artists. I liked the shape of the word on the page: "detective."

My friends are surprised when I tell them what gets me excited about my art as a memoirist. Most people think a memoirist writes biography, but it isn't like that. Memoirs are about a meaningful time or event in a person's life. I like talking to dozens of people about an incident that many of them didn't find significant. I enjoy reading old messages about trivial matters. I relish the little personal items that most people overlook, like how someone folds their clothes or how they eat their meals. I like watching what people do with their hands. You can learn a lot from just focusing on hands. Do they keep them still? Do the hands have a route (on the table, touch the face, touch the other hand, back to the table). Do the hands flutter like birds? Do they count out unheard rhythms? Are they tensed or relaxed?

And that is just the hands. I like watching what people do with their eyes. I like speech mannerisms. Posture interests me. How someone organizes their closet fascinates me.

Everything is a story, and if a story is about assembling meaning out of chaos, then that is what I do.

But my approach wasn't fruitful so far. Nothing that I learned about Mewlana helped. I needed to focus on suspects, the thirty-six poets, all who had a better chance at the festival with Mewlana ineligible.

Octavio found me in the meditation room. Up close, I saw his poems were programmable skin art. He could change the display's wording, color, or font. He could animate them if he liked. I didn't go for skin art myself. They say you can't feel the images moving, but the idea bothered me. His pants cut off the poems. I wondered how far down they continued. I wondered if he ever used that to his advantage. "Come back to my room to read the rest" or something like that. Instead he said, "Some of the poets are arguing that the festival should be canceled." He looked worried, but he met my eyes when he spoke. The limerick that crawled across his forehead and down the side of his face was distracting.

"Really. I would have thought you all would be happy to see her out of the way."

"You have a low opinion of poets then." He put his fingers against the viewing window. No reflection. Just the infinitely deep black beyond. "Some contend that because she was last year's champion we should show respect."

"You could ask her." I wondered why Octavio had sought me out.

"I don't like to disturb the virtual." He traced letters on the window. "We should do readings in here. A few chairs, and this as the background . . ." He indicated the blackness. ". . . would be perfect." He turned toward me suddenly. "I don't think one of us could do this. We're closer than you think. It's not a poetic thing to do, and it was Mewlana. Do you know her reputation among the writers? Her works are lessons in the craft. No, I don't think a poet would do it." His hands were still. There's an interesting behavior I know related to what someone does with their hands when they lie: they will cover their mouth. Octavio believe what he said about the others.

"I'll keep that in mind," I said. One of the articles I'd read said that sometimes the guilty person would try to become a part of the investigation. I wondered if he had other reasons to talk to me.

"Killing is a strange thing," he said. "It's everything and nothing."

"Excuse me?"

"It just is," he said. "You should watch yourself. If someone was willing to kill Mewlana, they might be willing to kill you too. Save yourself often."

He left. I was touched that he cared.

If Octavio was right, and none of the poets did it, then who would have motivation? Mewlana was loved.

While reading the historicals, I discovered that old time detectives had access to information that I didn't. They could do phone taps (I had to look up "phone" to see what that was), or record conversations secretly, or look at a suspect's financial records. Clearly they had no sense of privacy. Nobody would tolerate that intrusiveness. What was the point of living in civilized times if you couldn't keep your information to yourself? Still, I wished there had been a camera on the meditation deck, or cameras in the hallways. If I was one of the old detectives, I could rush in and say, "Go through the tapes for the last twenty-four hours." Then I'd know. There was no way to track anyone's movements. All I could depend on was what witnesses were willing to tell me.

I gathered my notes, checked the Directory for my dinner reservation, and headed to the upper level restaurant where the poets often ate. At the door, I scrolled for my name and table. I could see at a glance who else would be in the restaurant I knew, and I could invite myself to sit with them, which they would then be given a chance to accept, but I didn't want the conversation. I scrolled backwards. The board showed me who had sat with whom for several days before.

The restaurant's reservation board had never attracted my attention. The list of names and pairings slid up and down. How interesting! For a memoirist, relationships can be the whole story. The meaning of an event arises out of how the actors interact. The reservation list laid out connections. I could see among the poets that the Dismissives ate with each other, which made sense. No one likes to hang out with a negative person except another negative person. They can reinforce their opinions when they're together. The rest of the poets appeared to mix it up. I could see friendships, writing partners, and casual acquaintances. Then I saw a pairing that surprised me. Night after night for the last month, the same couple, and they ate breakfast together too.

I checked into the backup center on the way to my room. I would have hated to lose my progress so far, but what I'd heard was right. People were nervous. The imaging artist, a haggard, young-looking fellow, said, "We're booked, but the appointment I'm supposed to be doing now is late. You can take this slot or wait a couple of days."

The imaging took twenty minutes. I felt much better knowing I backed up.

I had a suspect, but I needed proof, and to get that I needed witnesses. Three of the four Committee members met me outside the apartment door. All philosophers, the two women, who spent a lot of time in the fitness rooms and looked it, and a man in a wheel-chair. "I broke my foot," he explained. "Being extant has risks."

"We must search his belongings," I said.

It took a lot of debating. Privacy trumps almost everything, but, as I explained, "Privacy depends on ethical behavior. If a single citizen flaunts society's rules, then everyone else's privileges are threatened. Since my suspect would only lie if we accused him, we need proof, which I believe is in his apartment."

In the end, they agreed. While we were searching, I worried we would be caught. I didn't want a confrontation without the proof.

We found Mewlana's poem hidden behind a painting on the bedroom wall. I held the sheets in my hand, the first cantos on the top page. She'd finished six more sections since I'd read it last. It was all I could do to not sing with joy.

"I couldn't destroy them," said Rheinhold. He stood at the bedroom door. "How did you know?"

The poem felt fine in my hand. "It was about Aphra, wasn't it?" I said. "You had feelings for her, and you thought if Mewlana couldn't compete at the festival, Aphra would win."

Rheinhold's gaze dropped to the floor. "Mewlana won last year. It would have made Aphra so happy to take the wreath." He looked defiantly at me and the Committee, crowded into his bedroom. "And she still might. This changes nothing. Aphra will be the best poet this year."

The Committee member in the wheelchair said, "This is disappointing, Rheinhold. Now we must decide on an appropriate response."

Rheinhold looked surprised. "Response? I'm guilty of bad behavior. I'm sorry. You have the poem back. I'm sorry for that too. What other response would be necessary?"

"You murdered someone!" I shook the poem at him.

He raised his eyebrows. "No one died. We can talk to Mewlana right now if you would like. She's no more dead than you or me. I've inconvenienced her at worst."

My face heated. He looked so calm, so assured. "Mewlana had not backed up for one-hundred and fourteen days before you put a knife in her back. That person, the one who wrote ten more cantos to her poem, the one who made memories and evolved and felt moments that are now lost forever, died. That's murder, Rheinhold, not an 'inconvenience.' You killed almost four months of her."

The Committee agreed. They decanted Rheinhold to the Directory. The more I thought of the punishment, the more I liked it. His personality was flagged, of course, so it was unlikely he'd ever be extant again, but rather than the timelessness of virtual life, he'd be accessed repeatedly by scholars, psychologists, historians and story tellers. They'd all want the same conversation from him, though. "Why did you decide to kill your victim, Rheinhold?" or "Can you describe the guilt you felt afterwards?" or "What failings in your own life were you compensating for?" No one would ask

him his opinion on consciousness or sensations. Every waking moment would be about his crime, and that was it.

The Akhmatova Festival went on without Mewlana. Aphra
withdrew despite the other poets' (probably insincere) protestations
that Rheinhold's actions were not her fault. Without Mewlana or
Aphra competing, though, the competition was the most entertaining in years. Multiple upsets. Octavio made it to the semi-finals,
while the wreath went to a third-year entrant who no one would
have predicted as the winner.

A month afterwards, I met with the newly decanted Mewlana.
Aphra was right. Normally Mewlana would have been virtual until
a proper vessel was prepared for her on Zeta Earth, but with Rheinhold condemned to the virtual, it seemed a waste not to use his
body.

Mewlana held her, now his, poem in his lap for the first time.
We sat in the guest area in his apartment. I'd grown quite fond of
his decorating sense. "Now that I finally have it, I'm afraid to read
it."

I smiled. Of course, he looked like Rheinhold. To be extant,
Mewlana accepted the Committee's offer of his body. He told me
that this was his third incarnation as a male. "It's a change of pace,"
he said.

This body's hands were much larger than what he was used
to. Clumsily, he thumbed through the pages until he reached the
seventy-ninth cantos. "This is the last one I wrote." He reread it.
Mewlana's hands trembled as he turned to the eightieth cantos. I'd
read them all. I knew the rest of the poem, while Mewlana, who
had written it, did not. At least this Mewlana did not. He read
halfway into the unfamiliar eightieth cantos, then turned the pages
over. "I didn't write this. It's not mine."

A gap in existence between a backup and restoration can be
troublesome. There are instances of a backup becoming extant after years of further life. The person who they were continued on
without them. They might have started a new career or married or

had children. A person does not stand still after being backed up. Naturally there will be an adjustment. "Of course it is," I said. "You wrote every word. They're brilliant words. You must keep writing. I want to see how the poem ends."

"So do I!" said Mewlana. "So do I. Here, you take these." He handed me the last ten cantos. "I never want to see them again, at least not until I finish writing the poem, my poem, not this . . . this masquerade."

So I left Mewlana in the apartment to write, and I took the ten orphaned cantos with me. They were so, so evocative. Really the best work he'd ever done. Would he be able to do them again? I knew he could not, at least not exactly the same as these. He was becoming a different person from the Mewlana who wrote these every minute he lived.

This Mewlana, the one I held in my hands, truly had been murdered. What a tragedy. Someone would have to write her story. Someone would need to write her memoir, and now I knew what my next project would be.

I clutched the fragment of the poem to my chest.

What do you write about after the obvious, autobiographical material has been handled? (Autobiography as an inspiration never goes away, by the way—it bubbles up all the time). One readily available source is the writing prompt. Give fifty writers the same prompt, and you'll get fifty different stories. Stan Schmidt's question about a society where technology has released humanity from the drudgery of working for a paycheck produced "Death of a Starship Poet" for me. I'm curious about what other writers would come up with if Stan had talked to them.

Someone said that science fiction explores the possible while fantasy deals with the impossible. Making those kinds of distinctions don't matter much to me because they are arguments about form. I'm more interested in purpose, and I think where the two genres cross boundaries is that even if the props in the story are scientifically possible, as they are in science fiction, or supernatural as they are in fantasy, they both use the materials in their worlds metaphorically to make points about being human. Spaceships in science fiction, horses in westerns, or ghost ships in fantasy are metaphorically about getting away or being taken away. No matter what, they are about journeys, and they are about the human condition.

GHOST SHIP

ARIMA PROWLED THE DECK IN THE DARK, STRAIGHTEN-ing a messy rope, carefully placing loop on loop until the coil was perfect. Fog covered the moon, but the mist glowed in its thinness, casting an imperfect light. She stacked scattered buckets next to the mops, replaced a belaying pin to its hole in the gunwale, put an awl and hammer she found under a bench into the tool cupboard, and straightened the restraining net over the hatches. When she finished, she went below deck to tidy the sailors' sleeping area. Arima didn't care that they'd raise a superstitious babble about lined up shoes and neatly folded shirts. She had to do something with her time. When she finished, she retreated to her hiding place in the hold to sleep.

The *Wild Swan's* sailors didn't look after Arima—she stayed out of their way and took care of herself. She had no memory before the ship when she woke up shivering under a wet blanket in the *Swan's* hold, rocking with the storm, listening to timbers creak and canvas snap. Beneath the flooring slats, bilge gurgled about drowning; and a rat perched on a burlap bag, its eyes black, shiny and dead. Her hands smelled like wet wood and sea weed. She knew her name and that she was ten, but she didn't know how she knew.

Soon after she'd first awakened, Arima discovered that everything on the ship besides her was dead. The dead sailors couldn't see her, but she was sure that the dead cat could. It hissed, sometimes when she passed, or it would stare.

She listened to ship sounds. The *Wild Swan* sailed in perpetual heavy seas or fog. That was a part of its curse. Within days, she accustomed herself to pitching decks, and salt spray that soaked her when she went topside, but she never got used to the wind's piercing cold, no matter how she bundled up.

Arima awoke hungry. She crawled from the nest she made for herself deep in the hold, behind the heaviest storage, where the sailors never went, and moved by feel until she came to the dim square of wavy light at a ladder's top.

"We'll play cards," said a voice above.

"We always play the damned cards," said another.

She crept up the ladder. Two sailors sat on stools under a swaying lamp, casting wild shadows around the room. Behind her, in the yellow light, full hammocks cradled other sailors, their arms or legs hanging out. Some snored louder than the ship's sounds. The stairs to the galley rose beyond the two card players, though. She'd have to go around them. Pressing her back to the hull, she sidled behind the bigger man who smelled of rum, nutmeg and sweat.

The small one looked over his cards at his partner as if trying to read his hand. Arima froze. It was if he was looking at her.

The big man shivered. "There's a cold spot, and I'm sitting in it."

"The ship is always cold."

"We're haunted, I tell you. A spirit's walking."

The small man scowled. "Shut up and play. We're the ghosts, mate. If there was another spirit, I'd ask him to sit down and bet. Better company than you. Put gold on the table."

Arima waited until the large man dug into his purse to continue to the stairs.

No one slept on the gun deck. A sailor carrying a rag and lamp wiped a cannon. Even with the gun ports closed, wave-driven water sprayed through. He tightened an oilcloth over the cannon balls stacked behind the gun. The hatches were battened against the sea, so it was impossible to tell if it was day or night outside, not that it mattered much on the *Wild Swan*. The sun never shined on her.

In the galley she opened the cheese bin. When she'd first appeared on the *Swan*, the bin had been full, but now a fraction of the last wheel remained. She cut a small slice. The other bins were equally low or empty. Over time she'd eaten the stores that would have fed thirty men for weeks. None of them ate, and the food never turned bad. No weevils in the bread. No maggots in the meat. The drinking water remained fresh. Fruit never spoiled. She wondered how ghost food sustained her, but it tasted fine and was filling. She decided a strange magic must be at work on board, maybe the same magic that brought her here.

On deck, she discovered low-hanging clouds almost brushed the crows nest, and huge rolling waves like great green walls advanced on the ship, but no rain and little wind. Barefoot, she grabbed a taut shroud coming off the main mast, then swarmed up the ratlines, the ropes between the shrouds like ladder steps, until she was high in the rigging. Resting a hand on the mast, standing on the topgallant, Arima surveyed the ship that seemed miles below. From here, she could touch the clouds. Moisture coated canvas, rigging and hardware, but she had been in the sails so often that the footing didn't make her nervous. Of all the places, Arima loved the rigging most. Being alone high above the deck seemed right, not sad. The sea and wind vibrated the lines.

Her second favorite spot where sailors were unlikely to stumble over her was the bow. She clamored over piled rope and folded canvas to the front of the ship as waves lifted the *Swan* skyward. Poised for a moment at the top, Arima saw waves behind waves that vanished into the corduroy sea before the *Swan* slid down the long, glassy slope. She looked back on the ship, where the first mate manned the wheel. Seamen clung to the rigging, adjusting sails.

Over time, Arima learned some of their names. Ship Surgeon Miller joked with the men and led them in song. Quartermaster Schmidt rolled dice by himself on the quarterdeck when he was awake. The boatswain, a dark-skinned, surly sailor who mumbled constantly, never came on deck. He wandered among the stores in the dark, taking inventory by candlelight. She wondered what he thought of the diminishing food supplies. And then there was the captain.

Even though the ship never berthed, it never made port, Captain Sheridan kept his crew busy making repairs and scrubbing the deck. He stood tall and broad with black hair and full eyebrows. He wore a dark-blue coat that he never buttoned regardless of the weather. Other than issuing orders and ship's busineess, Arima had never seen him talking to his men, and they didn't talk to him. He existed friendless on the ship. He often took the wheel or used his telescope; he strolled the deck with hands behind his back. The wind when it blew, ruffled his hair.

Captain Sheridan emerged from his cabin, looked to the sails, then walked toward her. She stayed still as he approached.

Arima's first day on board, she'd tried talking to the men. "Hello," she said to a sailor, "I'm lost. Can you help me?" But he continued carving a piece of bone he held on his lap. He didn't look up. He didn't seem to feel her when she tapped his shoulder to get his attention. The second sailor was the same. The third, though, sat on the deck, sewing a patch into a sail. That day, fog draped the *Swan* in dark, damp sheets. The sails dripped, and when a breeze stirred them, water shook loose like rain. "Hello," she had said. The sailor paused in his work and tilted his head, looking puzzled. Arima nearly jumped in excitement. "Can you help me?"

The man cast his gaze left and right as if he'd been struck blind, and for a moment Arima wondered if he was sightless, since he looked past her and around her, but not at her. Suddenly, though, he stopped searching, his eyes locked on her. "Mother of God," he exclaimed as he dropped his tools. He ran below deck, leaving Arima confused.

Later, long after she'd given up trying to get help from the sailors, she heard them talking about a ghost. The sailor who had run away wasn't the only one who glimpsed her. She heard tales about the spirit of a child who walked the ship. They argued about her. "How can there be a haunting here? We are the cursed ones. We are the dead," said the Master Gunner. "We pay for the Captain's sin."

The ship's carpenter said, "Plenty of guilt for all. No one shouted, 'Give that ship aid, Captain.' We wanted bonuses and the honor too. The curse is ours."

The Master Gunner snarled. "Only the Captain could have ordered us about. It didn't matter what anyone else wanted, but we are sailing forever in purgatory, never to set foot on land, never to be released. More than two hundred years at sea."

The Surgeon said, "We may be ghosts on a ghost ship, but that little girl, that apparition, is a demon. If she touches you, you will burn in Hell forever."

"Do you think Hell is dry?" asked the carpenter. "I might take dry over this water-logged tub."

The captain stepped over the same ropes and canvas that Arima had traversed to reach the bow. She pressed her back to the hull to stay out of his way. He gripped a rigging line, put his foot on the gunwale and looked to the sea. Above him, the forestay sail bulged in a breeze that didn't reach the deck.

"I want to go home, Captain," she said. He put out a steadying hand to compensate for the ship's pitching. She touched his leg. The pants were cold and wet with spray, but he didn't react. "I want to go home!" Arima pounded his leg with her fist. He didn't move. Finally, exhausted, she lay still and looked up at him. Absently, as if he had an itch, he slid his hand down his shin and rubbed it.

He said to no one, to the wind perhaps, talking to himself, "We're never going home."

Captain Sheridan turned back toward his cabin, walking as if he carried the crew's lives on his head. In the first weeks she'd been aboard, she tried communicating with the sailors. She wrote messages in the daybook. She spelled out her name in dried beans on the main galley table. She yelled in their ears when they lay down, but the things she left scared them, and when they did see her, they ran. Arima terrorized the ghosts. She was their bad dream. When she could get through, they became miserable and fearful. They talked in their hammocks about families they'd left behind who were long dead now. About girl friends who must have met others, fell in love, married, raised children, and forgot them. They were not cruel men. After she'd listened for many nights, Arima grew sad. They suffered for their wickedness they'd committed so long ago. She pitied them, so she straightened their belongs and found their lost tools.

The *Wild Swan* rode the waves like a carriage on a hilly road. Sails creaked. Tackle rattled. Ropes thumped against the masts. And behind the noisy ship, an even noisier ocean hissed against the hull, slapped at it angrily. Sucked and sloshed, splashed and sizzled, smelling of salt and clouds. Arima propped herself up, watching the sea. It would be easy to take the extra step, climb over the rail and drop into the immensity. She imagined the ship sailing from her until it became a speck atop a wave.

She shook her head, suddenly afraid of her own thoughts, then returned to the galley. In a fruit bin, she found the last orange, which finished the fresh produce. The biscuits would be gone in a couple days. She could stretch the cheese and salted meat for a month. Why was she on board? Who was she? Did she have parents who missed her? Was she cursed too?

The cook, a grizzled man who wore a dirty scarf over white hair, walked with a limp and whistled tunelessly, came into the galley after her. He opened an empty bin, looked sadly where food used to be, then said, "Most useless man on the ship." He slammed it shut before climbing down the ladder to the card game and hammocks.

"Ship ahoy!" called the lookout. Arima rushed up the stairs ahead of a handful of seaman. They seldom saw other ships. The first one she'd seen was a tanker that never came within hailing distance. This one, though, grew closer and larger every minute. A huge white ship, multiple decks that towered above the top of the *Wild Swan's* main mast. The waves that carried the wooden vessel so easily, passed under the great boat without rocking it. Orange-covered lifeboats hung from the ship's sides. People walked along the railings, too far for Arima to see their faces. A sign painted near the stern read ROYAL CARIBBEAN and the one at the bow said, INDEPENDENCE OF THE SEAS.

"We could give her a broadside," said the Gunner's Mate. He leaned on the railing next to Arima.

"They'd never even hear it," said a seaman. "What kind of ship is that? It's big as a city."

The Gunner's mate scratched his chin. "The world's moved on."

"That's your world, isn't it?" said the Captain behind her.

Arima leaned over the gunwale, straining to see. The huge vessel was only five-hundred yards away. "I'm here!" she yelled, waving her hand, but the ship powered on, leaving the *Wild Swan* in its wake. She wondered if she jumped overboard if someone would spot her in the water; or if a passenger, looking out on the ocean, a preoccupied passenger whose mind cut loose a little from the day-to-day reality on board, glimpsed the mythical ghost ship beside them, a tall-masted brigantine, sails full of wind, doomed sailors manning her deck, and one little girl trapped with them.

A voice in her ear whispered, "They're from your world, aren't they?" She turned. The Captain's face was only inches from her own. He rose, yelled up to the wheelsman. "Take her straight south. We'll follow that ship."

"We can't catch her, sir, even with the wind," said the Sailing Master, a large map rolled under his arm. "And what would be the use?"

"Do you have a better place to go?" said the Captain. He looked down directly at Arima, who was stunned. He was seeing her, speaking to her. "I'll be in my cabin," he said. "Visit me."

When she closed his cabin door behind her, he sat in his large chair by the stern cabin windows. "You're here, aren't you," he said, squinting at the door. "Sometimes I think I see you, and other times I know you are there but invisible to the senses."

"Can you hear me?" Arima said. Goosebumps jumped onto her arms and legs.

He turned his head. Maybe he did hear a bit of her, like a mosquito buzz just at the edge of perception.

"Or am I going crazy? Not that I think the gods would give me such a release. Insanity, I mean." He studied his hands on his knees. When he walked the deck, Arima thought he was too young to captain a ship, but in his cabin, the responsibility aged him. Suddenly he looked like a man who had been at sea for more than two hundred years. "We took on a challenge. Deliver letters in three days. No one made that trip in three days before, but the *Wild Swan* runs before a favorable wind better than any ship I've sailed. We could have stopped to save the foundering sloop; it would have delayed us just an hour to aid her, but they were close to shore. I was sure others would help. They could even have swum, I thought. We didn't stop. After we delivered our mail, while we celebrated and took on fresh stores, I heard that all on the sloop drowned. At the next port, in terrible weather, we anchored, took the dinghy to the dock, but we could not touch the ladder as if all we saw was smoke. We do not eat. We do not die, although God forgive us we have tried."

"I don't know why I'm on board," said Arima. She moved a map from the other chair in the room and sat. Captain Sheridan flinched when the parchment settled to the floor.

"You are adrift," he said, "but not like us. I think you must be a living person. Your curse must be terrible. What happens when you starve to death on a ghost ship?"

The Captain rose to study a map on a table in the room's center. He switched from map to map, including the one at Arima's feet. "I don't know where we are. We seldom see the coast and never stars for navigation, but the ship we chase calls itself the *Royal Caribbean*. There may be cause for hope." He used a magnifying glass to read the map's markings, and he didn't speak again. Arima grew tired and wandered in and out of sleep. When she opened her eyes, the Captain was gone.

She looked at his map of the Caribbean Sea that he'd left on the table, a vast stretch of water with islands to the east and north, and continents to the south and west, all with exotic names: Hispanolia, Barbados, Tabago, marked with the countries who ruled them, the Dutch, French and English. Someone else might be willing to starve to death, but she decided that it would not be her.

On deck the wind blew from almost directly astern, pushing the Wild Swan south at the best speed Arima had seen. Night had fallen. Spray flew from the bow as the ship plunged forward. Under the watch lamp, Captain Sheridan stood at the wheel, one hand holding a compass, the other keeping the ship on course. The best way to leave would be on a lifeboat, but she could see no way to lower one without help. She doubted she could row it even if she did manage to launch it. She could make a raft, figure out how to get it into the water, and then paddle or sail until she hit land. The ghosts might not be able to touch the shore. She wasn't dead, though. At least she didn't think she was. If she could make landfall, she bet that she could touch the sand. She would be able to walk until she found people. She could save herself, but she'd have to work fast. Her craft would have to be built and launched before the sailors awoke.

An hour later, she'd winched enough lumber from the hold to construct a raft. Difficult work to do in the dark. The cargo boom solved her problem of getting the raft into the water, though. It rotated so that when the raft was finished, she could raise it whole, move the structure over the rail, and then lower it. When the raft was in the water, she could climb down a rope, board her craft and cut it loose.

She laid out the boards and began to lash them together.

The Captain's voice startled her. "You are a brave one, I'll give you that." He sat on a barrel, a dark shape in the night, overlooking her effort. "Where will you row, child? What will you do when the ocean raises itself and dashes your hopes to splinters? I doubt that Vice Admiral Lord Nelson himself could navigate your raft across a country pond in a spring breeze."

He hopped off the barrel, pulled on the first board she had tied to another, which unraveled easily. "Wait until morning. Every day you are alive is a reason to hope for the next one. This . . ." he dropped the rope onto her raft, ". . . would be suicide."

Arima couldn't tell if the Captain could see her or not. In the moonless, starless night, anyone could be a ghost.

By morning, the wind had settled to a gentle push, slowing the *Wild Swan*, and a thick fog hovered over the sea, swallowing the top of the main mast. Arima saw hundreds of yards horizontally as if the fog and sea sandwiched the clear air between. The waves calmed. Sailors clung to the rigging, repositioning the sails. Captain Sheridan still steered. She wondered if he had stayed there since he spoke to her.

"We are too close to shore, Captain," called the Sailing Master who stood at the rail, a marked lead line in hand.

"Apprise me of the soundings as necessary."

Arima looked to the port side. For the first time since she had been on the ship, she saw land, a white beach with palm trees beyond, only a few hundred yards away. The air smelled jungle green. She ran the length of the deck and up the stairs onto the quarterdeck.

"You could jump," Captain Sheridan said, "if you can swim." He watched the shore closely, moving the wheel to adjust course. Did he know that she was standing beside him? "I think the ship we followed, the *Royal Caribbean*, must be here, but I have to be sure. Leaving you on a deserted island would only be another kind of death."

"Do you recognize it, Captain?" said a sailor in the rigging.

"Cozumel, I believe. We resupplied here long ago."

Arima stared into the trees. All she needed was a sign of human habitation. She didn't even have to be able to swim. If she took a board with her, she could cling to it and kick her way to land.

The *Royal Caribbean* came into view first, anchored in front of them, a great white mountain of a ship, but now hotels replaced the forest. On the beach, cabanas and furled umbrellas emerged from the fog.

"Drop anchor!" shouted the Captain. "Take in the sails."

Arima would not have to swim to shore. Captain Sheridan directed the men to lower a boat and drop a rope ladder to it. He clambered down. When he took his place at the oars, he looked up. "Are you coming?"

She sat in the bow of the boat as the Captain rowed. A stingray swam under them, a gliding gray shape longer than she was tall.

"I have learned that if I look to the side, away from you, I can see you most often," said the Captain as he rowed easily. He was a powerful man. The boat, as heavy as it was, jumped forward when he pulled on the oars.

"Thank you for doing this," Arima said. The Captain didn't answer, and soon she saw beach sand under the boat and Captain Sheridan rested on his oars.

"This is as far as I can go. You can walk from here."

Arima jumped out. The warm sea came to her waist.

The Captain reached toward her. "Take this, would you, to remember us? And if you ever dare to tell the living about your adventure, say that the Captain of the *Wild Swan* is eternally sorry to all whom I have hurt, both to the drowned and to my crew. I should have been punished alone."

He dropped a coin into her hand, a worn doubloon, a bit of tarnished gold.

Arima nodded, then waded ashore. When she reached the beach, she sat, exhausted, and watched as the Captain rowed away. She'd never seen the *Wild Swan* from outside the ship. The wood was dark and beaten. The sails looked more ragged than she thought they were when she climbed among them.

The Captain reached the *Swan*, climbed aboard. His men helped him over the rail. It was the only time she'd seen them aid him in any way. The Sailing Master clapped him on his back. Did the crew understand what the Captain had been doing? Did they know that he'd taken them into a port that none of them could ever enjoy, that he dangled in front of them the very thing they could not have to save their "ghost"?

She was dumbfounded.

The fog parted. Sun poured down on the brigantine for the first time in two centuries. The *Wild Swan* glowed as if on fire. Men looked up. Some raised their hands, palms out.

And then gradually, beautifully, the ship faded and swirled. A flock of seagulls flew through the old ship, beating their way toward shore. Their wings whispered as they cut through the air as they pivoted and flew along the water line. When she looked back, the *Wild Swan* had vanished as if it never had been.

Arima pushed herself off the sand and walked toward the nearest hotel. She fingered the doubloon in her pocket. She wondered if a restaurant would accept it for breakfast.

Another source for stories is what I've come to think of as the "noodling thought," which is an idle fancy that crosses my brain from time to time. "Ghost Ship" came from watching Pirates of the Caribbean *too often. It occurred to me during the third or fourth viewing to wonder what the crew of the* Black Pearl *did when they were in between their pirating adventures. How would they occupy their time? What sort of things might scare a superstitious ghost who was carrying the burden of a never-ending curse? What I've learned through experience is to pay attention to the noodling thoughts. They're the fun ones to write about later.*

Most people are familiar with the butterfly effect: the idea that the small-est of incidents like a butterfly flapping its wings on the other side of the world might start what will be a hurricane that hits America's eastern seaboard. What they don't consider, though, is that everything is the result of the least significant looking starting points. Your very existence depends on an innumerable series of seemingly unrelated events. And that's the way it has always been.

MARS, APHIDS, AND YOUR CHEATING HEART

IMAGINE THAT TIME, SPACE AND MOTION ARE CONTAINED in an ocean infinitely long, broad, and deep. And imag-ine further that you are God, and you know everything about your ocean. No part of it is unknown to you. The tiniest movement is known; the most minuscule detail is obvious. Beginnings and end-ings are equally known, and they have no difference. There is no cause and effect; there is only detail next to detail next to detail. Narrative, then, is an illusion created by ordering details in relation to each other chronologically, but the stories are illusions because they are already in the ocean. They don't "happen." They float, com-plete, unchanging, and within the context of the ocean's all-encom-passing existence.

Imagine, then, how difficult it would be to extract an infinitesi-mal part of the ocean and turn it into a story. Difficult, of course, but not impossible. You are, after all, God. Telling story means separating details, ordering them, sharing them a word at a time, imperfectly, because they really should be communicated at once. A story should be a black spot on the page where every letter is typed on top of the other. A book, a series of books, time's entirety could be within the dot.

But if seeing everything at the same time is what it means to be God, then seeing the beauty in detail should be possible too.

On Mars during a summer windstorm, on the floor of Valles Marineris, a single sand grain shifts from its place at a crater's edge, falling a tenth of an inch to lodge among the others. This grain has a shiny side, like a mirror, catching the sun perfectly. That motion alone, one moving grain is lovely in its uniqueness, in its power and grandeur. It attracts your infinite attention, as does every moving sand grain. On nearby Earth, a ladybug crawling on a purple iris, eats an aphid. All things in relation. The iris grows next to a sidewalk that runs from the front door of a yellow house to the street. The thirty-two-year-old policewoman who planted the iris eight years ago when she bought the house is fighting breast cancer. She doesn't know it and never will because her body's immune system will win. The cancer will be there her entire, long life, never expressed, never exhibiting a symptom. Cancer won't kill her.

It's night at the yellow house. Hiding in the policewoman's bushes for the second night in a row, sitting on a canvas camp chair, two feet from the iris where the ladybug attacks and eats an aphid, with Mars shining bright in the sky, a man, Jaydee Janac, watches the house across the street. He has a camera with a long lens on a tripod in front of him, a coffee-filled thermos beside him, and a tattered paperback in his coat pocket that he occasionally rereads. A man named Bennett who doesn't trust his wife hired Jaydee. Bennett has a mistress in Santa Fe he visits every summer when he tells his wife he's away on a work retreat. They've met for thirteen years.

Still, the idea that his wife might be unfaithful eats at the man. Bennett doesn't see irony between his behavior and his suspicions. The idea that she might be seeing someone distracts him at work. Twice he's missed meetings thinking about it. He takes antacids to counter the burning in his stomach which he attributes to worry.

Anxiety doesn't cause his symptoms. Bennett has an intestinal cancer that will kill him in seven months.

He doesn't know. You know. You are omniscient.

The aphid died not knowing that a ladybug was killing it. Aphids don't "know" things the way people understand knowing. In that sense, the ladybug didn't know what happened either. Insects aren't burdened with self awareness. This particular ladybug will live seven years, which will be a record, if ladybugs kept records. At the end, it will take off from a salvia, fly two feet and die. The death will be sudden, painless—not that ladybugs experience pain the way people think of pain.

Jaydee focuses his camera on the living room window. The wife went into the house thirty minutes ago. She's named Linda, a name that she always thought plain. No Princess Linda in fairytales. No heroines or famous artists or world leaders named Linda. As he did the night before, a man greets her at the door, a peck on the cheek and a quick hug. Jaydee clicks off pictures. Door closes. Lights behind the curtains in the living room dim but don't go off. He slips from the bushes, checks Linda's car that is unlocked. Finds candy bar wrappers in her trash. Nothing incriminating. He thinks it doesn't matter. With the pictures, he has all the husband needs, and Jaydee is convinced. People no longer impress him. He's worked this gig for too long. He's seen it all, like a terrible guilt chain connecting everyone: a wife cheating on a husband with the husband's brother, while the husband's brother's wife gambled online and lost their retirement fund to a bookie who lied to his parents for three years, telling them he was in college when he wasn't. He took the tuition money to set up a numbers game on campus. The gambler's partner, an underclassman studying botany, had dozens of hours of hard core pornography on his computer. One piece of film was a bit of revenge porn that the husband who started this chain had posted of him and his wife on their honeymoon, when they still loved each other. As far as Jaydee is concerned, everyone he investigates is dirty. Everyone has secrets.

Still, Jaydee makes two-hundred and fifty a day for this assignment. If he uses a day or two more to find extra evidence, he can bill for the extra time.

He takes a risk, sneaks across the front yard, presses a stethoscope against the window. Two voices too low to make out. He guesses foreplay. When lovers meet, there can be a passionate rush. Once he followed a man to a hotel where his secretary waited. They fell on each other like cats, tearing and unbuttoning, their mouths seeking each other, and in their explosion, failing to latch the door. It drifted open on its own. Jaydee shot beautifully incriminating photos from the parking lot. He didn't even get out of his car.

Jaydee knows Bennett is not interested in the truth if that truth doesn't support his belief that his wife is seeing someone else. The husband's bad stomach drives his desire. He must know she is cheating. He already bought a gun to kill her and the unknown lover when Jaydee names him.

Jaydee doesn't know about the gun. He suspects it. When he talked on the phone with Bennett the night before, asking if Bennett knew the address that Linda was visiting, he heard the gun in Bennett's voice. A private investigator develops a sense about such things. You in your omniscience know. You know the husband doesn't aim well. The first time he took the gun to a range and pulled the trigger, it jumped from his hand, fell to the floor, and when it hit, the husband saw the barrel pointed straight at him. The range instructor assured him that his gun, dropped the way he dropped it, could never fire, but the husband couldn't close his eyes without seeing the black hole pointed at his face. He flinched when he pulled the trigger every time he shot after that. Accuracy doesn't matter to him, however. He plans on putting the gun directly against her head. Boom! he thinks, and the matter is settled. To tell the truth, the idea excites him. He imagines how killing her lover will feel, how justified he will be. He even thinks he will call the police himself. Who wouldn't support him once they knew?

By the house's front door, a brass plaque glints in the darkness, unreadable, but Jaydee sees the glint, cups his hand around his phone to shield the light, and checks it out: MARK TIGGS, TAROT READINGS, PALMISTRY, SEANCES. Jaydee wonders if Linda isn't cheating after all. Maybe she's here for a reading.

On Mars, the single sand grain provides just enough weight to destabilize the slope. Other grains break loose, sending a handful sliding toward the crater's bottom. Dust and sand a half inch to a foot deep coat the windward side, and the crater is one-hundred and seven miles in diameter. The entire slope gives way at once sending thousands of tons to the bottom. No one observes the soundless avalanche. The newly exposed ground is several shades lighter than the sand that covered it. Mars itself becomes infinitesimally brighter in the sky. It would seem impossible that this tiniest of changes in Mar's luminosity would make a difference, but the repositioning of a single grain started the avalanche. All events in the ocean of movement, space and time start with almost nothing.

Inside the house, the woman rests her elbows on a small round table. Her eyes are closed, and she holds Tiggs' hands. Tiggs thinks about the information he found on the Internet before she arrived, the information he knew to look for after his initial interview with Linda the night before. He knows she lost her mother a year ago, and the mother's name, which came from the memorial announcement. He knows what the mother looked like and that she arranged flowers and volunteered at church. He knows Linda is the youngest of three children. He knows her husband's name, and what he looks like. This will help him give a more convincing séance. When Linda used his bathroom, he searched her purse, so he also knows she's an organ donor and that she uses the public library and that she likes candy bars and Starbucks. These last bits will be less helpful, but he's always pleased by how much a purse or wallet will tell him.

"You have lost someone close to you," the psychic says. He likes holding Linda's hands. She reminds him of his first wife, before their marriage went bad. He remembers their first year and how they laughed with each other.

Linda nods. She's skeptical. The reason she booked the session was that her best friend at work, concerned about her happiness, gave her Tiggs' address. "He's a wonder," the friend said. "You'll feel so much better."

She does feel poorly. Her mother's death hit hard, and Bennett has become distant. He doesn't join her for breakfast on the weekends. When they were first married, she knew that when she got ready for bed, he would drop whatever he was doing to join her. He said he couldn't sleep unless he was holding her. They held hands in public. Somehow all that drifted away. She suspected that he intentionally avoided her in the house. She wondered if he still loved her.

Linda doesn't believe the séance would connect her with her mother, but the idea glitters in her imagination like a jewel. She turned forty-two a month ago. Will she ever feel like an adult? she wonders. Needing her mother makes her feel weak. Still, she came. The psychic could be a charlatan and his business a scam, but if he is good, he could still comfort her. She is willing to play along. She thinks of it as a purposeful placebo. Accepting this as a con doesn't mean that she can't suspend disbelief. Lie to me, she thinks. I want it.

Mark Tiggs wonders if Linda will sleep with him. He knows a séance's atmosphere can be erotic if he plays it right. He's alone in the house with a grieving woman. Three candles flicker on the table. Incense burns on the fireplace mantle. A rain recording on a loop plays softly in the background. Once, he convinced a woman that the spirits would be more comfortable if she could release her tensions. He rubbed her shoulders, unbuttoned her top blouse buttons. Two hours later they'd advanced to massage lotions. Mark smiles at the memory. He starts his patter. "Say after me, spirits of the past, move among us. Be guided by the light of this world and visit upon us."

The woman sighs. She's glad that she's not paying full price for this.

Outside, Jaydee curses his cheapness. A stethoscope on the window doesn't give him anything close to the sound quality he needs. He hears voices without words, and there's background interference that sounds like rain. Is she cheating or isn't she?

He can do nothing except wait for Linda to leave. With luck he'll get a shot of a goodnight kiss or an embrace. That should be enough for the husband. Jaydee doesn't care what happens later. He doesn't think about the gun he hears in the husband's voice. If Linda is cheating on him. She's not innocent.

Jaydee didn't read much when he was young. He liked watching other kids on the playground and trying to figure out what kind of people they would grow up to be. He did read one book, though: a paperback called *A Princess of Mars* that he still carries with him. There is a moment in it that he often thinks about. John Carter, the hero, an ex-Confederate soldier, falls asleep in a cave, and when he wakes, he's paralyzed. Every time Jaydee rereads it, he guesses that Carter was dying, not falling asleep. He must have been shot and not recognized the wound. Suddenly, Carter stands naked by his own body. A literal out-of-body experience! Carter, naked, probably dead, sees Mars in the sky. He always loved the planet. So, in his need, he wishes to be there. Carter says, "My longing was beyond the power of opposition; I closed my eyes, stretched out my arms toward the god of my vocation and felt myself drawn with the suddenness of thought through the trackless immensity of space."

Jaydee thinks often about that passage. Now, with nothing to do, crouching below Mark Tiggs' living room window at night, Jaydee sees Mars low in the sky. He's never seen it brighter, and he wonders if this is one of those times when Mars is close to the Earth. He's right, it is close to Earth. It is bright, infinitesimally bright enough to keep his attention a moment longer than it would have, and it reminds him of John Carter, a Virginia soldier who became a great hero on Mars, who fell in love, rescued a princess and became a prince himself. If he could, he would wish himself there like John Carter. Sentimentality overwhelms him, and he feels like he did when he read the book the first time, wonder-filled and hopeful. What am I doing with my life, he thinks. How is this a noble thing to do? He pictures the god, Mars, striding toward him, sword in hand.

Inside, Tiggs moves deeper into his standard séance. He does voices. He triggers a mechanism that raps on the table as if in answer to questions. Curtains flutter and candles flicker on his command. "You miss a powerful female figure in your life," he says.

Skeptical as she is, Linda grips Tiggs' hands tightly. Sweat beads on her brow, runs down her back. "Yes," she whispers.

Tiggs doesn't know, but he is slightly psychic. You are omniscient and see the spirits in the room that Tiggs sometimes senses. The dead linger. Current science does not understand this. It does in a later time, not that time means anything to you, a god yourself. Linda's mother isn't in Tiggs' house, though. She is content elsewhere, but eager spirits, forceful ones, swirl about, trying to break through. They can't. They almost never do. Tiggs feels a presence just the same. A tingle runs along his arms. He closes his eyes and sees the figure of a war god, red and glorious, bare-chested, holding a sword. Tiggs' pulse races. His eyes fly open and he breathes hard. Suddenly he has no interest in seducing this woman. He wants her out of the house so he can open the Scotch he keeps above the stove.

For a moment, Tiggs bridges the gap between his mind and Jaydee's. It's Jaydee's vision he sees. No ghost. No god, but an ideal in Jaydee's head.

"We're done," Tiggs says. "The spirits are not aligned correctly." He releases Linda's hands. Tiggs returns her check. "Sometimes the dead are moody." The vision shakes his confidence, rattles him in a way he's never been before.

Confused, Linda gathers her coat, moves to the door. She does not know of the convocation of events: that Tiggs can sometimes read minds, that the mind he reads crouches outside the house, that Mars captures Jaydee's attention and causes him to think about an old novel he loves, that an infinite number of events have met to drive her from Tiggs' home.

She also doesn't know that a ladybug is flying right now toward the door she exits. The ladybug ate an aphid a moment before and had the energy to leave the iris. It could have flown any direction, but it only chose one, the one that existed in the ocean and has always existed.

Linda opens the door. The porch light comes on. At the same time, the ladybug lands on her cheek. She closes the door softly, afraid to jar it.

Jaydee hides only two feet from her behind the thinnest screen of leaves. The quickness of her exit surprises him. Linda moves her finger under the bug on her cheek. The porch light bathes her in a soft, yellow glow. Her hair, catches the light too, haloing her head in a nimbus. She is slightly twisted, one hand on the door as she turned away, the other moving on her cheek. She looks like a princess, not in her dress, but in her posture. Self possessed. At home within herself. Royal. Dignified. Jaydee sees the ladybug, red on her skin. He doesn't connect the ladybug's color with Mars, but his chest swells when he realizes she is saving it, the smallest of gestures, yet Jaydee nearly chokes on the tenderness. Linda moves her hand with the ladybug toward the bush by the door. She waits while it walks off her finger onto a leaf. Her eyes widen and lock on Jaydee only a foot deeper in the bush.

Jaydee says, "Don't go home. Your husband thinks you are having an affair. He will kill you."

"You have been watching me?" Her voice doesn't shake. The scene is too surreal to feel frightening. It is out of her experience.

"He hired me."

Linda nods. She reorders clues in her head: how Bennett talks to her, the questions he asks, his behavior. Too, she hears conviction in Jaydee's voice. She looks toward the street. Her car sits under a light. She will drive to her sister's who lives a town away.

"What will you tell him?"

"He doesn't want the truth."

"Tell him I went south."

"Are you going south?"

"Not if you tell him I am."

Jaydee nods, rises from the bushes, his stethoscope dangling from his neck. He wonders if he will curse himself for sentimentality later, although he doesn't think so. Linda walks to her car while Jaydee watches. She's not a princess, he realizes. There still is an aura about her. It's her humanity and her kind moment on the porch. It's Mars a little higher in the sky, a reddish beacon to an imaginary world where a man become a hero.

Jaydee doesn't really know why he did it. His client won't be happy. Jaydee probably won't be able to collect on the job. He's wasted several days, but he's not sad. Strangely, he's buoyant. He's almost to his car when a thought occurs to him. He returns to Mark Tiggs' porch, knocks on the door. Warns him.

It seems the right thing to do.

Jaydee hasn't done the right thing for a long time. The world's a strange place, he thinks. Who knows why anything happens?

You do, though. You know.

The ocean is vast. This story is a drop in it, almost impossible to extract from the rest of the sea since all is connected. Almost impossible, but not for you. You are God. You know that everything connects to everything somehow.

Like you know that on Pluto, a long sheet of water ice between two boulders in the stygian black cracks the entire length, shifting one boulder several inches. It changes a picture the *New Horizons* spacecraft takes of the surface. An astrophysicist notices, and later that impacts the Kentucky Derby. It stops a war. It cures a disease.

That's the way of the universe.

You are God.

You know.

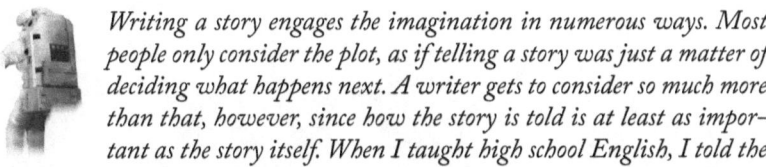 *Writing a story engages the imagination in numerous ways. Most people only consider the plot, as if telling a story was just a matter of deciding what happens next. A writer gets to consider so much more than that, however, since how the story is told is at least as important as the story itself. When I taught high school English, I told the kids who were getting ready to write their essays that what they thought was only as interesting as how they expressed it. That's a part of story telling too. For this piece, I messed around with point of view. What would happen if I chose a truly omniscient viewpoint AND wrote in second person? The longer I've written, the more I've come to realize that at least half the fun of telling the story isn't in the story itself at all, it's in the language and form decisions I make to shape the piece.*

The eternal question that an artist is asked is "Where do you get your ideas?" Sometimes the question is answerable, but only to a degree. Maybe the painter says, "When I was young, a tree grew outside my bedroom window, and the birds sang all day, so I decided to paint birds." But many children have trees with birds in them outside their windows who not only never paint birds, but never paint at all. Why does the idea for the painting come to one individual but to no others? It's a puzzler, so what if you could design an experiment to explore the question of "Where do you get your ideas?"

THREE PAINTINGS

HERE YOU GO, VINCENT. YOU'RE BACKED UP."

Vincent opened his eyes, checked his watch. Twenty minutes as promised. The back-up technician handed him his jacket.

The imaging center's reception area opened beneath him through the ceiling to floor window. It looked more like an airline terminal than a medical facility. Most seats were empty, but the people who waited watched videos or read. The early morning sun bathed the area in a mellow light.

Vincent's manager, Brian, met him at the door onto the street. He handed Vincent a small, heavy black bag. "The studio is set up." The energetic man checked his tablet. Dark hair fell across his eyes. He brushed it away impatiently. "The refrigerator room is stocked. You've got breakfasts and lunches for at least two months in the pantry, as ordered, and the catering service will provide hot dinners through the delivery slot at 6:00 each evening. I double-checked with them that they know they will be dropping meals off, not handing them to you personally. No conversation. Laundry goes in and out the same way. You already set up canvases and art supplies, so you're okay there."

Vincent surveyed the street. Morning traffic was light. A two-block walk, and he'd be at the studio. "What are the critics saying?"

"Who cares about the critics? The buyers are frothing at the mouth. We've got massive media attention that's built over the last forty-eight hours. Bids for the paintings are past huge. You'll be breaking contemporary art records."

Vincent nodded. They passed a bagel shop with an open door. The smells were too good to pass up. It would be the last time he'd interact with another human being or be in public for at least a month. He grabbed Brian's arm and directed them in. The barista, a petite blonde, smiled as she took his order. He noted her name tag, "Lisa." Underneath, she'd written in marker, "Coffee maker to the gods," which tickled him.

As they ascended the stairs to the studio, Vincent's mood was buoyant. A month of uninterrupted work! The art world was buzzing. Buyers already lined up. He could hardly wait to start. Brian opened the outer door. In the tiny foyer, they solemnly shook hands. "See you on the other side," said Vincent solemnly.

The second door, the one into the studio, was steel. It locked on the outside. Once Vincent started, he could not let himself out, but shutting the door on Brian positively relieved him. Brian handled the business end. Hustle and tension surrounded Brian like an aura.

The studio smelled of solvents. The blank canvas, a big one, stood on the easel where it caught the light from the windows best. Vincent put on his work clothes, sat before the clean fabric, a brush in hand, then thought about what he wanted to commit to the surface. He purposefully had tried to come to this experiment without a project in mind. Something bright to start, he thought, something bold. He mixed paints, chose a broad brush, then swept a vivid swath.

Day and night didn't matter. Vincent painted when he woke, slept when he wanted, occasionally collapsing on the floor beneath the work. Other times he staggered to the bed in the back. Mostly he toiled during the day, but the changing light changed the painting, and he saw it differently at night. Paint splotches covered his hands. If he would have looked at himself in a mirror, he'd see paint on his forehead and in his hair. His face was becoming a painting too.

Occasionally, he showered, mostly when thinking through a problem on the canvas. Running water could make contemplation easier.

He'd paint for long hours until the colors shifted before him, until it seemed that musical notes flowed from his paintbrush, and the image became three dimensional. Dark areas felt like step-offs into chasms, and light areas baked with their own heat. He sat still, sometimes, staring, until the only outside stimulus, a click at delivery slot told him his dinner had arrived.

For several days, although Vincent had ceased counting, he worked on one, tiny area in the painting. He'd add a brush stroke, sit back to think about it, then make alterations all through the canvas to reflect the small change. He considered light sources within the painting. What was illuminated? What was shadowed? What reflected? What absorbed?

Color, tone, shape, gesture, texture, all tumbled in his head, bubbled from his brushes, seeped into his dreams. The painting smelled like coffee to him, like warm baked goods. Yellows dominated. Yellow in the flowers, yellow at the green leaves' edges, yellow in his portrait's hair. If a mountain could be said to smile, then the mountain in the painting smiled. If a lakeshore could be said to be welcoming, then the shore greeted him like a lover. Elements appeared that he hadn't planned. A brush stroke went too long, or the color blended at an intersection in a unpredicted way. He looked at accidents as opportunities. The paint makes the painting as much as the painter. When you look at the canvas, the canvas looks back at you.

He painted in celebration and abstraction. Layers in the painting took on deeper and deeper meaning. Vincent loved what he was doing. He loved the work. In the end, a painting can be, should be, pure emotion, and this one was love.

On the last day, he added just a single stroke, a white line at one shape's edge. It completed an arc of highlights that drew the eye from the upper left corner through the entire painting. He smiled. Was the painting good? He didn't know, but the process was holy. He'd done the work the way he wanted.

Next to the door that he opened once a day to pick up his dinner stood a table with a phone. Beside that sat the unopened black bag he'd brought with him. He received no calls on the phone. It connected only to a single number. He hadn't touched it while he worked, but now Vincent picked it up. Brian answered on the other end.

"It's finished," said Vincent. He put the phone down, looked at the painting from across the room as if he couldn't quite believe himself that it was there, opened the bag, took the gun in hand, pressed the barrel against his forehead, and pulled the trigger.

The bagel shop blonde sneezed when she handed him his coffee. "Sorry!" She sniffed and wiped her nose with a napkin.

"Take lots of vitamin C," said Vincent. He wondered if the pantry had vitamins in it.

Fifteen hours into a session, music blasting, Vincent attacked the sky. He used a broad brush, slapping it hard into the canvas, pressing deep strokes into the paint. The music gave him a counterpoint, a rhythm, and an intensity. His shoulders burned with effort. Then, the brush broke, snapped in half. He looked at it dumbly for moments before he realized what he'd done.

*

He fired the gun. The sound deafened him, but he wasn't dead. High up on the wall, he saw where the bullet entered. Hesitation mark, he thought. I'm not really dying, but still I flinched. He smiled, held the barrel to his forehead firmly with one hand while pulling the trigger with the other.

The painting looked stupid, it felt stupid, and only stupid thinking had gone into it. Without ceremony, Vincent took it off the easel, faced it to the wall against the other stupid one, and then chose a fresh canvas to start again.

Vincent had never painted better. Every stroke found the perfect path. Every transition blended exactly the way he hoped. Proportions fell into the golden mean. He worked on a single canvas in a blaze of unflagging achievements. When the last paint hit the surface, he noticed the other canvases he hadn't touched. He chuckled. I only need one, he thought.

"You are done, sir. Your backup has been restored."

Vincent opened his eyes, checked his watch. Twenty minutes as promised. The back-up technician handed him his jacket.

He paused while putting it on. "Restoration? Not a back-up?"

"Yes, sir," said the tech.

"Wow." Vincent shook his head. "It's already worked." Way more than twenty minutes had passed. He felt like he'd been Rip Van Winkled. "Am I me?"

"As promised,' said the tech. "Movement may feel odd for a

day until you get used to the reset. Your body. Your face, and the you part of you is still you. Welcome to modern biotechnology."

Through the window, the imaging center's reception area opened beneath him. It looked more like a bus terminal than a medical facility. Most seats were full. People stood in line to complete their registration. A rainstorm darkened the windows. Water ran in rivulets down the glass.

"You look busy," said Vincent.

The technician already had the next client's folder open on his desk. He glanced up at Vincent. "What? Yes, very busy. You have a good day, sir."

Several people bumped him as he moved through the crowd toward the door where Brian waited. He handed Vincent a small, heavy black bag. "The studio is set up with supplies for as long as you need. Every night at 6:00, the caterer will deliver a hot dinner." They started the two-block walk to where Vincent would spend the next weeks working in isolation.

"They know I won't be answering the door?"

"Naturally." Brian checked his tablet.

"What painting am I on?"

Brian laughed. "I forgot for a moment. You don't know. This is the second."

"How was the first? What did I paint?"

Brian didn't answer.

Vincent said, "No, I'm being ridiculous. You won't tell me."

They walked, head down in the rain. Vincent thought Brian looked tired. There were bags under his eyes, and his step didn't have the same bounce that Vincent recalled.

They passed a bagel shop door. Vincent smelled the fresh goods, stopped and pulled Brian in. "My last chance for a human interaction."

"Minimum input will make this session as much like the last session as possible." Brian seemed impatient. "Those were your rules."

Vincent thought with eagerness about the time he had given himself in the days ahead. Finally, he could eliminate all distraction. In his twenties, he'd worked as a night hotel clerk. At 5:00 am, he staggered home, slept for two hours, and then drew or painted until it was time to work again. He yearned for the time to create, for the long, uninterrupted hours in his own head. Today, a pause felt like a luxury.

"I always have a bagel to begin my day," Vincent said.

The barista, a haggard looking, petite blonde whose name tag read "Lisa," with the handwritten addition, "The masses' downtrodden servant," stood at the counter. "Cinnamon raison, toasted with strawberry cream cheese?"

"Yes!" said Vincent. "How'd you know?"

"I'm good with orders. Is your skinflint partner paying again? A dime tip is from the 1950s."

"Did she say that last time?" asked Vincent.

Brian put a twenty-dollar bill on the eight-dollar tab. "Keep the change."

"You *are* a skinflint, Brian." Vincent laughed. "What's got into you?"

He shrugged. "Let's go. Your studio awaits."

Vincent wanted to finish his breakfast first, though, so they sat at a table next to the window. The rain continued, a dark, cold drizzle that made the passing cars splashing through puddles sound like viper hisses.

The idea for the experiment, a performance art piece, occurred to Vincent a year earlier. Over the past twenty years, he'd built a reputation for himself. A New York City and a Santa Fe gallery were devoted to his work. A busy catalog business and steady stream of orders for pricey prints flowed in, but he worried he was going down a commercial wilderness, losing touch with relevancy in the art world, turning into Kincaid or Rockwell, an artist who could do only one thing, a popular thing that sold well but meant he was stuck creatively. Last year he'd been the artist in residence at a retreat in the Wyoming Rockies. He remembered sitting outside on the main ranch house steps, enjoying the morning sun. Two young attendees, talking earnestly, passed him on the stairs. They nodded in his direction. For a moment, he felt like he had arrived. After all, they had come to this retreat to learn from him. They were disciples. But as they went through the doors, one said, "He hasn't been revolutionary since before I was born."

Vincent wasn't ready to join the old guard. So the question he'd struggled with for years came back to him: what is creativity? Where does it come from? To answer, he decided to do three paintings. He would backup himself just before the first painting, throw himself totally into the making, and then when he finished, die. The reset would be him again at the beginning. He'd do the second painting. Would the two paintings be the same? Would that mean his creative destiny was hardwired within? A creative fate? Or would the paintings be different? Given the same starting condition, would he wander into other creative areas? Did he have creative freewill?

Resets weren't cheap. Backing up a complete consciousness with all its memories didn't pose a challenge anymore, but preparing a new body did, especially if he paid for looking like himself instead of taking a generic shell. Still, he could afford it. The idea was a stunt, but an important one. He would be relevant again, pushing the envelope's edge.

Once Vincent proposed the idea, Brian turned it into an event. "Why not be *both* creatively valid *and* profitable?" he argued. So, the project became a media extravaganza.

"We have to move," said Brian. He tapped his fingers nervously on the table. "You're going to overhear something, or someone's going to walk in here with a newspaper. A headline you didn't see the last time could invalidate everything."

Vincent nodded, gathered the half bagel and coffee.

As they ascended the stairs to the studio, Vincent's mood was contemplative. The rain muted the city's sounds. Trees dripped. In the foyer, he shook Brian's hand solemnly. "See you on the other side," said Vincent.

Vincent was glad when the door closed, locking him in the studio. Brian's paranoia that Vincent might be changed by ten minutes and two blocks irritated him.

The studio smelled of solvents and something else. Vincent wrinkled his nose. There was bleach, a biting odor. A blank canvas, a big one, stood on the easel where windows would cast the best light, but the day was gray and the canvas shadowed. Vincent put on his work clothes, sat before the unmarked fabric, a brush in hand, then thought about what he wanted to commit to the surface. He purposefully had tried not to come to this experiment with a project in mind. He looked up at the windows. Rain spots and roiling clouds greeted him. He felt dark, so he mixed paints. His first stroke was a black, wide swath.

Day and night ceased to matter. Cut off from the world, without a clock or phone or radio or computer, the only regular rhythm was the clatter at the delivery slot at 6:00 p.m.

Vincent talked in workshops about getting into a creative zone, a place where outside concerns faded away, a place where the hand and the mind and the materials seemed to be one. "In the zone" became the place he sought, a Zen-like peacefulness that negated self and time, a place he'd wake from thirsty because he hadn't drank for hours, or where the pain in his wrist and back told him he'd been at the work beyond his body's capacity. Always, always, always, exiting the zone felt like rising from ocean depths. He'd break the surface and blink with surprise at the studio's reality. Walls, floor, chair, table and bed, all so solid and not related in any way to the painting and where his head had been minutes before.

Over the days, he layered the paint a dozen times. Black on black. Violet and grays, and deep, dingy blues. He'd painted clouds. Behind them, he imagined sun shining, but the clouds never broke. There were places, though, where a higher cloud's underside caught a reflection from a lower cloud hinting of light beyond. On the dark landscape below, brush strokes suggested shapes. Was it a human herd, their shadowed heads bowed below a hopeless sky? Was it an army fleeing a battle so vicious they felt only fear and death?

Off to the side among the seething mass rose a single tree, barely enough light from the clouds to separate it from the background. If your eye followed the branches, you saw they stretched the canvas's length, but you couldn't see them unless you saw the trunk first. Dark on dark were the branches, except on one branch where three leaves glowed larger than perspective would allow. When Vincent stood back from the painting, the three green lights were what attracted his eyes first. It was only after his gaze broke away that the darkness in the rest of the painting resolved itself into the clouds and bare branches, and the retreating army.

Was this what he painted the first time? Vincent sat before his nearly finished creation, spent. For days he'd been more in the painting than he'd been in the world. But now he thought about emerging. A few more strokes, he would call Brian, hang up, then kill himself for the second time. He didn't have to turn his head to know the black bag sat beside the phone, waiting.

For the millionth time, his eyes found the small hole in the wall by the door. It was the only imperfection in the sterile surface. He wondered about it. Insects? A bullet? It amazed him how often he caught himself staring at it.

He rested, the painting nearly finished. From his bed, he saw the morning light reflected on the painting, the darkest painting he'd ever done, or was it? What had he painted earlier? The time was gone, which was the experiment's point. He couldn't know what he'd done before, in his other incarnation. He was supposed to be the same person for each painting. How would subtle differences affect him?

Vincent moved to the painting. His hand, paint splotched, ached from hours holding the brush. Maybe a highlight would be the last touch. A light tinge reflecting from the tree trunk. He picked through his paints to find the white he liked, but he didn't put it on the palette. The tube rested heavy on his hand. He had used so few light shades. He turned it over. On the back, the company printed the batch number. If you knew what you were looking at, the batch number told you when the paint had been manufactured. Vincent read the number, put the tube aside, and then checked the rest.

When he lay down, he couldn't sleep. He laced his paint-stained hands behind his head, thinking about the experiment, his place in art history, bleach smells, and Brian.

Brian said the work would set records for contemporary art, and Brian would know. Brian knew art values. He was the money-man.

Vincent eyed the telephone and the black bag. He'd finished. He could call Brian, then pull the trigger. Brian said this was painting number two. The third one would finish the project. He would find out if creativity was preset, or if what he painted changed as he painted. Starting from the same place, would he paint the same canvas three times? Did da Vinci have a choice, or was the Mona Lisa his fate?

Michelangelo said he didn't choose the figures he carved. He said, "Every block of stone has a sculpture inside it, and it is the task of the sculptor to discover it." Michelangelo carved away everything from the stone that wasn't the sculpture. That idea always bothered Vincent. When he painted, was he making decisions, or did he lay down predetermined strokes? Did the sculptor control the stone, or did the stone control him?

Vincent opened the bag, took out the gun. Its solidity surprised him. Very utilitarian in design. He hefted it, then pressed it against his forehead to feel what it was like. He'd pulled the trigger before. A flick and the safety was off. Once he called Brian, he could go back to the beginning.

He didn't know guns well. It took a minute to figure out how to free the magazine, but after fumbling for a moment, the magazine dropped from the gun's handle. Vincent picked it off the floor.

It was empty, and so was the gun's chamber.

He thought a long time about what the empty gun meant before moving. He stalked the studio's perimeter. Paints, brushes, extra canvases, solvents, cloths, his clothes, a chair, a table, an easel and a bed. He kicked the chair apart until nothing was left but the four legs like clubs, and a splintered mess.

He called. "I'm finished," he said when Brian picked up on the other end.

Vincent waited by the door, a chair leg in his hand. When it opened, it would shield him from whoever came in. There were no clocks in the studio, so he had no way to measure how long he stood there, conscious that his heart pounded, twitching at every imagined sound on the door's other side.

Finally, a solid click told him the outside door had opened. A key turned the deadbolt in the solid steel door. Vincent held his breath, the chair leg over his head.

Slowly, the door opened. "Vincent?" said Brian. A gun and a hand slowly moved into view. It stopped. Brian could see the painting. "My god."

Vincent brought the chair leg down hard. He felt the wrist snap, and the gun spun away on the floor.

Brian shrieked, fell to his knees, holding his arm to his chest. "What the hell, man!"

Vincent put his foot on Brian's chest and pushed him over.

"You were going to kill me." He didn't feel rage. The gun was too far for Brian to reach. Vincent took steady breaths. "How long have I been painting? How many paintings have I done?"

"We're making a fortune," Brian gasped. "You've never done better work. The buyers are lapping it up."

"You got greedy, didn't you? How many?" Vincent rested on his stool, the chair leg across his knees.

Brian grimaced with pain as he sat up. "Just one as far as you know. This was the experiment, to paint a single painting as many times as you wanted, always starting fresh. I think you broke my wrist, dammit."

"You took the bullets. When did I stop killing myself? Did I ever kill myself?" It occurred to him maybe he'd lost his nerve from the beginning. With the backups in place, Brian might have shot him the first time (although, to Vincent, *this* seemed like the first time).

Brian closed his eyes. "After the sixth."

Vincent flinched. "Six? We announced I'd only do three."

"The buyers loved your work. I told them you'd extended the experiment. Who wouldn't? I thought I'd find your body like I had the first five times, but you had the gun. You were going to kill me. I talked you out of it, though. We were going to walk out together. It wasn't a big deal. You did three more paintings than you thought you had, but when you gave me the gun, I shot you. I've done the deed myself since. How did you figure it out? For five paintings, you followed the plan. Why'd you screw it up?"

"You stocked the studio with new paint each time. The tubes have a coded date on them." He picked up the white he'd used last. "This batch came out three years from now. How many paintings, Brian? How many times have you killed me?"

"Twenty-two. You paint fast. But you're thinking about it all wrong. You may have died all those times, but I've restored you too. This eight weeks or so in your life that you've had twenty-seven times could be the most brilliant you'll ever be. Can you imagine what other artists would give to be at the top of their talents all the time? No fading. No eroding vision. It's like knowing when in your life when you'd be the happiest, and rather than seeing it pass, you get to stay there. I've given you a gift, an awesome, profitable gift. Vincent, you'll never have to work again. You have become a legend."

Vincent looked at the painting's blackness. It truly was magnificent, or at least it seemed magnificent, but it was also a joke.

"You don't get it, Brian, do you? You never have. You don't understand art."

Brian shook his head. "What do you mean?"

"It's about growing. You know what I'm looking forward to? It's the painting I do next, with this one in my head. The big deal is all those other Vincents who learned from their paintings but never got to do the next one."

Vincent tossed the chair leg aside. "Art is about process, Brian. It's about leaving a trail. I'm going back into the world. I'll look at those other paintings. I'll mourn for the lessons lost, and then paint something new."

He thought for just a second about closing the door so it would lock behind him, to leave Brian with the gloomy painting, all the supplies he would need to maintain himself, and a loaded gun. How long would it take, Vincent wondered.

But he left the door open. Outside, the clouds draped across the sky in shapes and shadows. The street danced in perspective and lines and texture. A business woman walked by. He could see the tension in her hand holding the briefcase. Her neck struck a beautiful gesture as she turned to look up the street.

Vincent longed to paint her, to capture everything, to build on his last work and grow.

He smelled coffee and bagels and the urge to create.

Consider writing fiction as a game between the writer and the readers. Done well, it's a pleasing contest where both sides respect each other and play fair. The writer treats the readers as the intelligent folk they are, and the readers expect that the writer won't cheat them. Readers like to figure things out about the story as they go along. An easy way to see this is to look at characterization. If the writer says, "John made frequent witticisms," but John never says anything funny, the reader will feel robbed. Not only did the writer not trust them to figure out on their own that John was a clever speaker, the writer also didn't reward them with witticisms. It's better when the writer doesn't tell, but shows instead. What happens, you might ask, if the writer thinks he's shown something but he was actually too stingy with his clues? How does the writer know when the reader gets it? That's a good question. The way to answer it is to consider the story of the chief mechanic and his apprentice. The mechanic shows the apprentice a giant bolt on a hugely expensive machine and tell hims to tighten it. The machine's ability to work is entirely dependent on this bolt being as tight as possible. "How do I know when it's tight enough?" the apprentice asks. The chief mechanic says, "Tighten it until it breaks off, and then back up a half turn."

In mythology, Odysseus traveled the Aegean Sea and the Greek islands for years. His son, Telemachus stayed home. I wonder if Telemachus ever envied his father's adventures, and once Odysseus returned, if Telemachus wanted to travel on his own. One part of the young man must have been overjoyed to see his long lost father. The other part must have wanted to board a ship to see the world. Which part was more powerful?

WE HAVE ALWAYS LIVED IN THE HAMLET

TORY OPENED THE PICNIC BASKET FILLED WITH QUILT-ING supplies under the Green Granddad, a thousand-year-old yew tree on the edge of Tillton Forest. She'd spent yesterday choosing among the scrap fabrics, cutting the pieces, and then pinning them together so she and her sister could sew blocks today. She sighed anxiously. Leaves whispered above at the end of long, twisted branches. Carver Creek murmured below the hill. Warblers chirped and sang their complicated melodies all around, and Janelle was late.

The low stool Tory used was a sturdy one she'd made in the barn last year. She'd sanded the seat to fit her comfortably. Janelle had grown impatient with the project, so Tory finished hers. Now, Janelle's stool sat on the blanket under the tree, but no Janelle. Tory stitched together a dark blue, pinstriped block while she waited. The sturdy fabric had come from an old blouse with a torn sleeve Mom had worn when she was young. Tory's fingers moved quickly as she looked toward the forest trail. She'd see Janelle minutes before she got here, but she couldn't look away from her work for long, though. That was one of the reasons she loved quilting. The work required focus even when she made a stitch she'd done hundreds of times before. If the edges didn't line up just right, if the seam wasn't exactly the right distance from the edge, if the stitches were uneven or if she pulled tight or not tight enough, the block would bunch and have to be remade. Automatic, focused, meticulous, repetitive attention. This was why quilting was perfect for conversation. The hands and eye worked together to produce the blocks while the mind could wander. Tory always had her best conversations while quilting. If Janelle would arrive, she could have one of those conversations today.

"Quilting?" said Janelle. Tory jumped. As usual, her sister hadn't come the expected way. "I can't think of anything more boring."

"You mean 'meditative,' I think."

Janelle plopped onto the other stool. Tory thought Janelle was the better looking version of the two of them, and they both favored their Dad. Pert nose. Strong jaw. Blue eyes. Black, kinky hair. Tory was one day short of a year older, so each year they celebrated the day being the same number. This year was eighteen.

"You have to repair every other block I make," said Janelle. "Your patience astounds me."

Tory didn't want to tell her that she redid all of Janelle's stitching, but she liked her company enough that the extra work wasn't a bother. "Practice makes perfect. I'm doing that Texas Star pattern for Cousin Beth. It's just a baby quilt. I don't think I have the endurance for a full-sized one."

Janelle dug in the basket for needle, thread and a handful of cloth pieces. "I just slow you down. You'd get more done than the both of us if you worked on your own, but you didn't invite me out here just to work on Cousin Beth's baby quilt, did you? She's not even expecting, is she?"

Tory blushed. "She could be, sometime. She wants to be. No point in waiting for the inevitable."

The sewing required concentration. Tory bent over her work,

unsure of what to say next to her sister. Normally, she found the Green Grandad the most relaxing place in her world. His shade stretched for dozens of yards. What sunlight fought through the leaves, sparkled like emerald stars. And the air smelled moist and fertile. She once told Janelle that the hours quilting beneath the ancient Yew weren't subtracted from her total hours on Earth. If she never left, she would never die.

Finally, Tory said without looking up, "So, are you still going to go? We have always lived in the hamlet."

"We talked about this. Yes, I'm going."

"It will be hard work."

"It will be an adventure."

"You could die."

"Eventually."

"We might never see each other again."

Janelle didn't answer that. She ran a line of stitches through the cloth, counted them, then snugged it up. "There's weeks and weeks with nothing to do on the ship. I'll make a quilt for you. Maybe those darned blocks will come out even. I'll bring it back to show you."

They worked silently until the sun dropped below the horizon and the shadows under the tree were deep and velvety. Fireflies winked on and off in the tree's limbs and around the trunk. Tory couldn't see her stitching any more, but she didn't want to leave, and it seemed Janelle wanted to stay too.

Tory said, "I don't see fireflies here often."

Janelle sighed. "Mostly they hang around the cemetery. Summer nights and fireflies among the tombstones. I'll miss that."

She left the house at dawn.

The messages came regularly the first two months. Janelle chatted about life on the ship, about crew members, about her hopes. Tory talked about flowers she grew behind the house, about fishing in Carver Creek, about poetry she wrote.

But as the ship's speed picked up, communication became harder. Relativistic lag meant Janelle's signals took longer to assemble, while Tory's thoughts chased the ship going closer and closer to the speed of light.

By fall, communication stopped.

Over the years, Tory taught quilting to youngsters in the hamlet. She studied rural community management because she found it interesting. A small press put together a collection of her poems that won an award.

She took long walks among the yews and elders and oak. Eventually, she volunteered to serve on the hamlet planning committee. Her studies qualified her for the position. On her walks, she thought about the purpose of a technological society. What was the point in becoming civilized, in becoming a technological utopia, unless everyone's needs were met? The hamlet and communities like it all over the world proved the concept. When farming became automated, the only farmers were hobbyists. They no longer went to the fields like people of old, hoping to raise enough crops for the winter. The same with manufacturing and medicine and service industries. Working forty, fifty, sixty hours a week for wages with the hope of a brief rest at the end belonged to an era that passed. Technology and automation served humanity's pleasures and leisures. Finally, people could do what they wanted, pursuing efforts that made them happy. No one went without. There was room and resources for all. What else, then, would science be for?

Tory learned about herbs. She grew them, extracted oils, made fragrant sachets and lotions. She studied nature, mapped and named the limbs on the Green Granddad, found other venerable trees far back in the woods. She sat still for so long that she felt as if she was floating, becoming a part of the forest herself, like her own tree, a small one with flesh branches and hair leaves.

There were people, though, like Janelle who couldn't sit still. The world could provide everything to make them comfortable, but they needed to stretch their legs, so they left.

Tory helped to design better parks and wilder wilderness. She enjoyed the company of her friends. She learned to be at even more at peace with herself and with others.

Not everything was perfect. Despite advances in medicine, and the unending pursuit of the only medical challenge left unresolved, Tory aged. Compared to the bulk of human history, it was a slow aging, like the Biblical patriarchs.

It took longer to walk to the Green Granddad. Her poems became shorter. Sometimes she would speak them to herself just to hear the syllables roll. She realized a single word could be a poem. "Janelle," sounded out carefully, was a poem. A thought about the word could be a poem. All was poetry, just as the entirety of a quilt could be contained in one well-sewn block. She assembled the most difficult patterns and invented her own. Sometimes she thought about her sister. When they were sixteen, they had argued about heaven over breakfast. Tory said, "If I could go, it would be a place where I chose my own schedule, where I listen to my own rhythms. It would have trees and books and lots of spring afternoons. My friends would be there when we needed each other, and we'd leave each other alone when we wanted to be thoughtful. There would be waterfalls at the end of long hikes. There would be music every day."

Janelle wrinkled her brow, and then laughed. "That would be it? Trees and waterfalls? My heaven is a long series of hills with something wonderful behind each one. No matter how many I climb, there's another one afterwards. It's a place where I can build things like houses or cities or empires, and then abandon them to climb the next hill."

"Your heaven sounds exhausting. You'll want to come to mine to rest."

"What's rest?"

Tory looked at her sister and knew she didn't understand her, this creature who radiated impatient energy.

So Tory lived a full life, exercising her mind in the way that pleased her, and sometimes thought of Janelle, far-traveling Janelle, who lived in the night sky. Tory set a chair by the Green Granddad on warm summer nights, listened to the leaf choir whispering its protracted song to the wind, and looked up.

Tory roused slowly from a long dream. She'd fallen asleep while composing the last two lines to a sonnet she'd started years earlier. On the blanket beside her sat a basket filled with cloth scraps. She'd wrapped fruit for lunch and brought a thermos of hot tea.

She didn't know what woke her. Above, the yew's reaching, comforting branches focused first. Tory looked at them for a while before realizing she wasn't alone. A young woman wearing a worn, gray jumpsuit sat cross-legged on the blanket. Her hair was pulled back. A fine scar ran from the corner of her left eye to her ear.

"You came home," said Tory.

"I told you I would."

They embraced. Janelle hugged with strength, with youth.

"It's been over two centuries." Tory felt a tear run down her cheek that she wiped away.

"It hasn't been twenty years yet for me. You've aged well," said Janelle, "and the tree looks exactly the same." Janelle leaned back on her hands, breathed in the forests smells. "I have been places, but I was afraid I'd get back too late. Much happened."

"You climbed hills?"

Janelle's eyes shown. "Oh, if you could only see where I've been, Tory. You can't imagine what it is to watch another world coming toward you, what it feels like to take a first step onto a alien shore. I thought I knew what adventure would be like, but it was so, so much more."

"I have traveled too."

"I heard. I read your poems as we came in. They're beautiful."

Tory smiled. "Poems are like animal tracks. They show you

where I've been, but they don't show me. It's me who traveled."

"You look tired."

"I'm not. You look young."

"I feel . . . older. Maybe there has come a time to rest, to sit under a tree. I brought you something." Janelle put a quilt on Tory's lap. Texas Stars. It wasn't perfect. Some of the seams were crooked. Tory could see where Janelle had to compensate elsewhere in the quilt with larger or smaller pieces.

She ran her hands over the cloth that had been to other planets, that had traveled light years to find its way back to her. "It's lovely."

"I had a plan," said Janelle. She leaned across the quilt, held Tory's hands. "I would come back to the hamlet for you. I've done a thousand deeds, Tory. I climbed a volcano's throat. I sailed a silk-sheeted sloop on an ammonia sea. I raced from a supernovae, convinced for every second that we'd started away too late. My plan was to come back, to take your place beneath the Green Granddad, and see what you see here. I'm . . . full with other worlds. While I sat, I would send you on your own journey. There is much to see out there, Tory. The universe is huge." Janelle gripped hard. "Will you do it? Can you do it? Take a trip over a single hill while I wait for you here?"

Tory imagined the scene. She was old, very old, but not broken yet. She could climb aboard Janelle's ship and fly to worlds beyond this one. She could! And for the first time in her life, she felt a touch of wanderlust. The changes in Janelle convinced her. A flight, an exploration, a hike to cross a horizon rose up in her like a tide, like nothing she'd felt before. Then, when she returned, she could walk back to this tree. Perhaps twenty years would have passed for her, while Janelle would have lived through two hundred. They'd be together again, sisters who were the same age for a day once a year. They could talk under the tree about the things they'd done, and they'd live in the hamlet, as they had when they were young.

It was a beautiful vision.

Tory thought about it while holding Janelle's hands. She realized they were crying, silent silvery tears that made their cheeks shine.

Tory said, "I have a better idea."

Janelle nodded.

"Let's both go."

One of the most appealing aspects of writing fiction is in the writer's freedom to explore anything. Stephen King told a story about why he wrote the things he wrote about. He said that the brain is a sieve. All of life passes through it, but only some parts get caught. Every person retains different images. King said that if he and the western writer Louis Lamour stood on the edge of a small pond in Colorado, Lamour would think about water rights in a dry season. King would thing about a creature that crawled out of the pond in the middle of the night. Of the many bits that have stuck in my sieve, one is the relationships between my sisters. I started with two sisters, and "We Have Always Lived in the Hamlet" came out. If you wrote a story about sisters, it would be very different.

All literature addresses one or more of these three questions: Who am I? Where am I going? How should I behave? Any writer who deals with the question of where am I going eventually runs into old age and death. Advances in medical technology have done much to push back old age, but death still awaits. Someone once said that if you fear old age, you should consider how much worse the alternative is. Not everyone is as sanguine about the end of life though.

PRO LONG

EMY MET THE CONNECTION IN A LOWER DOWNTOWN Denver bar where scars marked tables, chairs didn't match, and the place smelled of bad malt and old kitchen grease. A joint you wished you'd brought your own glass, and if you danced, you wanted to spray your partner with disinfectant first, but he'd heard that the guy had smuggled Chinese proLong.

The college-aged kid put a fanny pack between them. He didn't open it. "Just so we understand. I'm not representing the product with guarantees or an endorsement of its efficacy. It would be illegal to sell you a prescription medicine without a doctor. It's for demonstration purposes only. You got the money?"

Remy nodded. He'd heard the speech numerous times. "It's the real deal, right? I'm not popping cash for sugar pills." He put an envelope by the bag, keeping his hand on it.

The guy leaned close. "Between you and me, the stuff's better than what you'd get straight from Mayo Clinic trials. How old do you think I am?"

Remy studied him. No lines in the corners of the guy's eyes, no gray, clear nails, unblemished skin, brilliantly white teeth. "Twenty-two," Remy said.

"Forty-one." The kid flopped a driver's license on the table. The date checked out.

"Sampling your wares?"

"Would you buy from anyone who looked older than me? It's an advertising expense. How old are you?"

"Sixty-six next month. Let me see."

The guy put the fanny pack on the seat next to him, hiding it from the room, not that anyone was looking their way.

The three capsules were called Lady Kisses or Ruby Slippers. Pink on one end and red on the other. Highly prized. Practically impossible to get. Most thought they were an Internet legend.

The kid reached for the envelope. Remy said, "You know if you were dealing with someone else, you could get killed."

Startled, the young man's hand froze, fingertips almost on the money.

"Those pills are as fake as your ID." Remy put the envelope into his jacket. "You trying to pay your way through school?"

"What are you talking about?"

"Steal bikes on campus and sell those. Less risk. People like me . . . well . . . we're desperate."

Remy slid from the booth and walked out into the rain and dark. A passing bus splashed his shoes. He didn't care. Another dead end. Another tick of the clock.

Outside his hotel, Remy checked his watch's medical readouts. Blood pressure, heart rate, O2 intake, white blood cell count, cholesterol, electrolytes, and thirty other metrics. The data streamed to an autodoc that adjusted his meds based on real-time data. It flagged problem areas, recorded everything he ate or drank, suggested diet and exercises, and synced data with his toilet that analyzed his waste products. He also waded through numerous screens filled with ads for drugs, nutritional supplements, athletic clubs, acupuncture centers, and yoga classes.

The watch picked up traces of immunoglobulins in his blood six months earlier, cancer's harbinger. It caught the beta-amyloids not long after, Alzheimer's calling card. He'd heard a joke once about an elderly man talking to his doctor. The doctor said, "I have bad news and horrible news. First, you have cancer."

"Oh, no," said the old man. "What's the horrible news?"

"You also have Alzheimer's."

The old man looked glum. "Really?" Then he brightened up. "Well, at least I don't have cancer."

The prostitute, knocked on his hotel room door at 11:30. Tina was plump, long-haired and perpetually late. She also had a shy smile, when Remy could get her to smile. Thursday night was their regular date.

"It's raining like crazy," she said. "If I wanted weather like this, I could move to Seattle."

"Colorado's changeable. Give it a couple of hours and something else will come along."

She hung her coat and unbuttoned her blouse. "You sleepy tonight? My kid's running a fever."

Remy looked around his room. Cheap nightshade on the one lamp. Clean but faded bedspread. Mold stain on the wall near the corner. Antiseptics in the bathroom didn't really cover the whiffs of whiskey and bad plumbing. Outside, busses and trams passed occasionally along Colfax Ave. "I'm sorry to hear that. You want to skip this week?"

"My sister is sitting. I'm good. She charges me the same no matter when I come in." Tina dropped her blouse on the nightstand and unbuckled her jeans.

Remy shrugged. "Just as well. I could use the company." He undressed, turned off the light and joined her in bed. Her back was to him. He pressed against her, draped an arm across to pull her close. She smelled like a beer, but in a good way.

She said, "No luck today?"

Remy rested his head on the pillow. "Another rip-off. I didn't even have to test the pill. He'd laminated something from his printer for an ID. He misspelled 'license,' for crying out loud. Put two Ss in it."

Tina laughed, rolled over, and massaged him for several minutes without result. Remy let her. He imagined it was working. He imagined the passion. Finally, though, he pushed her hands away. "I appreciate the effort, but things are falling apart in the old body."

She kissed his forehead. "Have you tried Viagra?"

"I took it before you got here. Aging sucks."

She rolled onto her back. "You're not that old."

Remy wrapped himself around her again. She was warm, soft and comforting. "I am old, and getting older by the minute."

He let himself relax. That's what he paid her for. Sleeping alone night after night became too creepy. His knees ached. His back throbbed. He'd lay awake, thinking about mortality, about not being able to run or jump or throw, about forgetfulness; and when the sun rose in the window, he would have not slept at all. With Tina, he could sleep.

Tonight, though, he faked the deep breathing and soft snore. After a half hour, she rose quietly, dressed in the dark and left.

Her kid was sick, after all, and needed her.

Remy ran into Mark Roundel coming out of The Turning Tide, an upper class gray bar near Coors Field. Nobody there was under sixty, and most were much older than that. Lots of canes, walkers and oxygen bottles. It was a hotbed for geriatric pharmaceuticals: anti-inflammatories, sleep-aids, anti-rheumatoids, heart stimulants, memory augmenters, industrial-strength vitamins and the rest of the shopping list for the aging. Folks swapped drugs like trading cards. Remy met Mark six months earlier when Mark had been the go-to guy for senolytics, a drug class that combatted aging by repairing eroded telomeres. The supply dried up when the FDA shut down the company for operating without approved regulatory oversight.

"Let me buy you a drink," boomed Mark. He clapped Remy on the shoulder and went back into the bar with him.

Remy liked The Turning Tide for more than the drug connection. They displayed posters from the '80s and '90s: *Sixteen Candles, Ferris Bueller's Day Off, Pulp Fiction*, and played music from the era. It was like a permanent reunion for the class of '95. Talking Heads' "Once in a Lifetime" started.

Mark led him to a table in the back.

"You're looking good," Remy said suspiciously. Mark's hair was no less gray, but it seemed thicker, and the last time they'd met, Mark walked with a cane. No cane and no unsureness in his step now.

"Beer first," said Mark. "I got a bit of a windfall."

They drank. Remy observed Mark's hands, how he held his mug without a shake. Mark told a story about fishing with his dad when he was fifteen, the same year as the Twin Towers. He told it without hesitation, without repetitions or digressions. When the waitress, a winsome blonde with an athletic step, came by with the second round, Mark flirted. He suggested he might help her manage school debt. He wrote his cell number on his business card and gave it to her. As she walked away, he eyed her appreciatively.

Remy whispered, "You scored!"

"I don't know what you're talking about."

Mark's posture, a tightness in his skin, his quickness, gave him away.

After the fourth beer, Mark started talking. He leaned in, kept his voice low. "Hypothetically, let's say I ran into a drug rep who was down on his luck. Gambling debts, you know, and kids who need education, he might be willing to part with a sample. Something he ordinarily sells to the elite. Something that costs a fortune. Let's say theoretically that he ran into a guy like me with a hefty retirement fund, someone who believes all the money in the world means nothing if you don't have the health to enjoy it. Then he might drop a Ruby Slipper on the sly. It's a sample. Not inventoried. Who would miss it? In the right hands, though, not trivial."

Billy Joel's "River of Dreams" played in the background. Mark wasn't the only winner he'd found, but the rest came to nothing. Their sources were one-time only or flukes. A drug rep, though, that could mean something. "Let me get you another beer." Remy flagged down the waitress and a fresh round. "Theoretically, where would someone find your drug rep?"

Mark peered slyly at him. "Let's say an older fellow was feeling his oats and had money to spend. He might trade information for pliable company."

Remy looked around. At other tables prescription bottles came out of purses and briefcases. Pills were counted out and swapped. Cash slid from hand to hand. The Turning Tide existed for gray trades. Everyone looking for an edge, a tool in the perpetual battle against age. Youth was the underground currency. They wanted it again. He could see it in their eyes, in their swelled knuckles. The Turning Tide was a market, and everything was a commodity.

"She's not like the barmaid," said Remy as he wrote Tina's number on a slip of paper. "Whatever she asks, pay double."

Mark took the paper. With the fragile care of a man who has drunk too much, he typed a number into Remy's phone. "Don't mention my name," Mark said. "We didn't have this conversation."

Harold the drug rep met Remy in the top row seats at the Pepsi Center during a Denver Nuggets exhibition game. The arena was seventy-five percent empty, and there wasn't a soul within twenty-five yards. Harold said, "It's an unacknowledged war, and you, my friend are cannon fodder."

Remy nodded. He kneaded his left calf that had cramped climbing the stairs to these seats.

Harold continued, "The way I see it is insurance companies, pharmaceuticals, lawyers, and government are in it together to milk money from the population while delivering the least compassionate care imaginable. Your role is to pay premiums, fork out for unreasonable deductibles, and then die without straining the system. I'm working for blood suckers."

Remy nodded. Harold was one of those people: the conspiracists who saw medicine through paranoid glasses. Remy met bunches of them at The Turning Tide.

"Look, I get that medical care is expensive. I don't mind that it's expensive. What I want is the medicines we're not being offered, the miracle pill. I want the universal cure. The fountain of youth. I heard you're a guy who can connect me."

Harold slumped into his seat and appeared to be watching the game. "It's a myth," he said after a while. "Who have you been talking to?"

"Friend of a friend." Remy's knuckles whitened on the chair rest. This was the make or break moment in the negotiation. If Harold didn't like the smell of it, all he had to do was walk away. No deal, and Remy would be starting over. "I have disposable income."

Harold looked him over. Remy knew what he saw. He saw it in the mirror every morning: hanging skin under the neck, age spots, watery eyes. His hands trembled. Nothing dignified about the vehicle falling apart.

"How much disposable income?"

"It really works then? It exists?" Remy's breath tightened in his lungs.

Harold leaned close. "It works better than anyone imagined. It doesn't just stop ageing; it reverses it, at least for a year before the effects begin to wear off. proLong eliminates cancer cells. It repairs joint damage, clears arteries, resets the metabolism. Dementia goes away. The body is reborn from the inside. One drug! Everything a snake oil salesman claims, proLong actually does."

"What's the downside? Why aren't the drug companies tooling up to release it? Everyone will buy; they'll make a fortune."

Harold laughed bitterly. "proLong is a job killer. This one drug eliminates the rest. You'll only go to a doctor for traumatic injury or cosmetic surgery. Hospitals will close. Other pharmaceutical agents will be obsolete. They'll never release it."

"That's awful. The world will lose a wonder."

"Only part of the world, Remy. It's too effective to be made generally available—just think what would happen to world population if everyone lived hundreds of years—but powerful people aren't going to let it disappear. No, there's a secret program tooling up right now. The pills will still be made, but you won't see them."

"I won't see them?"

On the court below, a player made a spectacular dunk. The small crowd erupted into cheers.

"Not through a legitimate channel. Just how big is your 'disposable income?'"

Remy named a figure. "A lifetime of working and investing."

"That'll buy one pill. You wire the money to my account. I make sure it's strings-free, and then I deliver."

Remy thought of the other sellers he'd talked to. Everyone a fake, a scam. "What guarantee do I have that you are legit? I can't clean out my account on a promise."

Harold nodded. "That's the beauty. I can give you a taste. The real deal works in stages. Sort of a time release mechanism, except that it imbeds itself in the system instead of sitting in your stomach. The effects accumulate. That's how it makes repairs. It's not instant, but I can let you try the basic drug without the long-term effect. You'll get a day or so to see what it does. If you're convinced, then call again and we can talk about a full dose."

He produced a small cellophane envelope from his jacket, dangled it from two fingers. "Mix it in a glass of water. Give it an hour and you'll start feeling it. Twenty-four hours before it fades."

"Side effects?" Remy took the envelope. A teaspoon of semi-clear crystals like table sugar shifted in it.

"Some people report depression. You taste the fruit of the vine, and you remember how good it was."

On the basketball floor, a player made a steal, raced up the middle with two opponents pursuing. The ball moved in a blur. Faster than Remy could believe possible, the breakaway player reached the top of the key, launched himself in the air a fraction ahead of the defenders. He rose, impossibly high, avoiding outreached hands, then kissed the ball off the backboard for two. Remy remembered when he played basketball on the driveway with a friend long gone now. Hours and hours of games to three, win by two. They never tired. Sweat flowed from them like rivers, and they laughed and strained and played again and again.

Remy tucked the envelope into his pocket and stood.

Harold grabbed his sleeve. "If you have a lady, this would be the night to call her."

Colfax after sunset. An evening thunderstorm rumbled through, soaking streets and sidewalks, leaving low, ugly clouds that hovered like great, wet vultures, but Remy felt good. The air smelled clean and moist. Water drops falling from a tree plinkcd as clear as fairy bells in puddles. Bikes whipped by on the street, tires ripping through the watery sheen. He took his glasses off to wipe away spray and realized he saw better without them. Two hours earlier, he'd mixed the crystals and drank. He'd started walking, too antsy to stay still.

Were the crystals just an upper? Was this a placebo effect? He wanted proLong to be real more than anything. He yearned for a do-over, a chance to relive wasted days, to absorb minutes as if each were a pearl. How much had he lost not walking outside, not visiting friends, not reading books he meant to read? How many chances had he passed?

It wasn't that he'd been lazy. Once he'd gone to Europe, toured castles and cathedrals. He'd spent a week on a Caribbean cruise. He'd gone skydiving another time. There'd been romances. But when he added up his accomplishments, they seemed small. A list small enough to fit on a tombstone. A poor epitaph. When he looked at them, none of them measured up to the moment right now. He turned his face to the sky to feel the mist, to fill his lungs. Nothing he'd ever done matched walking down Colfax this very second.

He crossed a street. Before him stretched a single city block, store fronts to the side, a rain-drenched street reflecting city lights to his other, like a runway, like a launching ramp. Remy picked up the pace, noticing the persistent ache in his hips had faded. His back didn't hurt. Faster he strode until he'd broken into a trot, arms swinging, chin high. He ran down the sidewalk, grinning. Air whistling. His feet left the ground, splash, splash, splash, like an Olympian, like a gazelle; and before he knew it, he reached the end of the block. The light turned red against him, so he stopped, bent over, laughing at the audacity. Oh, god, it felt good to run.

Then he coughed, a great wrenching cough. His lungs worked to expel thirty-year-old tarnish. He laughed again, dots swimming behind his eyes, dizzy for an instant, and then strong again, breathing evenly.

He called Tina. Offered her triple to stand up a client and see him instead. They reached his hotel door at the same time. "You're looking chipper," she said.

He kissed her before they'd closed the door. They didn't sleep, not once. The sun rose on them together in bed. He took her for breakfast before saying goodbye. It was only as he walked back to the hotel that he realized he'd figured an eighteen percent tip for the bill in his head. He hadn't felt confident enough with numbers to do that for several years. A fog had cleared. Memories crowded. His brain felt nimble, curious, questing; zinging on fire from image to image. So this is youth, he thought. This is what I took for granted most of my life.

By dinner, Remy couldn't walk. Every muscle in his back felt sprained, and his calves cramped on top of Achilles tendons that turned to marble. It took ten minutes to get to the bathroom where he had a bottle of Diazepam to relax the muscles he imagined were in the midst of an extended spasm, as if his entire body was trying to make a fist.

Harold met him at a Starbucks the next morning. "You all right, guy?" Harold asked.

Remy put his hand on chair tops to keep himself steady as they walked back to a table. Suddenly, he understood the necessity of a walker. He had a new respect for his old friends who relied on them to get around.

"I'll do it," said Remy. "Give me the details."

Harold nodded, knowingly, while opening his computer. Minutes later, it was done. Remy's entire retirement account had been drained. Harold handed him an unlabeled prescription bottle with one pink and red capsule in it.

Harold said, "How long have you been looking for this?"

"Seven years."

"It's effects last about a year, then whatever you suffer from today will come roaring back. You spent seven years and a lifetime of earning for one good year. Will it be worth it?"

Remy bounced the pill in the container. It clicked in his hand. "When I need it again, I just have to find you, right?"

Harold shrugged. "A lot can happen in a year. I might not be able to get anymore. I might be out of the business. I hear already that they're tightening up distribution. For all I know, they could find out that I sold some and kill me for it."

"No, surely not."

"Can you think of a secret more important than this one?" Harold looked pensive. "I'm a rebel, Remy. The system can tolerate a thief, but not a disbeliever. Besides, the price is the same a year from now. Do you think you can gather together a sum that took you your entire working career in twelve months?"

Remy put the bottle into his jacket. He hadn't popped the pill, yet he already felt immortal. A wise part of him said, "It's the over-confidence of youth," but the rest of him trusted, really trusted, that in a year he could do it. Nothing stops you when you're young. No mountain can't be climbed. No ocean can't be swum.

Remy felt the power aching to get out. He was young, or would be soon, and possibility is never ending.

 *Minor characters are fascinating, or at least they should be. If the protagonist is supposed to feel multifaceted and real, then it only makes sense that she/he lives in a world with equally real minor characters. Part of the fun in this story for me was in the creation of the kid who tries to scam Remy into buying fake proLong; Mark Roundel, the old acquaintance; Harold, the cynical drug rep, and most especially, Tina, the prostitute. The characters are minor, though. There's not much room to make them unique without making them distractingly too interesting and drawing attention away from the main character's story. It's a balancing act, but one worth doing. I learned a lot about minor characters by reading Charles Dickens. Pick up a copy of* David Copperfield *or* Great Expectations. *You've probably read them before, but look now at how he creates unique characters in just a line or two. He's instructive.*

At first when the thought of space flight entered our collective imagination, we saw a universe of possibilities. The urge to explore caught fire in our imaginations. But it wasn't long before we started to the think of the day to day existence in space. How could we survive the long trips? How much of what makes us human could we do without? What might we do to recreate our lives in environments that aren't conducive to our basic needs? In this story, Ethan's parents made a decision about what would make their lives complete.

ORPHANED

THE BOY SAT CROSS-LEGGED IN THE MIDDLE OF THE FLOOR, chanting names: Metis, Adrastea, Amalthea, Thebe ... He said them to calm himself. His mom told him, "Facts fight fears."

He climbed into Dad's chair by the communication console where he surveyed buttons, toggles, sliding switches, small joysticks and an array of lights. Some blinked, some were green. One was red. A countdown timer clicked off numbers methodically: "0D, 2H, 12M, 8S." The 12 became 11 while he watched.

He pressed a button. His dad always pressed buttons when he sat here. "Ethan to Dad and Mom," he said. The speaker above a small video screen that displayed nothing remained silent. Ethan tried his call again. Dad made calls too, except he said, "Captain Ramis to Relay Central" to talk to his bosses, or "Base to Mobile One" when he called Mom. She said the same thing when she sat in that seat, but she'd be calling Dad. Someone always answered when they called. Mobile One would answer on its own if Mom and Dad were in the habitat. It could explore independently. "It has a bright AI," Dad said.

But no one answered. He was sure he pressed the right button. He'd seen Mom and Dad use it a thousand times, but they also adjusted dials before making a call. He didn't know what the settings were. He murmured, Io, Europa, Ganymede, Calisto.

Through the tiny port beside the communication array sat Mobile One, eighty yards away on Io's uneven surface. Something happened to it: the six-wheeled car was canted to the side, lying on its single door, the top pressed to a rock, crushing the communications array. "Ethan to Mom and Dad," he said again. "Are you okay?"

Behind him, Mom had hung a "Happy Birthday" banner over the dining room table. She and Dad had been figuring out how to make a cake for him before they'd left. They'd wrapped a present that sat in the table's middle. "I'm five today," thought Ethan. "Today's my birthday." Mom would hold him close and call him her "little miracle." Dad bounced him on his knee when he sat at his workstation. He played games with him. He read to Ethan and said he was their "science project." He said, "You, my child, are a 'misappropriation of resources," then laughed and hugged him.

"Station, why aren't they answering?"

The station said, "The Mobile One Rover appears to be incapacitated."

"What if they're hurt?"

"My medical facility is top notch. It can print skin, major organs, eyes, and other desired replacements. It can also diagnose and treat most known illnesses."

"Call Relay Station. They'll help."

"Relay Station will not be within range for four more days. You will have to be brave."

"Shut up, Station." Ethan hated AI pep talks. It was always telling him to work hard or be happy or to "solve the problem."

Ethan went back to the port. In the distance, one of Io's numerous volcanoes spewed sulfur dioxide into the sky. Sunlight caught the flume, turning it into a sparkling fountain.

If he could call Relay Station himself, he would, even though

Mom and Dad warned him to never talk to them. They sent him from the room when they called. "They don't know about you," said Mom. She told him when he went to bed about their journey to Io, about how they were to man the station for seven years before coming home. "We were too lonely," Mom said, "so you came along. You're our secret child. You're a treasure and twice as precious."

Ethan checked the countdown timer again. 0D, 2H, 7M, 49S. It was the air supply in Mobile One.

"Are they okay? How's their telemetry?" No one told Ethan that he had a strange vocabulary for a five-year-old. In fact, it wasn't unusual for someone raised the way he was. He knew words like silicate, caldera, Colchis Regio, and he knew that Io was subject to tidal heating. He could disassemble and reassemble a space suit, and he could sort and store rock samples. He could name Jupiter's sixty-three moons.

"No telemetry data is available from Mobile One."

"Is there air in the rover? Has it ruptured?" Ethan swallowed heavily. He knew about vacuums. Outside the habitat was beautiful but empty and deadly cold. Jupiter filled half the sky, white, gray and orange striped, always changing and always huge.

"No telemetry data is available from Mobile One. But your parents wear space suits when in the rover. Even if there was a loss of pressure, they could survive."

Ethan grabbed handholds and propelled himself through the living area and work area, barely touching the floor in the light gravity, past hydroponics and the power plant until he was in the garage. Mobile Two stood under the lights, a duplicate of the rover marooned outside the station. Access covers were open. Wires led to panels on the walls. "Can we fix Mobile Two?" said Ethan.

"It has no AI," said Station.

"I don't need it to be smart. Can we drive it?"

"The AI controls the complicated gearing in the wheels, adjusts life support, and is the coordinator for all mechanical operations. Without the AI, the rover cannot be operated safely."

Ethan climbed up the vehicle's side to the cabin. "We're only going to Mom and Dad."

Inside the vehicle were two rotating seats and numerous control panels. Mom and Dad took him for rides many times. They used one set of controls to drive it and another manipulated the mechanical arms on the front and back. Once, Mom let him move the arms. He stretched them out from the rover, opened their clawed hands, and drug them through the sulfur dioxide frost that covered the surface.

"Is this strong enough to set Mobile One upright?"

Station said, "Mobile Two suffered damage in a quake five years ago. It cannot maintain cabin pressure. It cannot be operated safely without the AI. You will not be able to control it efficiently to effect a rescue. This line of questioning is not brave; it is foolish."

"Tell me how to get Mobile Two ready to move."

The Station didn't answer.

"Don't be such a baby!" yelled Ethan.

Ethan tried not to imagine that he was already too late. Dad told him once while they were doing one of their regular safety inspections, "The universe doesn't forgive mistakes." They were checking the motion dampers the station rested on. If one failed, any of Io's regularly occurring, strong quakes could shake the station to pieces. "Io is like a big ball of putty," Dad said. "Jupiter's gravity and the other moons squeeze and pull on it all the time. The surface rises and falls more than a hundred yards per cycle. It's like being in an elevator."

Maybe Mom and Dad made a mistake.

Themisto, Leda, Himalia, Lysithia. Ethan detached power cables like he'd seen his parents do before. The heavy connectors were hard for him to budge. He had to grip with both hands, brace a foot against Mobile Two and pull.

"How much time, Station?"

"One hour, twenty-one minutes. I have run diagnostics on Mobile Two. The cabin may not hold air. The heating units are off line.

The vehicle has not moved on its own power for one-thousand, eight-hundred and twenty-five days."

Ethan ran around the rover, disconnecting wires and closing panels. "Is it strong enough to push Mobile One off its side?"

"Yes . . . probably, but, Ethan, if you lose your air and freeze, you will not have saved anyone. Your parents will not approve of you doing this."

"What I need is a spacesuit that fits."

"One does not exist."

"Can you help me drive Mobile Two?"

"I can remotely monitor rover status. I can answer questions." The speakers whispered. Station hadn't finished talking but was deciding how to phrase its thought. "If you leave, I will be lonely."

Ethan worked grimly, silently. Station sang songs to him at night, read him poems, played word games. When Mom and Dad worked, Station was his friend. It cheered him when he was sad.

Station said, "If the cabin loses pressure, the liquids in your skin will boil away, lowering your temperature precipitously. This will be painful. The garage depressurizes in sixty seconds. It repressurizes in five minutes. A human being loses consciousness in fifteen seconds in a vacuum."

"If you can't be helpful, stop talking." Ethan opened a locker, pulled out a reflective blanket and tossed it into the rover.

Elara, Carpo, Euproie, Thelxinoe. The chanting quieted his breathing. He circled the rover. All the cables and wires were detached. The pathway to the garage door was clear. He started to climb the ladder, then jumped off and ran back to his sleeping area. In his toy box, he found the six-inch tall astronaut his parents had printed for him. Mom called it an "action figure." The miniature stood resolutely with his feet apart, hands on his hips, looking up as if he expected to rise on his own in a moment. Ethan called him Alpha-man. Alpha-man explored new planets, he made friends with alien creatures (Mom and Dad had printed them too), and Alpha-man always knew what to do. Mom told him Alpha-man adventures before he went to bed.

Ethan put Alpha-man on the mission specialist seat in the rover, while he fastened himself into the pilot's seat. A push of a button, and the door closed with a pneumatic finality, popping his ears as the cabin established its own pressure. He threw a switch that turned the garage lights to flashing red. Air rushed from the space. At first the pumps sucking the air away sounded loud. Then the noise faded. Ethan listened intently. Was there a hiss? Of all the sounds on the habitat, leaking air was the one he feared most. Twice he'd discovered leaks after large quakes. As powerful as the motion dampers on the station were, a heavy shaking strained the structure. Doors automatically closed to isolate compromised areas. Mom and Dad sprinted to make repairs. In every room, sealant and patching material stood ready.

The panic always started with a hiss.

No hiss. Just steady fan noise. The garage doors opened outward, revealing Io's dim surface. Dad told him that the sun lit Io's surface about the same brightness as on Earth right after the sunset. Ethan had seen pictures of Earth. The sun's brightness during the day didn't look as weird to him as a sky without stars or Jupiter's looming presence.

Controls on Mobile 2 were straightforward. One joystick steered while the other changed speed. The AI adjusted power to the wheels depending on the traction. Mom told him that driving across Io was like navigating a field of concrete bubble wrap. Lava flow created the moon's surface. Gas-filled cavities and lava tubes formed beneath the elastic rock before cooling, some very thick, but some parchment thin. Broken bubbles, like cracked egg shells, scattered across the plain, monstrous gaping holes rimmed with silicate rock, iron and iron sulfate teeth.

"How much time?"

"Thirty-seven minutes."

Euantha, Helike, Orthosie, Locaste.

Ethan slid the joystick forward. Electric wheels clicked into motion; the rover lurched and then stopped.

Station said, "You must continue to press the joystick forward or Mobile Two will halt. I'm detecting a slight air leak in the cabin. The rover will automatically compensate by pumping in more air."

Ethan felt good. He was three feet closer to rescuing his parents, seventy-nine yards to go, so he pressed the joystick, following the path Mobile one had taken.

"Why did they fall over? They've driven this way a thousand times."

"Without readings, I would guess an undetected sinkhole."

The rover cleared the garage doors, jerking forward, allowing Ethan to see more of Io than was visible from the habitat. A second volcano sprayed beyond the horizon, marking Jupiter with a silver haze.

He wrapped the blanket tightly around his shoulders. Without heating units, the air that blew into the cabin was already cold. Beyond that, the heat he carried with him quickly dissipated. His breath blew out in frost.

"Your air leak is increasing, Ethan." Station sounded desolate.

A slight whistle sounded from the door, and the blowers redoubled their efforts, but Mobile Two advanced steadily. Now, it was only twenty yards away. He saw a light from Mobile One's cabin that he hadn't been able to see before. It glowed on the rock the rover had fallen against, so it still had power. The wheels on the left side had broken through the brittle surface. What had been a level path yesterday now had a pothole large enough to tip Mobile One.

The whistle raised in volume. Ethan swallowed to clear his ears. Praxidike, Harpalyke, Mneme, Hermippe.

Ten feet from the crippled rover, Ethan slowed Mobile Two. He gasped a little for breath, and he realized his nose was bleeding. His face and hands lost feeling. The forward arms took a minute to unship. At first, they wouldn't move. Ethan shoved the control forward that should have extended them, but they only whined. Then he remembered and threw a toggle that released them. A heavy thump from the rover's roof told him they were free.

"If you lose air pressure, you will have fifteen seconds of consciousness," said Station.

Ethan maneuvered the arms so he could scoot them under the fallen rover. "That is not helpful." He wished there was a window in back that he could see through. Were his parents okay? If he could right the vehicle, and the door wasn't jammed shut, they could walk to the habitat. Dots swam in front of his eyes. He tapped the joystick that moved Mobile Two forward. The hands slid through the yellowish frost, under the metal. He pulled the lever back. If the hands held, if Mobile One wasn't too heavy, if his parents were alive, this could work.

Servos inside whined in protest. The arms were designed for medium to light tasks, like collecting samples or moving rocks, not picking up an entire exploration vehicle.

Station said, "Oh, no. Be brave."

With a pop, an entire section of seal around the door gave way. A whirlwind stirred dust and a scrap of paper. Alpha-man flew off the mission specialist's chair. Stuck to gap in the door for a second, then fell. Twin ice picks jammed into Ethan's ears. He screamed but couldn't hear it as his lungs emptied themselves. No air came in when he inhaled. His eyes burned. Bubbles formed on the backs of his hands. Everything in him shrieked with pain, but Mobile One stirred! Ethan held the joystick back. His face, his arms, all of him seemed to swell.

Fifteen seconds is what Station said. Slowly Mobile One tipped toward upright. Time slowed. Surely fifteen seconds had passed, but he could still see what was happening. Ice crystals formed in his mouth and nasal passages. Pain. Pain. Pain. He held on. He held on.

Thyone, Ananke, Herse . . .

*

A flicker . . .

He dreamed.

Mom leaned over him.

Aetne, Kale, Tygete . . .

I'm awake, he thought.

A flicker . . .

Dad examined Ethan's arm. "His skin is freeze dried. Muscles ruined." Dad pulled on the skin. It flaked away. Broke off in chunks. Ethan felt nothing.

A flicker . . .

His arms were naked metal rods that ended in shiny metal skeleton hands. Ethan couldn't move.

"We'll reprint the damaged parts. We can build him again."

Mom said, "Is the AI intact? Is he still Ethan?" She looked down on him. Ethan tried to show her that he was there, but nothing moved. He couldn't even blink.

Dad thought for a moment. "I think so. A rover's AI is built for abuse. A freezing wouldn't wipe it clean."

Ethan saw Mom's hand coming down. She must be touching my head, he thought.

"So he'll still be my little boy?"

Dad smiled. "Far as I can tell. He's come a long way from being a wiped rover AI."

Station said, "He's not dead? You can make him again?"

Mom and Dad nodded.

Station sobbed.

 *Most "surprise" stories don't work. Either the surprise wasn't all that effective, it was too earlier telegraphed, or it wasn't worth waiting for. There was only one O'Henry, and darned few successful imitators. So, hinging the entire payoff for the reader on the surprise ending isn't the best strategy. An easy way to avoid this problem is to make the rest of the story interesting on its own. Then, if the surprise doesn't work, the story still has payoffs. That's what I was trying for in "Orphaned."*

The world's first stories are the mythologies we study now. The ancients told how the world was created and explained natural phenomena. They created heroes who exemplified the way they wanted to see themselves. Humans use narrative for so many purposes, including the tales we tell our loved ones to make them feel better.

THE LIES

BRI TOLD ME THE LIFT SHIPS TO TERRA STATION TOOK off Tuesday and Friday mornings from Campbell Field. They made the cabin look like an old-time luxury liner, like a zeppelin crossing the Atlantic, with wooden wainscoting and brass fittings. She said stewards in white jackets and white gloves served champagne in souvenir flutes engraved with your takeoff date.

The ship held five hundred colonists, chosen by an international lottery, but because separating loved ones was cruel, the lucky could choose three people to go with them. It could be family members or friends. Lottery winners had all debts paid, and if their leaving deprived a family of income, the corporation provided absentee pensions to prevent suffering.

Much of the ship's hull became transparent during the flight so passengers could see the flame that enveloped them at takeoff, and then the ground receding so fast that before they knew it, the sky grew dark and the horizon curved. What a joy, she said, to discover for yourself Earth's true size. In one way, the Earth was huge. The continents and oceans unrolled beneath you. Day became night and cities glowed like Christmas lights. The size, the grandeur, startled you and filled you with awe. At the same time, you saw Earth all at once, a blue and white marble, a falling soccer ball, a crystal sphere that shrank as the ship rose to its high orbit. That tiny planet held humanity, held within its history all that had happened to man, and if you raised your fist, you could eclipse it, the Earth was so small.

I told Bri that doctors had found cures for human suffering. While I traveled to the stars, diseases were being eliminated. Accurate genetic testing guaranteed medicines custom tailored. Cancers, of course, would vanish first, followed closely by communicable disease and inherited conditions. Finally, they would remake the deformed. The lame would walk, the deaf would hear, and the blind would paint new glories.

Bri's lungs would inhale fully and suck in flowers and mountains and summer storms. She'd stand from her wheelchair. When I returned, I'd put my hand in the small of her back and twirl with her on the dance floor. She would tell me about Earth's advances. Not in the whispery, painful way she spoke now, but with a full voice. She'd laugh and not cough. She'd learn to sing.

She held my hand and told me about Zeti Prime, the Earth-like planet orbiting Zeti Reticuli. Oceans lapped silver beaches circling tropical islands. Lizard-birds nested in the blue trees, and at dusk took off as one. She said they filled the sky, then swept low over the waves, hunting the tentacled fish. Zeti Prime enjoyed a lighter gravity. Colonists reported the spring in their step lasted for months before they grew used to it. Zeti Reticuli's light healed depression and it didn't promote carcinomas. Crops grown there contained more nutrients and vitamins. No one on Zeti Reticuli had died of old age yet. Colonies were small. Wherever you walked, in a few minutes you would be in the frontier. Rivers, mountains and lakes were yet unnamed.

Hike twenty miles, she said, throw seeds on the ground, then stand back.

Will there be a stream there?

Oh, yes. What will you call it?

The Tumbling Bri.

She smiled.

You'll go to a golden hospital on a hill, I said, where the nurses speak seven languages and have studied under the greatest doctors in the world. The medicine there is so powerful that healthy people are cured. Each doctor controls a ward where their breakthrough treatments are miraculous daily. The hospital's chaplain only leads services of praise. He never comforts the grieving; there is no grief there.

I have your ticket to Terra Station, she said.

Bri reached into her pajama pocket, the skin on the back of her hand as thin as tissue. She took two tries before she brought out the paper slip. Her bald head rested on my shoulder. Her ribs and backbone pressed against my arm. She closed her eyes.

Around us, other patients lay on cots. Some coughed. Some cried. No one comforted them. Light came through grimy windows. The air didn't move. At one end, a net still dangled from the basketball rim, but the backboard above us had been broken long ago. They told us there would be medical trucks coming every afternoon, but they didn't come yesterday or the day before. I gave Bri a sip of water.

Bri said, what is the hospital's name, the golden one on the hill?

Grace Taylor Hope.

I bent close to hear her.

That's funny, that your name is on it.

I have to go to work, I said. I'll be back when I finish.

No, today is your flight. You won the lottery.

Of course. I kissed her on the forehead. They'll move you to Grace Taylor Hope. I'll find you there.

I'll be better before then.

I walked in the middle of the street because bricks strewed the sidewalk. Trash filled the alleys. At University Blvd., a burned out bus on its side blocked the path. Inside, dogs growled as they fought over a hunk of meat. I didn't want to know what kind. The city smelled of scummy water and burning tires.

At Veteran's Park, I checked out rubber gloves from the foreman. They didn't put the bodies in bags anymore. There were too many. I took a girl wearing a yellow sweater from the back of a flatbed truck, put her in a wheelbarrow and pushed her up the ramp overlooking the pit. She rolled twenty feet before she stopped against the dead at the bottom.

Back to the truck. An old man with scabs on his face. Back to the truck. A small boy wearing a Cub Scout shirt. I was glad he didn't weigh much. Back to the truck.

The sun set. Diesel generators ran the lights. When one truck emptied, another took its place. At the pit's far end, an earth mover pushed dirt over the bodies. Tomorrow, we'd move to Denver University's practice fields.

My arms ached until finally I stopped under one of the angrily buzzing lights, and pulled the paper from my pocket. One edge was ragged. Maybe Bri tore it out of a book. Barely legible in pencil, it read TICKET FOR ONE TO ZETI PRIME.

Beyond the arcing whiteness, the city was dark. A fire burned to the west, too far away to worry about. Supply ships to Terra Station run every day, Bri had told me. They ride on flaming fingers to the stars, and sound like God clearing his throat. Look for them, she said.

But I looked for Grace Taylor Hope instead, the hospital on the hill. It's out there. They have a bed for Bri. Even now, they are picking her up. She'll ride in an ambulance on silk pillows. A steward in a white jacket with white gloves will offer her a soothing tea, and the driver will miss every bump in the road.

I put the ticket back in my pocket. Tomorrow things will be better. Tomorrow Bri will be strong. Tomorrow the world will turn around. She told me so.

I have a ticket to the stars.

The writer Bruce Holland Rogers wrote a completely brilliant story called "The Dead Boy at Your Window," which won a Stoker Award and a Pushcart Prize. He said that he wrote it in response to a workshop writing prompt: Start a story with a lie. I loved Bruce's piece, and I thought the starting point was wonderful. One way I use to provoke stories is to challenge myself with a writing suggestion. You can find them online if you're interested. Just do a search for "writing prompts."

Special places in the world exist for almost everyone. Sometimes those places exist for only a moment. Some places are there every time you return. And every once in a while, there are places that find you, when you're in the right state of mind.

FALLING OUT OF DOWNEY

IGHTLY ROLLED NEWSPAPERS FILLED BOTH BAGS, BUT I didn't recognize the street. One moment I was rounding the corner onto Elm, ready to start my route, and the next the street changed into something else.

I nearly wrecked!

Pedaling slowly, I inventoried. Mountains to both sides, check. I-70, loaded with traffic whining a bit above town to the north, check. Familiar houses before me, nope. Nothing I recognized. By the block's end, I knew I'd fallen out of Downey, which would be a catastrophe. Trianna, who I'd had a crush on since seventh grade, said I could come to her house to hang out tonight.

People said the secret to getting to Downey was establishing the correct state of mind. Mr. Lambert, who publishes (and writes, photographs, designs, and sells advertising for) the *Downey Pica-yune* told me he'd been driving to Denver for a friend's wedding when he took the Downey exit. He said he hadn't been thinking of anything in particular. He didn't need anything. The exit sign looked like any other, although in retrospect, he'd never noticed it in the many times he'd driven this stretch. He saw the visitor center, where people stop who almost get to Downey, but the town beyond looked tempting. Four days later, he owned the *Pic* and he stays in town, mostly.

All the new folk get to Downey that way. I'm a native, though. Downey born and raised. Never left, until now. I swallowed a bit of panic. People tell stories about life outside Downey. Not good ones. I check out CNN on the Internet. I know about cities and wars and stuff.

To get back, I needed to keep moving. That was clear. Travel gets you places. Standing still gathers dust. The houses to both sides were typical mountain homes. Most were well-tended Victorian cottages. Lambert called them "painted ladies" when folks took extra time with them, painting the trim different colors, putting flowers on the porches. Many sported low cast-iron fences next to the sidewalk. No garages or driveways. They parked their cars in the alley behind the homes just like they did in Downey, but this wasn't Downey.

A woman in a broad-brimmed hat, pruning roses, waved as I went by. I nodded her direction. She didn't look like a monster, but you can never tell.

It felt weird to go down a street without delivering papers. If this were Elm, I'd be flipping them onto porches left and right. Lambert says that outside of Downey, newspapers are dying, but pretty much everyone takes the paper. You can't get local news on your computer. The lesbian vampires in the yellow two-story take the paper. Big tippers. The accountant next door likes me to put the paper in the mailbox. The werewolves keep a big dog in the front yard, so I have to phone them ahead of time before I collect their subscription. I thought it would be funny if the werewolves' dog turned into something else on the full moon, but it just stays a dog. A retired tooth fairy subscribes, as does the giant, the elves and the witch, along with the guy who sells hardware, the electrician and the mayor. Everybody. Lambert called the *Pic* the "the community's heart."

My favorite customers are in the cemetery, though. They set up trust funds before they died, so I never have to collect. There's real peace in pedaling on the path by the tombstones, flipping a paper next to each marker.

A street sign said I was on Virginia Street. Cutting down a block took me to Colorado Blvd., and a block later was Miner Street, then Idaho Street. Then, the interstate. The town was only four streets wide, sort of like Downey, which was also way longer than it was across. I rode Miner Street, checking out the businesses. Lots of little shops. Very touristy. A pizza place called Beau Jo's smelled particularly good, but this was no time for food. I had to get back.

"Hey, son. Sell me a paper?" An old guy wearing a baseball cap held out a dollar. "Keep the change," he said as he walked off. I wondered what he would make of the *Pic*. The front-page story featured a piece on the difficulty in enforcing noise ordinances when banshees lived close to town.

I know we deal with stuff that guy wouldn't recognize, but nothing as scary as on this side. We don't worry about global warming, for example, or terrorists or Amber alerts. When Downey fell out of the world, it escaped a lot, and took everyone with it. I closed my eyes and tried thinking Downey thoughts, about crimson sunsets, and how the creek that ran through town sounded like laughing bells, and how every once in a while, travelers who were time shifted and lost wandered down the street, wondering where they were. Sitting on a bench in Silver Park by the library could be very entertaining. That's where I was with Trianna when she leaned over and said, "Do you want to hang out at my house?" We were guessing where strangers came from. Displaced miners were easy to spot, as were Indians. Once a troop of Confederate soldiers marched through, looking confused at the buildings. But they never broke formation. They're like most everyone else in the world who slip out of their time and place occasionally.

We sat on the bench side by side. Every once in a while her bare arm would brush up against mine. She wore a white sundress that showed off her tan. We'd run into each other several times since her sixteenth birthday in June. I'm a June birthday too, so we talked about how lucky we weren't born in December. A June birthday divided the year up nicely. You get Christmas, and six months later, more presents. We agreed it was the perfect birthday. I bought her ice cream at Papa Shutlz Scones and Cones, and she thanked me with a kiss on the cheek.

I had to get back! If I stood her up, that slimy Bob Castile who smoked cigarettes and played a guitar would make a move. I don't know what anyone sees in him.

The historic business section in this town was only a few blocks long. I crossed a bridge over a twenty-foot wide creek, passed Ace Hardware, then circled a roundabout with a statue in the center. That's why the two boys I almost ran into surprised me. I didn't see them until I was already close. They straddled their bikes in the parking lot of a store called Climb High or Die that featured coiled ropes and a big carabineer display in the window. My front wheel was only inches from the kid on the right, who was about my size. His partner was huge. A shock of black hair tumbled over his forehead, hiding his eyes. Both bikes sported canvas bags to carry papers dangling from the handlebars. The logo on the side said CLEAR CREEK COURANT. My bags said DOWNEY PICAYUNE. The smaller guy looked me over. "Who the hell are you?"

"I'm the paperboy," I offered.

"The hell you say," said the small one. His breath smelled like bad vegetables. "We're the paperboys."

"I'm a little lost." I edged myself backwards.

"You're a little dead," said the big one, getting off his bike.

I pushed my bike forward, smacking the little guy's leg just as he leaned to dismount. He and his bike loaded with newspapers pitched into the bigger kid, and they went down. I didn't wait to see what happened next. Miner Street headed downhill from the roundabout, which helped me build momentum.

Paper bikes are solid, heavy, single-geared contraptions with big tires, built for cargo, not for speed. I'd been delivering papers for two years, so my legs were strong, and I was motivated. Behind me the boys yelled and cursed at each other. I didn't look back, but I imagined they disentangled themselves, dumped their papers, and were pursuing. Each bag on my bike held about thirty pounds of today's Downey Picayune, which was the complete print run except for what went into the stands at the Rachael Café, and the Gold Nugget Coffee House. Hesitation would kill me. I reached down and dumped the bag on the left. Papers scattered on the street behind me, and the unbalanced load almost threw me off. The right bag went next, leaving a handful of papers, and now I was sixty pounds lighter.

So, did the two Clear Creek Courant thugs ride better downhill, or were they climbers? I took a hard left, up the steep connecting street. The boys trailed by a half block with the little one leading. The big one had his head up, glaring at me, but clearly the little one was the danger. If he caught me and slowed me down, the big one would have time to arrive. His bike clanked like a deranged cricket. Maybe his chain was messed up, but it didn't seen to slow him.

The street rose steeply. I stood on the pedals, leaned forward, pushed hard. A gutter, a flat crossing of Colorado Blvd, and then up again toward Virginia. At the intersection, Virginia sloped downward slightly from left to right. A rutted path continued up the hill and curved into the woods. I turned right, down Virginia and glanced back. The smaller boy trailed the big one now. Evidently he was a sprinter, but the big guy came on resolutely. Clank. Clank. Clank. He was the one I had to wear out. His weight would give him an advantage going downhill. I flew down three blocks, whipping past houses. Two little girls sitting on a swing set in the front yard watched as I went by.

I turned right again. The mountain shaped the town, so what had been a hard slog uphill became a dangerous speedway going down. Did the cross streets have stop signs? A truck beeped at me as I slammed through the Colorado Blvd. intersection, and I caught air on the bump that was Miner Street. The only way to make the turn right on Idaho was to ride the brakes. Gravel squirted from under the tires. I leaned hard, risked the bike sliding from under me. Straightened, then built up speed again. Panicked a cat that froze, then sprinted under a car. The big guy had gained a few feet, while the little one lost another twenty yards.

I had a plan.

I turned right after covering two blocks. Now the street sloped up the mountain again, but this time I had three blocks to climb instead of two. Everything depended on gaining ground during the climb.

The wire baskets in back rattled. I was glad I'd filled the tires this morning. If they were low at all, the race would have ended in a block. Air burned in my lungs. Now, my whole body pumped to drive me up the hill. My hands and arms ached as much as my legs. At Colorado Blvd., a block short of the top, I turned left. The big guy was just crossing Miner St. I needed more separation! Everything depended on crossing Virginia before he turned right off Colorado Blvd. and could see me.

Here's the weird thing. Adrenaline flooded my system, but I never got out of my head. As I bruted out each block, I thought about not being in Downey. How Trianna didn't live in this world. About school shootings and drug wars and job outsourcing. Pretty strange, huh? I had to get home.

Now I reached Virginia, the highest paved road in town. My legs trembled on the edge of cramping. If I couldn't shake the big guy now, I'd never hold him off through another downhill stretch. Instead of turning right like I had before, I charged up the rutted road. My bike bounced under me. If I could make the curve, I had a chance. If I didn't, though . . .

Dirt roads in Downey ended at abandoned mines. All were dead ends. I'd have no place to flee.

The ruts bent left into the screening trees. As soon as I was out of sight, I glided to a stop and lay the bike down, gasping for air. Were they coming? Did they see me pedaling up this road? When they reached the top and couldn't see me, would they assume I went around the block again?

Weeds tickled my neck. Tiny bees hummed in the wildflowers. The death rattle from the big guy's bike sounded louder, paused. He shouted something to his partner. Then the clanking faded. He'd turned down Virginia again.

The ground felt warm and comforting against my back. Clouds moved leisurely above pine and aspen, and that nice polleny afternoon fragrance washed my face. Gradually, my breathing calmed. My legs quit shaking. I could have slept.

I looked down the road. An iron gate stood at the rutted end, only another fifty yards. In an arc across the top, iron letters spelled out THE KNIGHTS OF PYTHIAS. Beyond, tombstones poked out from the mountain grass, reminding me of Downey's cemetery.

The gate wasn't locked, which wouldn't have mattered because there wasn't fence attached to it. I could have walked around, but I unlatched it and rolled my bike through. In some places, young aspen stood in front of the stones, and in others, wild roses had overgrown the plots. I read the names and dates as I moved toward the cemetery's high end. Side by side stones showed brothers who died in 1884, Tunis and William Block. Tunis was twelve. William was seven. I wondered what happened to them. A clumping of small stones of children under three were also dated from 1884. Was there a disease? Lambert told me that people suffered from sicknesses outside of Downey. Medicine, he said, was better than it used to be, but not everybody could afford it.

A short granite bluff marked the cemetery's far end. Above that, the mountain rose steeply. Mine tailings in a long yellow spill marked the slope above. The cemetery spread out below me, but it didn't seem a sad place. I liked it better than the town. The dead could rest easy in this setting.

My paper bag held the last six copies of the *Downey Picayune*. I wondered if the dead here hungered for news too. I mounted up, pushed off, and clattered down the rutted path, tossing papers as I went. They flicked easily, thwacked against the tombstones, and dropped into the grass. This was practiced motion. I sighed contentedly as the last paper sailed toward its resting place.

I didn't feel the shift, but now the sun felt brighter, more comforting, and the trees' green stood out more intensely. I smelled river and meadow and pine. A giant bee, as big as a plum, hummed overhead, and I knew I'd fallen back into Downey. I recognized the stones. In five minutes, I could be back in town. I'd pedal to the *Pic* to explain to Mr. Lambert what happened to today's paper. He was a cool guy. I bet he'd understand. The phone would start ringing, though. I'd be handling complaints for days. My tips this month were history.

I smiled anyway. Tonight, I'd go to Trianna's house. We'd hang out. Maybe stream a video. We'd sit side by side on her couch. I'd put my arm around her. With luck, tonight, we'd kiss. The thought made me squirm a little. We'd look into each other's eyes. My hands would be on her beautiful, tanned shoulders. Our breath would be so close that they'd be a single one.

I was home. I'd fallen back into Downey, and I hoped never to fall out again. It's scary out there in the world beyond our magic place, in a universe where the highway leads to despair, but where every once in a while, when people have drifted into the proper mood, they see an exit from the road, a regular highway sign that says "Downey." Most don't stop, but perhaps for a second as they drive by, they feel an inexplicable joy. Hands on the wheel, they smile for a second, not knowing why. They breathe more easily and see a slightly different sun, smell a brighter wind, hear bees in a distant glade, and then go on and on.

Every once in a while what comes to mind isn't a plot or a character or a setting. What sticks in the head is a single situation. For years I've had in mind a scene I called "the apocalyptic bike chase." I just needed a story to write it into. Some writers put those snippets into notebooks. I have a file on my computer that's titled "ideas." That way the stuff that isn't a full story isn't lost. Occasionally I open the file up and one of those ideas catches fire.

Being able to use magic, to command supernatural powers, sounds attractive until you follow the logic to the end. How can a magic user's abilities be controlled? What does it mean for one person to wield unchecked dominion over unseen forces?

APPRENTICE

MASTER JEPTHE, ADEPT OF A THOUSAND GESTURES, kicked his apprentice in the back.

"The movements must be exact," he thundered. "Unless the spell's cadence and enunciation are perfect, you will be a fool waving his arms and speaking gibberish. Your body must know even when your mind does not. Do it again."

Wedge gritted his teeth, adjusted his posture so his shoulders aligned in the prescribed fashion, crooked his fingers just so, then moved his hands through the complicated weaving that shaped the space for the spell. At the same time, he chanted the incantation. An inflection on the second syllable stressed just right, a slurring of sibilants, the staccato rap of hard ending consonants and then the rising trill that culminated the chant. On the table before him, the squirrel lay in a crunched bundle.

Jepthe sat on the stool behind Wedge, arms crossed. The old man had only grown crueler through time. Wedge felt the scowl.

He swayed to the spell's rhythm, then he found the shape. It was like dropping his hands into an invisible groove, and power flowed through him. Spell making embarrassed him at first. He remembered how aroused he'd become the first time, a simple casting that closed a door. His face flushed and he breathed hard. When he'd finished, a nap sounded like the best idea, but he couldn't wait to try a spell again. For weeks he opened and closed doors with a quiet word and a practiced wave.

Now, the power arced in his forearms. Sparks snapped from his elbows, at his ear tips, and language welled from an inner cauldron. Command crackled in the room. With a rush, the energy crested, overflowed, then released in a sensual flood. The squirrel twitched, jumped up, looked at Wedge and dashed for the open window.

Wedge sagged on the stool, exhausted. Jepthe swung his hand through an evil motion and barked a jagged, thorn-filled word. The sprinting squirrel died in mid leap, hit the window sill, and dropped lifeless to the floor.

"Do it again," Jepthe said.

Fifteen years earlier, when a ten-year-old Wedge began his apprenticeship, he asked Jepthe why the spell to kill was so short but the spell to resurrect was so long. Jepthe contemplated the boy for a moment. Wedge felt proud that he had asked a question that gave his new master such pause. Jepthe reached out with his bony finger and pushed a crock off the table. It shattered into dozens of pieces on the stone floor.

"Reassemble that so it is as good as new," the old wizard said.

Pieces had sprayed across the floor. Not a one was larger than Wedge's thumb. "But that will take hours," the young boy said.

"And so you have an answer."

The afternoons belonged to Wedge now that he'd nearly reached his magical majority. The wizard's apprentice became the master on his twenty-fifth year, and the old master joined the ranks of previous masters buried in Magus Field. Jepthe had prepared the internment slate years before, a black slab of stone the size of a small dinner table. Twenty-three slate stones lay in the wizard's cemetery, and even though the groundskeeper kept the stones clear, the oldest ones had sunk into the ground so that rain turned them into rectangular pools. It was said that the face of the dead wizards could be seen in the water's reflection by lightning flash, but Wedge had never witnessed this. Jepthe showed Wedge his death robe made entirely from crow feathers that he would wear on his last day, which would be Wedge's first day as master.

He wondered why wizards did not die like ordinary men. The apprentice studied for fifteen years, and then at the end of that time, the master died, always. No extended deathbed for a wizard. Their candle blew out on schedule. Jepthe told him that when the day came, he would don the death robe and perform the ending spell. How was it to know that your days were so numbered? Did Jepthe hate Wedge from the beginning because in him he saw his hourglass draining?

Wedge turned toward the athenaeum as soon as he passed through the city gates. His free time, what little he had, was spent there, not just because of the scrolls, parchments and learned tomes, but because of Charlotte, an assistant bibliothecary.

She sat on a long bench in the research antechamber, a pile of slender leather-bound volumes beside her. He smiled as he approached, but Charlotte frowned.

"How many more times until you quit visiting me?" she said. She'd gathered her hair into a braid that hung like a rope down her back. Silver embroidery in her maroon doublet caught the afternoon's light that sliced through the room's high windows.

"When I am wizard, I will be free to come whenever I want." He tried to sound jovial. Of late, Charlotte had seemed progressively sad.

"I don't think so." She picked up one of the books. "This is the miller's wife's personal journal from sixty years ago, when your master graduated from his apprenticeship. She confesses herself honestly in these pages."

Wedge sat beside her. The athenaeum's air felt cool after the long walk down dusty streets. Paper, ink and aged leather scented the building. "Why do we care about a long dead miller's wife?"

Charlotte turned the book over in her hands. Wedge admired her long fingers, the strength in her wrists. "She tells about her daughter who loved Jepthe when he was young. They were inseparable, and the miller's wife thought they would marry when he became master."

Wedge could not picture Jepthe as a young man, and certainly not as one in love. The idea felt alien. Jepthe angered easily and hardly tolerated human company. "What happened to the them?"

Charlotte put the book back onto the stack. "The day Jepthe became master, he slapped the daughter down in the marketplace. He kicked her. It broke the daughter's heart. Her mother said that she never recovered. The daughter's spirit was destroyed."

That sounded more like Jepthe. "That's horrible, but Jepthe has always been loathsome. What does this have to do with us?"

In the main room beyond, a student sat at a table, taking notes slowly from a book that lay open before him. His quill scratches were the only sounds.

"The miller's wife wrote pages about Jepthe before he became the master. He courted the daughter for years. By her account and by others . . ." Charlotte picked up two more books. ". . . Jepthe was the kindest of men. Compassionate. A poet. A dancer. The day he . . . ascended, he turned into the man you know now."

Wedge took her hand. "That is not me. When I ascend, nothing will change between us. I am who I am."

Charlotte shook her head. "Writings go back eight hundred years. Journals. Daybooks. Reminiscence. Every apprentice who takes the wizard's robe turns cruel."

Nothing Wedge said could dissuade Charlotte or stir her from her misery. When he left and the city streets had grown dark, he kept his head down and kicked a small rock in front of him disconsolately.

*

"The king calls," said Jepthe. "Where were you?" When he was young, he must have been huge, but now he bent while holding his staff, and his robes were too big.

The master's traveling bag rested by Conjury Hall's entrance.

Jepthe's voice was raspy but he didn't sound as irritated as he sometimes did. This summer, his viciousness muted. Perhaps this close to the end, he was coming to terms with death. Whatever anger drove him was running dry. Surprisingly, though, when he chanted spells, the old man's throat found volume he never attained for conversation. "Squiring the librarian again, I expect. I don't like her looks. Too skinny by half. You will have no interest in her when I am gone. If you are going into town, the least you could do is waste time fruitfully." By which Jepthe meant practicing invisibility. He sent Wedge to spy out plots. More than one merchant who'd cheated the wizard, or town elder who spoke against him, fell ill and died after Wedge reported what he'd overheard.

Wedge picked up the bag and slung it over his shoulder.

"The king's usual problem?" said Wedge.

Jepthe spat on the ground. "Of course. You'll do the spell, and you better get it right. The king needs magic to perform as a man, so we'll give him magic."

Wedge reviewed the chant and motions in his head as they trudged toward the king's chambers. "Why does the spell wear off? We should only have to do this once."

The wizard laughed, an evil sound when he made it. "It *would be* permanent, but the queen pays me for another spell after a couple days. A manly king disturbs her rest."

The king didn't want what Wedge rehearsed. His highness sat on the steps before his throne, the vast room lit only by torches above the door and beside the king. At his feet, an old dog stretched on a blanket barely raised its head when they entered.

"I have had many hounds," said the king. His eyes were rheumy and red. He petted the animal's ears. "I grow sentimental with age."

Jepthe handed his staff to Wedge, then gingerly sat beside the king. "There are no spells to reverse years. The old die as they always have."

"I have heard of another spell," said the king. "The body may die, but the essence can live elsewhere."

Wedge's attention perked. He didn't know of such a spell after spending fifteen years with the master. It occurred to him that there could be many spells the master had not shared with him that he would have to teach himself once Jepthe was gone. The old wizard's private library held numerous scrolls he had never unrolled.

Jepthe nodded. "There is such a spell, but your long-time friend will not know his old tricks."

The king looked hopeful. "If he can be saved, we must do it."

Jepthe gave instructions, and the king called a page for the errand. They waited after the boy left in the dark room while the torches hissed and sputtered, and the dying dog wheezed. Very soon, the boy returned with a young dog on a leash.

Wedge helped the wizard stand.

"Your dog will pass on. He will pass tonight, but I can move his life to this other animal. He will be your dog, and he will remember you, but he will not know what has happened to him. He is a dumb animal and will be afraid. He might even become mad, and then you'll put him down as you would any mad dog."

Jepthe dug into his bag. "It will be easier on him if we cover his eyes and bind his limbs."

Wedge took the ropes and cloth shroud and approached the king's hound.

"Not him, you fool," said Jepthe, "the other dog."

Wedge's ears burned as he bound the dog and covered its head. Then Jepthe closed his eyes and chanted. His hands moved through a complicated pattern. Wedge concentrated on the movements.

What an interesting and useful spell this one could be, if it existed. He suspected that Jepthe lied to the king, though. There could be no such spell to transfer a being into another. Jepthe would make magical sounds for a few minutes, and then sneak in the death spell, killing the old dog. He could claim the spell had worked when all he'd done was to put the old dog out of its misery.

Somehow, the quality of torch light changed. Wedge gasped. This was not meaningless words and arm motions. An ominous pressure built in the room. In the distance, dogs howled, and the young dog whimpered under the cloth. Jepthe's voice grew deeper and hollow. His hands and arms glowed, but the king cared only for his dog, and continued to pet him. Jepthe had never taken so long with a spell. Its complications were many. Wedge saw the wizard's movements, and the spell's motifs in his hands' dance. He read the gesture's grammar and heard the incantation's tonal complexities, and in the complexities, verses and bridges. Air swirled in the chamber, bending the flames. Then, the king's old dog sagged as if it had deflated. If Jepthe had slipped in the death spell, Wedge did not hear it. The young dog whined and choked. Its legs quivered.

"Go to it," said Jepthe. "Your hound will respond to your voice. Your voice and touch will be all it recognizes of itself."

The king looked up, his hand on the dead dog's skull.

Jeptha said, "Do it now. Your animal suffers."

The king held the young dog in his lap until it quit whining. When he removed the shroud, the dog nearly jerked out of his arms, but the king commanded it to be still, and it remembered its master's voice.

"This is really my favorite still?" said the king.

Jepthe nodded. "As it grows accustomed to the new body, it will show itself to you more and more. But it will not have memory in its muscles to do what he used to do. The dog will have to teach its body the old tricks. It will have a young dog's enthusiasms, so think of how your dog behaved when he first came to your house."

The king nodded. "You have given me a great gift."

Gathering the young dog in his arms, the page took him away.

"Now," said the king, "we can attend to that other matter."

Jepthe nudged Wedge. "My apprentice will fulfill the spell, sire. This is his fifteenth year as my student. He will be the master soon."

Wedge set himself up before the king. "Are you ready?"

Conjury Hall was the second oldest building in the kingdom, preceded only by the castle keep. The first wizard, whose magic guarded the people and whose wisdom guided the first king, designed Conjury Hall as a fortifiable structure, a site for large gatherings, and a repository of mystic literature. Butted against a cliff, the building did not appear imposing on the outside. Plain crenellated walls jutted from the cliff, made of the same stone, not a hundred strides wide. The interior, though, burrowed into the cliff, above and below. Rooms high on the cliff wall with secret windows looked into the kingdom's valley, and hidden entrances on the mesa above the hall concealed the wizard's comings and going. The first master had even constructed stables and weapon shops. In the fifteen years Wedge had lived there, he had not explored it all.

Laying in bed, his hands behind his head, he pictured Conjury Hall becoming his. He would invite committees from town to visit, both to find ways that his art could make their lives easier, but also for camaraderie and companionship. Jepthe might have liked the old building filled with creepy echoes and ghostly whispers, but Wedge imagined music and laughter. The wizard's treasure room overflowed with precious metals, jewels and coins. Wedge would be charitable with it. The poor could look to him for help.

And there was Charlotte. He could see the day, soon, when he would lead her into the master's archives. Scrolls lined the walls. Maps filled drawers. Books of arcane matter stood side by side on stone shelves. She would be ecstatic. They could hold hands and read by candlelight. Jepthe may not have been romantic, but Wedge would not live a hermit's life.

Wedge's room overlooked Conjury Hall's courtyard. A full summer moon bathed the stone with its cool light. A square of it fell on Wedge's floor, revealing dimly his wardrobe and study table. Tomorrow, he would go to the archives and find the spell that Jepthe had used on the king's dog.

What a marvelous magic it was. Sad, though, that the young dog died to save the old one. Wedge asked Jepthe as they walked home where the young dog went. He thought that there must now be two dogs' minds in one skull, fighting for possession, or that the minds switched places. Jepthe laughed. His laugh always sounded sardonic and bitter. "We sacrificed the young dog, you cretin. That is the price of such a spell."

All magics had a cost. Something traded or altered or destroyed. That was magic's first lesson. Wedge sighed. How many lessons would he have to learn on his own when Jepthe joined the dead in Magus Field? For a moment, in the dark of his moonlit room, he almost pitied the old man.

Later, when the moon square had traveled the floor's length and crawled part way up the wall, Wedge had still not fallen asleep. He kept seeing the moment when the king's old dog quit breathing, and the young dog's shock at that second. Jepthe told the king that magic could not prevent aging. It could not turn back the clock. The old die. Magic could resurrect the dead from other causes, but not old age. Wedge had revived the squirrel that very day a half dozen times before Jepthe finally let the poor creature go. How frustrating to have the power to revive the dead, but no way to prevent your own, inevitable end.

These were the thoughts that kept him awake. Anticipation, questions, the insecurities of a young man, and the moment he kept returning to was Jepthe performing the complicated spell for the king. He truly was the master. The old dog's body died, as it would have soon on its own, but the dog himself lived on.

Wedge suddenly felt cold. He rose quietly from his bed. Jepthe's chamber was just a door away, and the wizard slept lightly.

Barely daring to breathe, Wedge gathered his clothes, opened his door with a wave and muttered word, and crept down the passageway. He didn't relax until he was outside Conjury Hall, put on his cloak and boots, and sprinted toward the town.

Charlotte lived with her parents in a cottage near a stream. The full moon lit the fields, and a breeze rustled the dark trees. Wedge tapped on Charlotte's window until she opened it for him. He'd crept to her window before, and they'd whispered to each other until dawn, but tonight he didn't pay attention to her night clothes, and his heart pounded for other reasons.

An hour later, she unlocked the athenaeum. At first she'd laughed when he'd insisted they go right then, but his urgency swayed her. Soon, she'd gathered the books she'd shown him earlier. "We need every record you have of when the apprentice ascends to master at Conjury Hall."

They pored through journals and town records and letters and histories. By dawn, they'd found mention of nineteen of Conjury Hall's twenty-three previous masters, and the pattern seemed clear.

"This is monstrous if it's true," said Charlotte.

"I don't think becoming master changes the apprentice's character," he said. "The power, of course, and the responsibility are heavy burdens, and surely they would make a young man more thoughtful, but he wouldn't become a different person."

Charlotte nodded. "Each new wizard behaved the same way. The apprentice doesn't become the master. The master never changes. Jepthe is eight hundred years old."

The enormity of this staggered Wedge. "No apprentice survives his fifteenth year with him."

"What will you do?" Charlotte asked.

"I can't kill him."

She grasped his hands, and he saw in her an intensity he'd never seen. "Why not? He's going to kill you."

"He's too powerful. He has wards and protection spells all around. Knives turn to powder when turned against him. Archers catch fire and burn to death. Poisons only sweeten his drinks. Besides . . ." he held Charlotte's hand. ". . . I think that killing him would make me become him. Not the same way, but surely if I murdered him I would taint myself, and I would lose you."

Charlotte looked away. "You must flee, then, where he will never find you."

"He would only choose someone else."

The antechamber echoed their words. Perhaps Wedge could defend himself magically from Jepthe's power. In his time with the master, Wedge had learned hundreds of spells, and he could find ones he didn't know in the archives. "I have to go back."

"You are giving yourself to him?" Charlotte looked stricken "What if he comes to me in your form? I could not bear to know that you are gone."

"I might have a plan," he said. "Besides, he thinks you are too skinny."

Charlotte didn't smile. "When will it happen?" She closed the book in her lap. "The wizard always dies in the summer. The leaves turn in weeks."

"I don't know, but I will be ready."

Jepthe's archives were not like the well-organized and neat stacks at the athenaeum. Also, the rooms had no skylights or windows, so Wedge dug into the scrolls armed with a candle lantern. He knew two spells that cast light, but one revealed ghosts, and the other attracted night gaunts like giant, leather-winged moths. Also, Wedge didn't know what to look for. Was there a spell that removed a wizard's powers? Was there one that made one immune to the transfer spell? Was there a general spell immunity spell? Or how about one that made a wizard forget a spell? The possibilities were uncountable, but if the spells were there, they were buried in irrelevant arcana. Here was a history of well digging in the southern valley. Next, variations on a spell to tan rabbit skins. Then, a treatise on cosmetic uses for berries and fruits. Scrolls detailing harvests. A book naming hand movements for "oddity" spells: one that turned walnuts white, another to turn frogs into cottontails, one to trick bats into flying at noon. Why would a wizard want to turn leaf mulch to dead ants?

Wedge knew defense spells. Minor warlocks occasionally challenged Jepthe's supremacy. The last one, Jepthe ordered Wedge to dispose. How humiliating was it to be defeated by the apprentice? Wedge had long ago protected himself against sleep, illness, blindness, deafness and pain enchantments. He also warded himself against love spells, depression, madness and confusion. Of course, so had Jepthe, who was practically invulnerable to attack. How else could he have survived for so long? In eight hundred years, the kingdom had suffered plague, fire, drought, famine, and disastrous weather—much less than the surrounding realms—all made easier, of course, by the presence of a powerful wizard. Despite Jepthe's distaste for anyone other than himself, the kingdom had surely benefitted by his presence. Wedge wondered if he should just yield. Could he defend the kingdom as well? Wasn't it horrifying arrogance on his part to believe he could do the job as competently as an eight-hundred-year-old sorcerer?

He closed his eyes. When he walked to town in the afternoons, he loved how the late summer grain rippled in the breeze, how cattle grazed with contented calm, how the city gates opened for him when he spoke the spell. He loved when the seasons changed. Charlotte's face when he surprised her at her work, made him smile. When her face rose to his and their breath met in the middle. This could be gone forever in the next few days. Jepthe's spell would end him.

The next parchment was written in a language Wedge didn't know, but it looked by the illustrations to be boat-building instructions. He dropped it to the shelf in despair, stirring dust and frightening a mouse.

That night he couldn't sleep. There was no bar he could put on his door that Jepthe couldn't shatter, and to do so would reveal his suspicions, but with the door unlocked, every creak sounded like its opening. Another night in the archives revealed little. Wedge fell asleep, his head resting on a five-hundred-year-old tome. When he woke, the candle had burned out, and he found his way from the dark room by feel.

"You look unwell, boy," rasped Jepthe. "Have you discovered the joys of the taverns, or is it your scrawny town girl who distracts you?"

The only reason Wedge didn't run was because the transfer spell was a long one. He would have warning if Jepthe started it, and unless the old sorcerer had a secret way to bind him—and he might—Wedge would have time to move out of range. He could bargain with Jepthe. Perhaps there was a way that didn't kill the apprentice or anyone else.

"I have been studying. There is so much I don't know yet to be master."

Maybe there was something frightened in Wedge's voice, or perhaps Jepthe knew him too well, but the old man looked at him with suspicion.

Jepthe came for him that night. Wedge went to bed as he normally did, planning on returning to the archives later, but the young man had stretched himself too thin and fell asleep. Jepthe had reminded him time and time again during his training to not rely solely on magic. Diplomacy could settle disputes without spells. Illness could be treated with medicines too, and an arrow would stop a man (but not a wizard) as effectively as a deadly enchantment. So Wedge didn't use magic to warn himself; he leaned his staff against the door between his room and the master's. When it clattered to the stone, he awoke.

Jepthe stood in his death robes, silhouetted by the torch in the sconce behind him. The crow feathers fluttered.

"You know, don't you, boy?" said Jepthe. "I didn't think you were so clever, but you're not the first." He raised his hands into a new position, not the beginning of the transfer spell, something else. Wedge didn't wait to see what it was. He shouted a word and waved his hand. The door between the two rooms slammed in Jepthe's face, while Wedge leapt from his bed and out the door to the hallway. The intervening door exploded. Splinters flew behind Wedge as he ran down the hall. Despite his thinking, he had no plan. He'd pictured a dozen ways this encounter would go. In all of them he remained calm. He was, after all, a well-trained magician, but now he was running, as frightened as he had been the first day he'd come to Conjury Hall when he was ten.

The wizard's home contained rooms and stairways and secret passages, but a spell of finding was the most elementary of tricks. Hiding would be impossible. Jepthe, though, was old and slow, while Wedge was young. As the apprentice ran up a flight of stairs, his heart shuddering and breath like fire, he knew he would have to stop. But now, like a child, he ran in a panic. What could he say to save his life?

He skidded on the slick floor as he turned and dashed into one of the many trophy rooms, a long chamber lined with art and armor and gifts from kings long dead. Jepthe stood in the doorway at the other end.

How could the old man have beat him to this spot? Spent, Wedge stopped, his hands on his knees, gasping. Jepthe wasn't even breathing hard. He'd said that Wedge was not the first to guess his fate. Had other apprentices, as young and fit as he also fled into Conjury Hall? Who would know the house's passages better than Jepthe? Perhaps, even, it was designed to confuse the panicked.

Jepthe raised his arms, the crow feathers dangling, his hands already glowing with the spell's energy.

Wedge sat, defeated. He couldn't run. He couldn't allow Jepthe to kill someone else in his place. He would join the unbroken line that was Jepthe's eight-hundred-year-old life.

Then, Jepthe smirked, an expression he wore often. He smirked and mocked and laughed at people. His superiority surfaced in every expression.

It was the smirk that provoked Wedge. If he was going to die, he didn't also want Jepthe's smug face being the last thing he saw, so Wedge spoke his first word of power, waved his hand in his most practiced gesture, and slammed the double doors on Jepthe.

Jepthe screamed. The door trapped his extended wrist, shattering it.

And so Wedge became master of Conjury Hall and the kingdom's twenty-fourth wizard. Many people wrote in their journals and letters about his kindness and charity. Charlotte became the first woman to occupy Conjury Hall in its history, learning magic of her own, teaching it to their children when they came.

The people wrote too about Jepthe who had once been their wizard, but who didn't die when his apprentice ascended. He sometimes came to town. They saw him in the tavern, bitter to the end, crippled, unable to make an enchanting gesture, haunted by life as no old man they'd ever seen.

When Wedge, adept of a thousand gestures, died after a full life, he left no apprentice, although his children were said to have learned some things from their parents. And after time, the kingdom became much like the others: stricken by plagues and famine and drought and disastrous weather, along with the fine seasons where the grapes came rich and the cows were plentiful and marriages and births were plenty.

Happiness and misery was doled to them in the same proportion as everyone else, and after a long, long while, when the writings had crumbled to dust, they only talked of wizards in stories, and they didn't remember Jepthe or Wedge at all.

 *Writing stories can be hard, particularly when you are beginning. There's so much to know! Still, new writers start all the time, feeling their way along, trying to tell stories the best they can. For me, I spent several years handicapped by my literature teachers. They were the only story experts I knew at first. It was from them that I first heard about setting and characterization and dialogue as separate subjects, which was helpful. One way they screwed me up, though, was when they talked about conflict. They said it was central to every story, and that it was identifiable. They'd even classified the kinds of conflicts in stories: Man vs. Man. Man vs. Society. Man vs. Nature. Etc. They told me that stories had to have conflict, but I couldn't make my teachers' definition help me. How in the world does knowing that my story is man vs. whatever guide me in the writing? It wasn't until I realized that there was a definition for conflict that helped writers that I was really able to solve my own storytelling problems. A writer's definition of conflict has three parts: Somebody wants something. Something stands in the way. And something of value is at stake. Once I knew that, it became much easier to write. All I had to do was to answer those three questions. If my character wants something, what does he do next to get it? What prevents him from getting what he wants right away? Why is his goal important to him? I needed to decide what the answers to those questions were to be able to write the story.*

The singer Rod Stewart said, "Every picture tells a story." People are natural storytellers. If you see a toy on a sidewalk, and there are no kids around, you start to wonder about the child who left it. Is the child sad? Does she/he miss their plaything? If you see skid marks on the highway, you imagine the accident. We create the stories implied by the clues that remain.

TITAN DESCANSOS

I F YOU'RE NOT FAMOUS, YOU THINK THAT FAMOUS PEO- PLE experience a different sort of life from you, that they don't shop at convenience stores or they don't get haircuts. You don't think about them spending time, just like you, driving their car. But they do. Even if they were an astronaut, even if they'd been to Titan, they still might have a dead brother. They still might have their little traditions, same as you.

The roadside memorial came up on my right: a wooden cross wreathed with decayed flowers next to a barbed wire fence. A weatherworn cardboard sheet with a photograph taped to it leaned against the cross. I pulled the car onto the shoulder, as far from the traffic as I could get it, but a semitrailer rocked me as it blasted by. Highway 50 is straight here. Grand Junction to the northwest, Delta to the southeast. Colorado residents sometimes call this stretch the "stinking desert," but it's semi-arid at worst. Dry grass and scrubby brush that drops down to the Gunnison River about a mile from here on one side, and the same, maybe a little drier land that rises toward the mesa on the other. Beautiful country at sunset or sunrise when shadows cut across, making what is green a dark and mellow shade and highlighting the rolling landscape, but at noon, when the sun blasts down, it's flat and dusty, a lot like our old home in Santa Fe. You would think an accident would be impossible here. A truck veering off the road would hit nothing more substantial than a three-wired fence or scrub oak as dry and insubstantial as toothpicks for hundreds of yards, yet this is where Gabriel rolled his truck. State Patrol said he probably fell asleep, dropped a wheel off the shoulder, then over corrected. They found the truck fifty yards from the highway on its top. Gabriel landed another fifty yards beyond that.

I pulled the cardboard off the cross. The picture was of the two of us camping eleven years ago. Gabriel sat on our cooler, a beer in one hand and a frying pan in the other. I stood behind him, holding a fishing pole and looking glum. Nothing bit that morning. We had pancakes again. It was my last vacation before the Titan lift-off.

The staple gun stuck the new cardboard with the same picture to the cross. I'd laminated it so it would last longer.

Gabriel knew I walked on Titan. He sent a congratulatory message. I sent a thank you back. At the speed of light, he had to wait three hours for my reply. No real personality in the messages, of course. He couldn't very well say, "How the fuck are you?" in an e-mail that everyone in the world might read, but that would be more like him. We'd save the rudeness for when I got back, when we could buy each other beers and remember when we played astronaut in the back yard.

Mamá called roadside memorials *descansos*. It comes from an old New Mexico funeral custom where the coffin was carried from the church to the *camposanto*, the cemetery. When the pallbearers needed to rest, they put the coffin down. The stopping was the *descansos*, a resting place before the body reached the final destination. Mourners might leave flowers to mark the spot, sometimes with a little wooden cross among them. Like a *descansos*, roadside memorials commemorate the body's rest before reaching the cemetery.

It was an unremarkable piece of land. The state hauled away the wreck long ago, and a rancher repaired the barb wire. Saturn would have been visible that night. I checked. Clear sky, dry, deserty air, no city lights. Gabriel might have looked my direction that night, before he crashed. Now, I smelled sage and the river, which was out of sight. The sand, brownish red and fine grained, slipped from my fingers.

According to the mission logs, I was on an EVA in the Titan rover when he died. I wouldn't learn about it for almost twenty-four hours. No real night sky on Saturn's largest moon. It's a hazy, dark, orange air during the day with the sun so far away. At night, no stars. Even Saturn, that great, ringed giant, isn't visible. I couldn't see the Earth, of course, not that I had the luxury. Driving the rover required constant attention. Liquid methane puddles and ponds dotted the area around the habitat. They weren't deep, but the ground became viscous at their edges and could bog the rover down. We'd used the second rover to extricate it several times. I was investigating a radar blip a couple thousand meters away, behind a low hill we called Mount Olympus.

They built the rover's cab like a Kansas combine. Enclosed against methane rain or wind, but not air tight. The atmosphere on Titan is thicker than Earth's by about half, so no need for a pressure suit, but we needed thermal protection. All that concerned us was keeping the temperature in. The weather on the surface was almost minus 300 degrees Fahrenheit, and a light breeze whispered past the windows.

There's a lot to like about Titan. Sound, for example. I'd been to the moon, Mars and Ganymede. All silent except for human and machine noise. Titan, though, had a voice. I imagine during the equinox, when the winds picked up, that it positively roared. Rain hissed as it slowly settled at a sixth of Earth gravity. Methane creeks made happy bubbly noises when they over-spilled their basins. Rocks clacked against each other when I kicked them. Occasionally there was thunder.

Planets have a smell, too. Regolith from the moon smells like burnt gunpowder. Mars smells like sulfur. Titan reeks. We decontaminated the suits when we reentered the habitat, but the methane and ethane stench lingered. It was hard to believe that Earth's atmosphere might have once been a rich, hydrocarbon soup like Titan's.

A smoggy late dusk under heavy cloud cover best described a drive at noon on Titan. I steered by headlights and found my way by the nav screen. The radar blip could be a rock situated the right way to bounce the signal, or a mineral deposit, or nothing at all. We'd investigated dozens of radar anomalies. We liked doing it. NASA scripted so much or our mission. There were science experiments to be set up, samples to be gathered, observations to be made. Responding to anomalies meant that we were human. That's why we came instead of self-directed robot explorers.

The Rover handled the rocky-strewn terrain easily. The hill tilted me a little, but that meant I was above the liquid, hydrocarbon muck below. Not much chance of getting stuck. Up here, the rover crackled as it fractured the thin crust on the surface. Underneath, the soil was a soft sand.

The headlights revealed a hump in the surface that I steered to go around. The blip was close. As I approached, the lump resolved into a cairn, but not just rocks on rocks. These seemed organized and fitted. The cairn stood stark in the rover's lights; a long shadow cast behind it. A breeze caught dust from under the wheels and swept around the rocks. I climbed out, put my suited hand against the stones. The pile was nearly as tall as me, and this close, the artifice was clear. How could this be a natural formation? I went around it, dragging my hand as I went, and on the far side, a low opening appeared. On my knees, I shined my light inside. Partly buried in sand, metal objects glinted back at me. My breath quickened. I knew I should call it in, but I wanted to make this moment last. Two, small metal boxes and what looked like a helmet. I reached in, brushed dust from the helmet's front. Beneath, it was a clear faceplate, too small for an adult human, and way wider than it was tall. We had not left it here. Ours was the only expedition to this area on Titan.

I had discovered the first sign of extraterrestrial life.

Somewhere around the time I knelt in front of a cairn on Titan's surface, within an hour or two, when I was about nine hundred million miles from home, Gabriel rolled his truck. Time of death was hard to pin down. A guy in a jeep spotted his overturned vehicle mid-morning. But by then, our news had already reached Earth. I'd been broadcasting a live feed, the now iconic, grainy picture of my gloved hands pulling a strangely shaped helmet from the dark. Anyone on Earth watching knew we weren't alone about an hour and a half after I did, after the signal flew at the speed of light across our solar system.

By the time we returned home, the space budget had tripled. New expeditions were scheduled to all the planets. Ambitious plans to explore the asteroids were being finalized. Who left the helmet? No one believed another space-faring species lived in our solar system. They had to be extra-solar. How did they get here? Had they mastered the power of faster than light travel? If they could, we could.

Then, the specialists went to work. What could we learn of the others' metallurgy, their manufacturing techniques, their engineering, their biology? You'd be surprised how revealing a helmet could be.

The two boxes were less helpful. One contained four small metal discs, about the size of a quarter. Each had a design etched on the front and two small hooks on the back, like a clasp. Were they coins or buttons? What did the design mean? The second box contained nothing. Had whatever been in it degraded in Titan's hydrocarbon atmosphere?

We found no trace other than the cairn, but Titan's surface changed with the seasons. Winds reshaped hills, wore away features, and covered what was once exposed. Unlike the moon, our footprints lasted only a day. By our best estimations, measuring wear on the stacked rocks, the cairn might only be a hundred years old. Had the others been visitors like ourselves? Or did they have a more permanent presence buried beneath one of Titan's migrating dunes?

Earth asked a thousand questions, and they all ended with who were they? Did we share enough with them that when we met, for surely we would, that we'd have a way to communicate? Discussion about the others circled the globe.

I think, though, that they're a lot like us. We have speculated why the cairn existed, but no one has an answer. Behind me, another truck passed on the highway. It was loud and filled with its own momentum. The driver probably didn't look my way where my car was parked beside the road, and when I left, even fewer would notice Gabriel's tiny cross. None would stop to contemplate his photograph or wonder who he was. Still, if you drove down any highway, if you looked, you'd see the roadside memorials, the *descansos* that mark the memories of the ones we loved. Because we honor the spot where the dead rested, we reveal something of ourselves, something about our hope that we will not be forgotten.

I wish I knew the name of the other who wore the strange helmet on Titan. I do not know what the disks in the box were, or what vanished from the second box, but I'll bet they meant something personal to whoever left them. I'll bet the others on Titan stood in the methane rain and placed these small items in memory. I'll bet they loved like we love, and the loss they felt burned like it burns in us.

Because they are alien, we believe they must be different, that their lives cannot be like ours in any way. We don't think about them living from moment to moment, working their routines, finding reasons to go on, just like us.

We don't think that they might have the equivalent of brothers, and that they might miss them.

The dead flowers crumbled in my hand. I scraped them away from the wooden cross. God, Gabriel, the days are lonely without you.

The road between Grand Junction, where I live, and Delta, forty-five miles away, is mostly straight, mostly flat and entirely unchallenging. Yet too many times in that short distance an attentive driver notices crosses and cairns and faded artificial flowers that mark the spot of someone's last moment. I can't see those markers without sharing a stranger's sadness. They're emotional. For this story, the emotion came first. The science fictional idea came much, much later.

In the old Norse poem, Beowulf fights the monster Grendel and kills him. Normally this would be enough of an adventure, but Grendel's mother comes to avenge her child, which causes another battle. What's horrifying about Beowulf's story is that monsters have children, and they love them.

THE CHILDREN'S COLLECTION

NOTHING PLEASED ME MORE THAN ESSEX COUNTY PUT-ting me in charge of the children's collection at Kingsport Public Library as my first job after grad school. Most of my classmates at the University of Arizona hadn't found positions, but I could have lucked out because I'm male. I'm an oddity. Several times I was the only man in my classes. It didn't matter to me. I believed what the university said, that my job was to "empower and motivate young people." Librarians have missions to fulfill.

I exited Route 128 and then lost time deciphering the confusing road signs and shoulderless two-lane blacktop that took me toward Kingsport before parking my over-packed Volvo on a scenic overlook that encompassed both the Atlantic, a gray seething mass that matched the clouds overhead, and the town itself that spread across the Miskatonic River valley. What a glorious view, so different from Tucson's bare mountains and cactus-strewn desert: high pitched colonial houses, steep narrow streets, dispirited trees that should have been brilliant with late fall colors but instead had turned blotchy brown, long wharves lined with boats, their bare masts gently swaying in the bay's swell; and on top a low hill that rose over the rest, a church and steeple that seemed like a land-locked ship with its own mast pointing skyward. Seagulls floated on a breeze that swept up the cliff. Their lonely, repeated cries played counterpoint to the ocean's sad lapping against the rocks below.

My GPS lost its signal before I crossed the city limit. Fortunately, I had printed a map to the cottage I had arranged to rent. The landlord wasn't there, but he'd left the key in the mailbox. The living room was small, and the bedroom not much bigger than a walk-in closet. I didn't care. It was my first home of my own after years in dorms. Painters had left masking tape on the trim, but acrylic couldn't cover the ocean's smell. I threw open the bedroom window that looked into a tiny, weedy yard. On the other side of the fence, twenty feet away, two little dark-haired girls played in a sandbox, one child with her hair cut short, and the other wearing it long. Both wore short-sleeve shirts despite a steady, cold wind. Beyond them, their huge house cast a long shadow. I suspected my cottage might have once been its servants' quarters.

Maybe the girls would come to the library, and I could show them the picture books. Children were my clientele. Through them I would advance my mission to "promote and nurture the habit of reading."

The short-haired one piled sand in a mound with a plastic, yellow shovel. They giggled when they sat back and watched. The sand moved, then slowly, painfully, a bedraggled animal dug its way free. It might have been a hamster. The long-haired girl grabbed it, shook sand from its fur, then held it down. They both dug a new hole to bury it in.

I turned away, sickened by the children's casual cruelty.

"We are really a branch for the Miskatonic University Library upriver in Arkham," said Delilah Mason, the head librarian. I'd talked to her on the phone about the position, and imagined her as tall, severe and dressed in black, but she was petite and wore a brightly-colored print blouse and blue jeans. "We get quite a few calls for books from their collection, mostly genealogy and local history, while their students ask for whatever bestsellers we've added. They don't have a popular fiction section at MU. Sometimes they'll request work from the children's collection. Picture books for faculty with families, mostly."

We sat in the children's section in child-sized chairs with our knees above our hips. The previous librarian had covered the walls with framed elementary school artwork. Book bins at kids' height filled the floor's middle. One wall devoted itself to chapter books, and another to young adult. A separate room labeled "Teens Only" held beanbag chairs and computers in a row. The entire library, a new building surrounded by a rundown neighborhood of seventeenth- and eighteenth-century houses, shone like a glass and steel beacon in a wilderness.

"We have Saturday story hour with adult volunteer readers, and I expect you'll work closely with the elementary school teachers. They don't have a library at the school since the budget cuts." I smiled. Collaborating with educators was on my list from the university. Delilah handed me the November activities calendar. They'd scheduled presentations and clubs most week days too: Preschool Story Time, Kids Game Club, Infant and Toddler Story Time, Little Artist Café, Puppet Show Thursday, Jr. Scientist Science Entertainment Night, Charlotte's Web Tea Time, and several others. I'd written a paper on children's library interactive learning, and had ideas that I was eager to implement. Every library had a unique population with unique needs. I wondered what Kingsport's unique needs would turn out to be.

Delilah left me with a large key ring, library procedures in two binders, and a tutorial for inventory and reordering.

Holding the material under one arm, I surveyed the children's collection. Ten o'clock on a Thursday. A mom pushed a baby in a stroller while showing books to her three-year-old son. A ten-year-old wearing wire-rimmed glasses took notes from a history text open on his lap. At the computers, two boys played games. One of our missions was to "introduce children to electronic resources." It would take a while to wean them off the games. I wandered the stacks, familiarizing myself with the organization. The first time I'd come to a library, the librarian had been so helpful. She issued me my first library card—made a bit of a production of it, really—and I felt as if I'd been given the keys to a castle.

A door by my office said, "Local and Regional Authors' Special Children's Collection." Underneath that a small typed notice said, "See the main desk for access." None of my keys fit the lock.

It was good to see my old friends, Dr. Suess, Susan Cooper, Madeleine L'Engle, J.K. Rowling and the books on dinosaurs and spaceships and deep sea creatures. I met several children during the day, pointed adults toward leveled readers, collaborated with a team leader for a home-school community, and read an Amelia Bedelia story to a preschooler whose mother was in the adult section looking for books on home canning.

After closing, I surveyed my domain. My first library! I didn't realize how keyed up I'd been until the last patron left and I breathed easily. The windows were dark. Lights switched off in the main library. For the first time, I really looked at the art my predecessor left on the walls. Little kids' drawing. Lots of crayon and colored pencil. Mostly trees, boats and stick figures, not all that different from Arizona in style, although desert kids drew mountains and cactus for their stick figures to live in.

A more sophisticated picture drew my attention. A forest on one side crept down to the sea on the other. The child used black crayon and purple, a bilious combination that made the forest a brooding presence. In the forest, the outlines of a house peeked out, also in black and purple so as to be nearly invisible except for a tinge of light seeping from a single window. The child's boldness in strokes struck me, as if she'd drawn the scene quickly with a strong hand. A single figure, also in black, stood near the ocean, looking into it. The ocean seethed, not like a wave, but as if something was about to emerge. I stepped back. It was repugnant. The repulsive power of it startled me, the ichor of its imagination. A child with nightmares might draw such a picture, if she could render her nightmares so vividly.

"I try not to look at that one," said Delilah. She leaned against the children's library door, wearing a heavy coat. "Amazing the creepy things a kid will draw." She bounced her car keys in her hand. "Come on. I'll buy you a beer and you can tell me about your first day."

I sat at my desk the next morning when a little girl named Allison suffered a seizure. Her scream rose into the library's quiet like a siren. The short-haired brunette girl who lived next to my house rushed away, a picture book tucked under her arm.

Allison lay on the floor beside the puppet theater, arching her back, gasping now and gurgling. Her mother tried to hold her, but the little girl had grown rigid, her eyes wide open. "She wasn't doing anything. She was just reading!" the mother cried. I didn't see a book on the floor.

Delilah rushed in and knelt beside the hysterical mother and child. "I've called 911," she kept saying.

Other children formed a semi-circle and watched. A weeping kindergartner held his mother's hand. Some children looked blankly, as if this were television, but a couple leaned in and smiled. Maybe one of them had drawn the black forest and the looming sea. My neighbor girl wasn't in the crowd.

I shepherded them back. "We need to give her room to breathe."

When we closed in the evening, the hospital reported she hadn't regained consciousness yet.

I took two books home with me, both local histories. I needed to know more about where I lived.

Fog eddied through Kingsport's streets as I walked. My Arizona coat failed to match a New England November. Its chill air seeped through everything. To my left, the old buildings rose, black and poorly lit. Side streets were cobblestone and too narrow for cars to pass each other. I imagined Kingsport in the 1700s, before the American Revolution, when people walked or rode horses, and nothing wider than a fish cart traveled the town. To my right, the hill sloped to the wharves where rooftops and crooked chimneys poked through the mist, but gray shrouded the sea. I held my coat close. Something skittered away in the gap between two houses, and a figure walked down the sidewalk toward me, his hands jammed into this pockets. When he passed, he didn't acknowledge my nod. His eyes reflected the hazy streetlight as he looked my way. I thought for a second he was deformed. His face seemed strangely long, as if his head had been squeezed in a vice, pushing his features forward. He parted his lips, revealing pointed teeth.

A half block further, I dismissed my perceptions as an illusion of bad light.

The first book didn't tell me much. Lots of chamber of commerce type pictures of sunsets and picturesque fishing boats along with a cursory history from colonial times about the coastal trade, ship building, fishing, and the challenges of farming rocky land. The only item of interest was a one-paragraph mention of the Salem witch trials and four witches who were hung in Kingsport. When dawn leaked into my window ten hours later, I reached the end of the entertaining but ridiculous second book, *Mysteries and Legends of the Miskatonic River Valley,* which contained as much fact about this little section of north-eastern shoreline as a book called *Famous Sightings of Chupacabra in the Southwest* would tell me about Arizona and New Mexico. The author footnoted extensively, referencing diaries, journals, oral histories and private letters held in Miskatonic University's special collections. Surely all fake, of course, but I made notes to look up some of the more interesting titles to see if at least that part of the fiction was valid.

That morning from my desk, the door next to my office clicked open then closed. I'd forgotten to ask Delilah about it.

Whoever had gone in locked the door behind them, but voices murmured on the other side. I knocked, and they fell silent. After a moment, I knocked again. The door cracked open. A middle-aged woman with dark hair streaked in gray, peered at me, half her face hidden by the door. "We have the key," she said defensively, and held out a key attached to a wooden plate, like a key you'd get to a gas station bathroom. The two dark-haired neighbor girls looked around her legs at me.

I didn't know what to say to that. "I'm the children's librarian," I finally offered. My name badge hung in plain sight from its lanyard around my neck. "May I come in?"

"You have to have the key." She shut the door.

Delilah sat at the main checkout counter, scanning codes from the backs of returned books and then putting them in the reshelve cart. Her face darkened when I asked about the room. "Oh, I forgot to talk to you about that. It's not used much."

"What is it? Why is it in the children's section?"

"I've been in Kingsport for seven years now, and I've learned that there's weird stuff about this part of the country. Did you know the town started in 1689?"

"I read up last night."

"I'll bet your reading didn't tell you the old families who go back over three hundred years have an . . . undemocratic . . . amount of influence. They get what they want. This library, for instance came about because the Kingsport families didn't like that MU's library was the region's book and research center. It's simple jealousy."

"So what about the room by my office?"

"MU's library doesn't have a children's collection. That room holds children's books by local authors. Some are the only copies in existence. Others are long out of print. I don't go in there much. Not to my taste. The old families check them out occasionally for their children. Mostly we just hold them. Not much scholarly research on kids' lit. Still, it's something Kingsport has that MU does not."

"My next-door neighbor and her daughters are in there now. They're darned territorial."

"I was going to ask if you'd met her yet. That's Emiline Smith-Armitage. She donated half the collection. Emiline's a single mom, great granddaughter of Henry Armitage, the head librarian at MU back in the day. She's estranged from the Arkham Armitages."

"I've seen the daughters."

Emiline Smith-Armitage marched from the children's library, the room key in hand, her daughters following. A short woman with a narrow face and firm stride, she slapped the key to the counter, gave me a dismissive look, then left.

A minute later, Delilah opened the mysterious door. "As I said, we don't come in here often. Most of the books are on loan."

The room smelled fishy, like bad salmon left out too long. One wall held books and a document bureau, while three reading desks, each with a hard plastic chair and reading lamp took up the other wall. A long, narrow space, it looked like a converted janitor's storage area. A row of thin, similarly bound books took up the highest shelf. I pulled the first one down: *The Founders Parade*, written and illustrated by Amias Basil, 1882, reprinted in 1927.

"I believe we have the only complete set of those," said Delilah. "He was popular in the region for a while. I don't see the appeal myself."

The leather cover had a slimy feel, and the image on the front had nearly worn off.

I have always loved children's picture books. *Polar Express, Owl Moon, The Garden of Abdul Gasazi, Knuffle Bunny,* the classics. My first editions of *Where the Wild Things Are* and *The Mysteries of Harris Burdick* are my most treasured possessions, but *The Founders Parade* appalled me. A hand-colored wood cut appeared at the top of the first page with the text below.

The Founders found our marshy shores
And built their homes from stones of black.
They sealed the walls with oaken doors
And dreamed of oceans that they lacked.

The picture felt unbalanced, as if Basil drew from an unfamiliar geometry. It's hard to explain the unease that arose from his illustration, and each page after was as disturbing. The story told about the founders celebrating a holiday. Snow appeared in some pictures, and the sea revealed its gray, stormy look when it appeared, but it wasn't a Christmas book. One picture showed fish-faced children with webbed fingers holding seaweed or entrails—I couldn't tell—while a shape watched in the background, a tentacled shadow with too many eyes and a mouth that fell away deeper than the page. I shuddered when I closed the book, and what terrified me, what woke me up that night with my heart pounding and my sheets sweat soaked, was the impulse not to close the book. To keep staring until the eyes stared back, until the mouth moved to swallow me and everything I loved. I wondered if Allison, the girl who'd had the seizure, had seen something from the special collection.

Twenty-one books made the Founders series: *The Founders Friends, The Founders Happy Day, The Founders Hold a Dance.* The worst was called *The Founders Feast.* I almost dropped it in disgust.

I swallowed hard. "Kids read these?"

Delilah nodded. "We also have children's diaries, children's artwork."

"Like the stuff on the walls?"

"Oh, some much worse. Therapists use children's art to reveal trauma. There's damaged psyches in those drawers." She looked at the document bureau.

"Do you know a book called *Mysteries and Legends of the Mis-*

katonic River Valley? There's illustrations in there that look like the Founders imagery."

"I've read it, yes." Delilah ran her finger down a book's spine. "I thought it was silly. Of course, that was before I'd spent a year here."

"How many children use this room?"

"Fifteen or so. They don't come in often. All old family kids. All home schooled. There's probably another hundred I never see. They don't get out much."

"Could you make a list?"

It took courage to travel the long walk to Emiline Smith-Armitage's front door. Her house stood three stories tall, and the poor illumination from the street lights revealed that her windows were open despite the thirty-degree temperatures and a steady breeze off the harbor.

She clearly had no interest in inviting me in, but when I didn't take her obvious hints, she held the door wider. Soon, I sat in her dining room, a broad space with a long, bare table in the middle. A candelabra turned low suspended from the high ceiling provided the only light so that shadows dominated in the freezing room. Now that I could see her close up, she was much more peculiar than she seemed from our brief encounter in the library. I thought she was about forty earlier, but up close she appeared younger. No lines on her narrow face. No color either in her lifeless pallor. When she wasn't talking, her lips parted every few seconds with a slight pop.

"I understand that your family has been in Kingsport for generations," I said.

She nodded.

I wondered where her children were. A set of heavy footsteps crossed the ceiling. Not a child's. She lived in a huge house. Delilah said she was a single mom. Several doors opened into the dining room, all black pits beyond. Something could be standing just out of the light in anyone of them, watching us.

"As the children's librarian, part of my mission is to provide engaging activities for young people."

She looked at me, but I couldn't read curiosity in her eyes or any human emotion. Her expression remained blank, her only sound the steady pop, pop, pop of her mouth opening and closing. Deep in the house, someone laughed, but it didn't sound sane, and it cut off abruptly.

No one knew I had come to visit. I hadn't told Delilah of my plans. I wondered if I could find my way from the house if the candelabra went out because it seemed to me that Emiline Smith-Armitage would have no trouble in the dark. I was sure she preferred it.

I said, "I'm glad to see your children use the library, but I understand that there are other children, children of Kingsport's oldest families who never visit."

The mention of her children caused a flicker of interest. She turned toward me, and I explained my plan.

When the library closed at 9:00, two weeks later, I walked the building to be sure no patrons remained. I unlocked the children's special collection door and went from table to table, leaving two or three picture books on each. Not just the Founders books, but the other ones with illustrations just as disturbing as the ones I'd seen. The language in some wasn't English or formed from English letters.

At 9:30, Emiline Smith-Armitage's children arrived with their mother. "Thank you for coming," I said.

Soon, other parents walked up the stairs into the library. I greeted them. Many were odd looking, as if they were related to the man I'd seen walking in the dark the first night I'd arrived. Many shared Emiline Smith-Armitage's odd habit of popping her lips, but the children they brought were eager. They ran from table to table, peering at the books, opening them, turning page to page.

I met with the parents to announce the new after-hours reading program for their children. They could read the books and not worry that someone who shouldn't see them might catch a glimpse, someone like Allison. Their children too could enjoy the library.

I went to the children's section, sat in the storyteller's chair, and gathered the children around. They sat at my feet like any other group I'd ever read to would. The book I chose, *The Founders Name the Stars*, was a big hit. I showed them the pictures on each page, the awful, mind rending pictures that hurt my eyes to look at. They sat rapt. The tiniest child, a two-year-old, sat near me, and as I read, he grasped my pants cuff in his little fist. He sucked his thumb and watched me read, hanging onto my words.

When I finished they begged for another. Their parents stood behind them, watching, it seemed, as if in judgment. When I finished the second, I felt that I'd been exonerated, and I didn't even know I'd been on trial.

"How many of you need a library card?" I asked.

Hands went up. Some were webbed. Some were clawed. It took until midnight to give them all their cards. I thought about my mission as the last child left, to help the children develop as learners. The library would be a part of their growth.

Every library had a unique population.

I'm here to serve.

 *Like "In Memoriam," this story was written on location (thank you, Grand Junction Public Library Children's Department). A writer really only has three resources to write from: personal experience, experiences borrowed from others (research, books, movies, television, your friends and family stories, etc.), and imagination. All are important, but too often young writers seem to ignore personal experience. In a story that doesn't work, the author might write about sadness, but it's as if the writer has never been sad. Or there might be a moment where the character is scared, but it's written by someone who hasn't truly remembered what it's like to be afraid. Going to the setting where the story takes place, talking to the kind of people the story is about, building up personal experiences to write from, are all activities to be encouraged. Nothing makes for more convincing fiction than a healthy dollop of reality.*

For all but the outdoor enthusiasts, weather has become increasingly unimportant. Our houses, schools and offices shelter us, protect us, and turn weather into a remote phenomena to look at through the windows. Weather hasn't always been so remote, though, and if the situation changes, it could become immediate again.

WRITING ADVICE

NEVER START WITH THE WEATHER. BUT WHAT IF THE weather is the whole story? Solar weather to start with, but also the weather as I write this? Wind rattles the windows. It whistles, moans and whispers like sheets sliding on sand. Rain taps its fingernails against the glass. Electricity went out hours ago. I find matches in the drawer by the stove, but it takes a while to locate the candles stored in a box with the Christmas decorations behind the suitcases and winter coats. Good thing the phone has a flashlight built in, as long as its battery holds out. No phone signal though. Turning off WiFi and Bluetooth to save energy. It's funny how useless a building feels without power. Wind stole the house's voice. Family is away visiting back east. No kids. No fans. No refrigerator. No television. Although, to tell the truth, I don't miss continuous disaster coverage. Magnetic storms. Coronal mass ejection (a CME). That's what they said before the lights went out, but they said the event would be just a few hours, and it shouldn't affect cars! I don't think the authorities know what's going on.

Show, don't tell. Drama is in action, they say. So my actions stretch to two days and then to three. I chop down the maple tree in the back yard for the wood stove. Have to clean out the flue. Haven't put wood in that stove for fifteen years. It's a gas-heated home, but the gas isn't flowing either. Dropped below freezing last night. Shut the upstairs doors and placed rolled up towels to block cold air. No radio. Car still won't start. Neighbors are testy. I'm not going to show my emergency supplies in the basement to anyone. I certainly won't tell them about the bagged rice and cases of canned goods. Let them laugh at my survivalist habits now! Ride my bike a few miles through the neighborhoods. People stay inside. It's a suburban ghost town, except for the inner-city refugees. People who live in apartments and condos aren't survivalists I guess. When the food from their cupboards go, they're done. Supermarkets near downtown must have emptied in a day. Now they're on the move.

Only one coincidence per story, and it can't resolve the conflict. That's easy to say for writing fiction, but coincidences happen all the time. Everything is a coincidence, if you think about it. So, what if there was a CME at the same time as an enemy EMP? The magnetic effects caused by the squashing of Earth's magnetic field would run a charge through electrical lines, frying transformers and anything plugged into a wall socket, while the EMP would knock out everything else that's electrical, like cell phones and cars. Are we under an attack?

Or maybe this is the situation: before the electricity went out, when the news warned of a violent sun event, they said that in 1859 a CME hit powerful enough to knock out their highest tech device, the telegraph service. The current built up in lines shocked operators, and sparks lit papers on fire. But the sun kicks out CMEs all the time. Most miss the Earth. The news said that if you imagined the sun as the size of a basketball in the middle of a football field, the Earth would be about 1/40th of an inch and orbiting in the outside lane of the track around the field. We're a really small target, even though the CME expands from the sun like a shotgun blast.

So the coincidences are these: the CME might have been way more powerful than the 1859 event, and the Earth just happened to be directly in its path, and now we have technology that is particularly vulnerable.

If the event is more powerful, it is also faster. The plasma could have reached the Earth in twelve hours. Figure a couple of hours for scientists to recognize what is happening on the sun. Another couple for world leaders to decide what to do, and now you have to hope that they get the power grid off line and protect fragile systems in time. Do you believe they would respond that quickly and make the right moves?

Or maybe these are the end times. I've never seen the aurora borealis in Denver, but tonight it is bright enough between the clouds to read a book. Weird green and purple lights cascading behind the storm.

Avoid detailed descriptions of characters. I am the story's voice, though. That's what history lacks, the character, and I'm recording this, me, not to tell you of America's fate, or the Earth, for all I know, but of mine. My name is Jim. I write science fiction and fantasy. Sometimes end of the world stories. When I was little, I loved apocalypses, especially empty-Earth ones where the buildings stood, but the people were gone. Imagine being ten and locked in a mall. You run through the hallways or ride a skateboard you took from the sporting goods store. You load your tray with anything from the food court. You sleep in the furniture store. You're ten, and the empty mall is your playground. I imagined nice, hygienic apocalypses that weren't populated with starving people who tear away at the boards over my windows and doors.

But my appearance? The advice is right. Does it matter to picture me, sixty-one years old, medium build, gray hair, wire-rimmed glasses. Maybe it would be more helpful if I tell you a few days before the lights died I sat in the gym watching the college kids play pickup basketball. They reminded me of my playing days. The young men ran fast, jumped high. Passes blasted crisp and hard, and they never tired. If I joined them, the first layup would strain my back. I'd twist an ankle. I don't have that easy wrist flip that sends the ball arcing toward the basket. I can't play with them.

And now, those same fast, strong, violent men want into my house. Whatever fantasies I've had about holding my own in a fight are a joke. Even the baseball bat I clutch won't stop them if they get in. I huddle in the dark behind my barricades, and shout threats. I hope they find an easier house to break into. The only description you need of me is that I'm helpless.

Tie the ending to the beginning. Which end? The one where the boards are torn away and I'm beaten to death for hoarding? Or a different one where the military trucks rumble down the street with emergency supplies before the fierce men burst through? Or the one where the lights flicker and turn on a day after they failed? Or the end where the refrigerator hums to life before the ice cream has really begun to melt?

I'm in present tense. I don't know the end. It's raining hard, and I'm alone while in the breaks between the clouds the sky bleeds purple and green. I'll go to the basement to look for candles soon. They're stored with the Christmas village and the glittery wreath and the ribbons and bows.

 *Multiple award winning author Connie Willis once told a room full of people at a convention that what sometimes motivates her to write is anger. Somebody did something so silly or so stupid that she had to react. I listened to a group of editors in a panel where one of the editors offered a series of pronouncements about writing as if they were all the holy word come down from high on gold tablets. He made me angry. It wasn't that the advice was bad; it was the way he presented it as hard and fast rules. So, of course, when he said, "Never start with the weather," I had to write a story that started that way. As far as I can tell, the only real rule for writers is this: It has to work. If what you write doesn't reach the readers, then it failed. If it does, even if it broke a "rule," then it's okay.*

The Declaration of Independence guarantees the right to pursue happiness. It doesn't say that we will get it.

THE GOLDEN DAFFODILS

NO ONE SHOULD GET DRUNK AT CARNIVALS. THEY ARE drunk already with rippling tents, cotton candy, rollercoaster, and always, always screaming children. Carnivals reel on their own. To be there is to wallow in revelry, to be sucked in, to surrender.

Ruth, drunk, weaved with dignity, a rum and coke thermos in one hand and a white teddy bear clutching a heart that read "I Love You" in the other. She couldn't get the lights to settle into one place, and a calliope belched a harsh, flinch-inducing song.

Bitter thoughts about happiness filled her head. The Friday morning meeting had been about happiness in the work place. The company brought in a speaker who gave them "resilience drills," and they did an exercise to practice "letting go." The expert handed out index cards. Ruth's cards said "grudges," and "jealousy." The group stood on their chairs to drop their "baggage." For a second, the meeting room looked like an index card snowstorm. "Find happiness in the process, not the product," the expert said. Ruth wasn't sure what that meant, but she was pretty sure that the process of the meeting pissed her off.

She shaded her eyes, huddled against the carnival's sound, then pushed into the fortuneteller's booth where the noise dropped by half and was blessedly dark. The fortuneteller sat behind a sable-covered table, cards waiting, an old man wearing mirrored sunglasses. Later, Ruth tried to remember the conversation, what the soothsayer said. Most was too foggy. She remembered they talked about happiness. He put his hands on hers, shocked her. "Tag, you're it." Then, a taxi driver woke in front of her apartment. "You're here, lady." Had the fortuneteller called the cab? She couldn't recall. When she fell into bed, the room rose and fell and swirled, like brightly-painted horses going round and round.

The next morning, Ruth put her briefcase beneath her desk. The breakfast eggs sat better than she thought they might, and out of habit she opened the filing cabinet for the aspirin bottle, but her head didn't hurt. She closed it.

At work, a chubby, balding, middle-aged loan closer named Art took his desk in the cubicle across from hers. "Mondays make me twitch," he said without irony.

"How'd your bowling tournament go?" Ruth smiled, which she hadn't done for a while, but she felt good, like a benign cloud surrounded her.

He looked at her suspiciously. "You've never been interested in my weekends before."

"It's an innocent question. I have a life. You have a life. We work together. Nothing odd about idle chitchat between coworkers. Did you win?"

"Tenth frame with the game on the line, I left a Greek Church. Nobody gets those, and I didn't either."

"Greek Church?"

"Two on the left, three on the right. Worst split you can get. Bad first ball. Impossible second."

"You'll beat them next week," Ruth said, and she meant it.

"Bah!"

Ruth shrugged her shoulders. Paperwork filled her inbox. Four complete mortgages to assemble, a closing to schedule, and two reminders for a morning meeting over changes in Federal loan filing procedures, which she normally loathed with a black dread, but she found herself humming.

Art glanced at her; Ruth didn't care. Before the meeting, she'd cleared over half the day's work. The doughnuts tasted delightful, and the slideshow, normally a complete bore-fest, contained helpful tips that would make the afternoon tasks easier. At lunch, Ruth opened her "to do" file, which she'd been avoiding for weeks, inventoried what could be finished by the weekend, and then in the time she had left, followed links to an Ireland travel package she'd been interested in a year ago but hadn't had the spirit to care about since. Castles, cliffs; rolling, green hills.

At 2:00, as she answered e-mails and finished off a particularly tricky deal that involved transferring ownership on two properties for one, she stopped to look at the lower right drawer in her desk. She hadn't opened it at lunch—she hadn't really considered it until now—and that made her thoughtful. Behind the vertical files was a three-quarter full vodka bottle. Over the course of the last few months, she'd been hitting it more often during the day, but a drink didn't sound appealing now.

Maybe tonight would be good for redecorating her bedroom. She picked up color swatches at the paint store, compared them to her drapes for ten minutes before deciding the drapes would have to go. At 9:00, the announcement that the fabric store was closing surprised her. She took her purchases to the counter, and by midnight, she'd cut the fabric the way she wanted. Tomorrow after work she would sew.

A glass of warm milk sounded better than wine to top off the evening. Ruth stood at her stove in her bathrobe, stirring slowly. When she was six, her grandmother used to warm her milk for bed. Ruth remembered grandma's arthritic hands holding the spoon, how the moths beat against the back door screen. She remembered a summer night, standing on the porch with grandma. In the field across the road from the farmhouse, a carnival set up. Burly men working by lantern light hammered in thick tent stakes. A lion in a cage roared. Just as she had then, Ruth shivered, then a hand caressed her own. The sensation was so vivid that she stepped back from the stove. It felt like the fortuneteller's touch from the night before.

Ruth fell asleep easily, dreamed pleasant dreams and woke up before her alarm, feeling better than she had for months. It was if the night had peeled years from her. The reflection in the mirror didn't look different, though. Belly a little poochy. Flabby arms. She added renewing the gym membership to her to-do list.

Ruth knew exactly when she lost her happiness. It wasn't during breakfast, when the sun fell through her kitchen window like honey butter, or when she stopped by the T-shirt shop on the corner, and it wasn't on the downtown bus when she scooted over so a ragged street person had room for his cat in a cage. No, it happened in the office. She went to the break room and found a roll of gift wrapping paper in a cabinet above where everyone hung their coffee mugs. Wrapping a T-shirt without a box always produced a lumpy, wrinkly package, but she smiled at the result anyway when she put it on Art's desk.

Art arrived five minutes late as always, and looked at the package for a moment before checking the office. Ruth glanced away and pretended to be busy at her computer. Finally, he opened it, took out the shirt, a bright purple cotton short-sleeve with a picture of two bowling pins standing on the left and right, and a bowling ball in the middle beside a couple pins that were down. The text on top said, "Smile!" and underneath, "Splits happen."

Ruth walked behind him and put her hand on his shoulder. "I guessed at the size. I hope that's okay."

"You didn't have to do this. I've never gotten you anything."

She shrugged. "I was in a mood."

"It is pretty funny," he said and put the shirt in a drawer.

When she touched his hand, they sparked, like static electricity, but stronger and more liquidy. Ruth drew back with a laugh. As she walked to her desk, though, she fought the pull from the floor as if gravity had turned up a notch. Her unanswered e-mails suddenly intimidated her. She sighed and opened the first one.

By the afternoon, Art whistled while he typed. He'd put the T-shirt on under his jacket during lunch. Ruth hunched over her keyboard. Spam infected her mail, but company policy was to open every message, as if a "dear sir or madam" message from Nigeria might be a legitimate customer. Art's good humor grated on. She wondered what could possibly be happening with him. It's Tuesday. No one whistles on Tuesday!

Before he left for the day, he dropped an envelope on her desk. She almost snapped and snarled, "It's not a game of tag," but managed to extract the venom from the comment before the words came out.

Art said, "One good deed deserves another. It's just a poem I like. Thanks for the shirt."

For a moment, Ruth recaptured the morning cheer. The envelope had gold filigree on the edges. Inside the card pictured a field of glowing, yellow flowers. The poem sounded vaguely familiar. It might have been one she'd read in college. The poet said he'd been wandering one day and came upon "A host, of golden daffodils; beside the lake, beneath the trees, fluttering and dancing in the breeze." He said that afterwards, whenever he was "in a vacant or pensive mood," he would think of the moment, and his "heart with pleasure fills and dances with the daffodils."

She thought about the poem on the bus going home, but her mind kept returning to "It's not a game of tag." It nagged at her while the car started and stopped along the route. People climbed on. Others left. She wondered if they were happy. Most carried nothing in their faces, but occasionally, one laughed or smiled. A young woman sat in the bench across from her, rapt and joyful, looking out the window as if she'd never seen a city before. Ruth wondered if she touched the woman that a little of her delight would rub off, then she remembered the fortuneteller's hand. "Tag," he'd said, "you're it," and she knew when she'd touched Art, he'd taken her happiness.

Ruth found his address in the employee directory, an apartment on the other side of town. Two bus transfers later, she stood on the street looking up at his building. He didn't answer the buzzer until she'd pressed a third time.

"Do you have it?" she asked at his door.

She could see in his face that he knew what she meant. Art crossed his arms across his chest, clearly struggling with what to do. He moved aside to let her in.

Surprisingly, Art's apartment was sparse and neat. Ruth had imagined he would be sloppy. Photographs hung from his walls. No portraits, only landscapes. The one bookcase contained poetry in thin volumes. She didn't recognize the authors. He liked incense.

"It's gone," he said. "What did you do to me?"

"Somebody did it to me first." She sat on the couch. "Who did you touch?"

Art's expression change to hope. "That's how? I thought I felt it in the office." He leaned toward her, desperate. "Touch me again. Give it back. For the first time in years, I had hours and hours without darkness. I thought the coffee was drugged, or I was having a weird anti-stroke that starved the part of my brain that processes the world. I was scared—really I was—I was losing my mind."

She recognized the symptoms. "I went to a carnival Sunday. A fortuneteller passed it to me. He knew. He told me about it, I think. Who did you touch?"

Art hung his head. "Standup room only on the bus. Someone bumped me on a stop. A jolt, like static electricity. I didn't realize what it meant. It could have been anybody."

Ruth fell back against the couch and closed her eyes. Maybe it would have been better to have never gone to the carnival. Her life didn't seem that bad before she woke up on Monday. She had a job that paid well. She lived in a nice apartment. What was there to be bleak about? But she remembered night after night, not even turning on the television because nothing sounded good. Not calling her family because she had nothing to say, and she didn't care about their lives. She held the bottle, poured one glass after another until she fell asleep, her chin on her chest.

"We have to go to the carnival." Art opened a closet and grabbed a coat.

On the bus, Ruth studied him as he looked out the window. Streetlights played across his face. Why wasn't he happy? In the years at the mortgage company, he'd seemed self-contained. Sometimes she saw him staring into the distance. He was grumpy occasionally at worst. Maybe whatever the fortuneteller gave them transcended happiness. Perhaps no one had experienced the world the way they had.

The bus dropped them two blocks from the fairgrounds. The Ferris wheel spun gaily against the cloudy sky, lights blinking. Kids yelled. The calliope moaned. A popcorn wind stirred papers that skittered past them on the sidewalk. Ruth clutched her coat tight against her neck.

She lead them past the ring toss booths and the octopus ride, past the funnel cake stand and the house of horrors. A line of couples holding hands stood outside the tunnel of love. Ruth's chest tightened. What had the fortuneteller said to her on Sunday? She'd tried recreating the encounter over the last two days, but her memories were fuzzy, and even sober, the carnival had a surreal, otherworldly vibe that set her on edge.

A padlock held the heavy canvas closed at the fortuneteller's tent. Ruth pulled at it in frustration.

"Are you sure this is the place?" Art pushed his hands deep into his pockets. A string of lights swayed in the wind above them.

"I'll find out where he is."

The target booth facing them had a single patron, shooting down metal rabbits one after another. A lanky blonde wearing a baseball cap and holding a roll of tickets said, "We haven't had a fortuneteller for two weeks. Saddest character I ever knew. Wife died. Kids died. His dog ran away in the spring. Wouldn't surprise me if he offed himself."

"But I saw him Sunday. I was in that tent Sunday. Is there another fortuneteller?"

"I didn't work that night. Maybe he popped in for old times sake." The woman shook her head. "We're looking for a replacement. Not much of a carnival without a card reader."

Art's voice rose. "Ruth talked to the fortuneteller here, Sunday night."

Ruth thought he looked a little crazed. She followed him as he stalked the fairground, looking down every row of booths. "Where's the card reader?" he asked at every stop. No one knew.

Later, Ruth took him to a coffee shop a block from the carnival. They sat in a back booth.

Art gripped his coffee cup. "He's out there somewhere."

"Maybe, but what does it matter? The happiness is only good until you touch someone. Then they have it. Whoever you bumped on the bus might have been happy for just a second before they bumped someone else. Last one on the bus to get it took it. Say it was a man coming home from work. He's joyous as he walks from the bus stop to his house. He can't wait to see his wife. He hugs her. She laughs because there's a shock. For a minute, the world feels better to her, but she touches her daughter who is eight. She takes it to school the next day. Person after person, skipping along, the happiness is transient."

Art took a bill from his wallet and put it on the table. "I don't believe it. If he gave it to you with a touch, there must be a way to give it to you permanently. I'll find him. He's a carny. They don't know any other life than the road. I'll bet he left because other people at the carnival suspected him. Their lives are empty, living like gypsies. Hoping the next town brings enough customers, but when someone touched the fortuneteller, they saw it differently.

You know what it feels like. Have you ever been better in your life, even once?"

Ruth shook her head.

"They drove him away. Imagine the carny folk slipping into his tent at night. 'Touch me,' they'd say. He'd have to leave. But I'll find him. He'll go from carnival to carnival because that's all he knows how to do. I'll find him and make him tell me the secret."

The middle-aged man pushed himself from the table, a haunting in his eyes. "He can't have gone far."

Ruth stayed after Art left. He could be right about the fortuneteller, but she didn't believe he'd ever be found, not by someone like Art. That's not how you get it—happiness, that is. You can't hunt it down.

No, Ruth found her moment when she wasn't looking for it. Happiness came to her unexpected. Thinking about her one day made her pensive. She remembered standing in her bedroom on Monday, the new cloth for the drapes in hand. The wall would be the fresh color. The drapes would filter sunlight just so. Ruth recalled the pleasure the project gave her.

The poem Art gave her had been right. The memory alone lifted her spirit. It was like the flowers pictured in the field. Her mind filled and danced with daffodils.

 *Someone once told me that most stories were simple reversals. If the characters start the story happy, they'll end up sad. If they start healthy, they'll end sick. He used Dickens' "A Christmas Carol" as an example. He said, "At the beginning, Scrooge is so miserly and miserable that his name has come to be a synonym for greed, but at the end at the end of the story he is generous and kind. The man who said of Christmas, 'Bah, humbug,' honored the holiday more than anyone." Stories can be about reversals, but it seems more accurate to say they are about change. Even stories where the characters end where they started as Samwise Gamgee does in* The Lord of the Rings *when he returns to the Shire and ends the tale with a simple, 'Well, I'm back,' have become different somehow. The story's events change the world of the story.*

In brightly-colored letters at the entrance to many elementary school librar-
ies, a banner reads, "Books are your tickets to adventure." This is true for readers
young and old.

THE SILK SILVERED
SKULLS OF MILLEN MIR

NOTHING BEATS A GREAT BOOK," SAID LES BULLARD. HE
waited below Miss Rhonim as she stood on the lad-
der, searching the upper shelf. Remarkably fit for a librarian. Solid
upper arms, well muscled legs. A statuesque Amazonian in black-
framed glasses. She fit in with the library's décor, which leaned toward medieval armaments.

"You know you read the title when you were young?"

"Fifth grade or maybe sixth. I went through a long heroic fantasy phase. Tarzan and Conan and John Carter and Elric of Mel-
niboné. The eternal champions. I wanted to be Doc Savage. God, I
loved those books."

"This one, though, it wasn't part of a series?" She pulled on the
shelf to move the ladder a couple feet.

"Nope. Just one, medium-sized book. Mine had a red leather
cover and gold-edged pages. Nicest book I ever carried in my backpack. A maroon ribbon sewn into the binding to mark my spot."

"But you don't know the author?"

Les wrinkled his brow. "I can tell you how the book smelled. I can tell you what it was like to lay on my grandmother's freezer in her cellar during sweltering, summer Ohio days, reading the book by the light of the open door. I can tell you about starting the book after breakfast, and reading until it grew dark. I walked from the cellar up a little flight of stairs and into her back yard where fire-flies winked over the vegetable patch. But I can't recall the author's name. It was three words, I think, like Jaime Fitz Mason or Robin Trait Curran. Something with that rhythm."

"I can't do a search for an author's name by rhythm."

"Maybe I'm misremembering the title." But Les was sure he wasn't. He closed his eyes and saw the book in the cellar's dimness, could feel the weight in his hand. Black letters embossed on red leather with a silver vine woven through them: *The Silk Silvered Skulls of Millen Mir*. He loved the opening line: "The swordsman's horse carried the weary warrior down a stony path."

Miss Rhonim ran her finger across the books' spines, one after another. "You came to the right place for hard to find books. The Orne Library at Miskatonic University is world-renowned."

Les looked down the long, poorly lit shelves. Small fluorescent fixtures hung from the ceiling at ten-foot intervals, but only the lights within fifteen feet of them were on. Darkness shrouded the rest. The cement floor reflected nothing. He couldn't see the wall at either end. "I heard your library had the best collection of uncata-loged titles in North America. I've been looking for this book for decades."

"That's dedication. Heroic fantasy, fairly contemporary lan-guage, you said."

"I didn't have trouble reading it when I was twelve, but I read well above grade level. I finished *All Quiet on the Western Front* the next year. Most depressing book of all time. I swore off fine litera-ture for years after that."

"So probably written in the late 1800s but no later than 1965 or so. We're in the right section, but we have thousands of titles, as you can see. It might take a bit." She glanced at her watch. "This is the restricted collection. There are irreplaceable texts stored down here. One of a kind. Patrons have to be accompanied."

Les bent to inspect the bottom row. His back creaked. "Why aren't these titles in a database? How do you find anything?"

She stiffened. "The Orne Library is the largest gathering of rare and historic texts in the northern hemisphere. In the general collection there are several million titles. Only Harvard contains more works than we do. Our Pickman Archive holds the finest examples of early Americana in the world, including settler diaries, journals and ledgers. We have letters from the original pilgrims. I think we do very well considering the complexity of our collection."

"I wasn't criticizing."

Miss Rhonim continued scanning book titles, clearly taking a few calming breaths. "Sorry to sound defensive, but you don't have to work in the Orne long before you realize the value of these books. Besides, the deeper collection is . . . difficult."

"What do you mean?"

"The books aren't always where we leave them. They . . . um . . . rearrange. Like this—" She held a black volume in her hand. "—is from 1788. It's misplaced. The faculty has learned to take a book when they find it. It might not be there again."

"So my title could be anywhere?" When they'd come down the long, stone stairway to this level, Les had thought they were going to a reading room or display area, but what greeted them at the bottom was a corridor formed by the ends of bookshelves that reached ceiling to floor. The lights must have been attached to motion sensors because they turned on as the two approached and blinked out behind them. At each junction, more neatly shelved books greeted him, row after row, until he lost count. They made several turns to reach the area they were in now, and not all were right angles. Some books stood in large circular shelves, like roundabouts, and others were stored in triangular formations, twenty feet to a side. Periodically they came upon a chair with an attached writing surface or a study table, but he hadn't seen another person. "I'm not surprised you lose books. The way this place is built, you could lose librarians."

"If your book exists, we have it. Looking is the only way to uncover anything; the loose organization down here is a feature, not a bug. The restricted collection is less about finding and more about discovering, Mr. Bullard. Our researchers and the books they need eventually cross paths." She replaced a book firmly on the shelf. "Imagine coming down here in the 1800s when you would have been holding a lantern."

The idea made him shiver.

They searched for another hour, Miss Rhonim using the ladder for the high shelves, and Les reading the low ones. He examined beautiful books, some with illustrated covers. One showed a burly savage wrestling an alligator, jaws open and stretching back, trying to kill the muscular human. Broken pillars, like a coliseum's remains stood in the misty background. He liked the style, but the artist was unfamiliar. "Can I check this out?"

Miss Rhonim nodded. "Twenty-four hours only. You have to sign a waiver and leave a deposit."

That night, Les made himself comfortable on the motel bed, turned on the reading light, then opened the book, *A Jungle Crown at Katung Pass* by Sideon Wayte. It had a faded inscription in pencil he hadn't noticed before: "To Beatrice, my jungle queen. Raymond, Christmas, 1908." So, written before Burroughs published Tarzan.

Twenty minutes into the book, Les climbed from the bed to stretch his back. When he'd retired two years ago, he'd looked forward to long periods of uninterrupted reading, a return to his youth. But now he couldn't stay in one posture more than thirty minutes before his back or neck hurt. Even holding the book made his elbows and fingers ache. He wondered if arthritis might be kicking in. And he could never find quite the right position for his bifocals. He kept adjusting his head to focus properly.

In junior high, he carried at least a couple novels in his backpack, waiting for class to begin so he could sneak one out. Mr. Crutcher, his 8th grade history teacher would turn his back to write on the board, and Les would have his book open. Then, like the snap of his fingers, class ended. For forty minutes, the teacher and his lesson faded away. When the bell rang, Les had to shake himself back to reality. He walked the halls in bewilderment because the literary world felt so much more real than the school. By the end of the day, he would have finished the book and started another. He read at night, long after he was supposed to be asleep so that he reached the new book's end.

Reading connected him to his youth. He didn't have to be able to run and jump like a fifteen-year-old if he could read like one.

Les sat on the bed's edge, reopened the book. The story wasn't bad, even if the language stumbled in places. Sideon Wayte couldn't turn a phrase, but he wrote with a cheerful, testosterone-soaked cheesiness. The villain was particularly black-hearted, the jungle animals "snarled with wild ferocity" and the women were slender, "small-handed" creatures who swooned on cue. In other words, *A Jungle Crown at Katung Pass* was a book of its time. It certainly didn't measure up to *The Silk Silvered Skulls of Millen Mir*.

If he could just find the book again! His gnawing obsession. For years he'd haunted used bookstores and antique shops, hoping he'd spot the familiar red cover. The summer at Grandma's house in Ohio, that had been his only title. He couldn't remember where he got it. Maybe he'd found it in her living room bookcase where she kept a collection of *Reader's Digest* condensed classics along with a few others. Surely his parents hadn't given it to him. They favored cheap paperbacks.

He'd always been a fast reader. Other books he finished in a day (even the fat and deeply depressing *All Quiet on the Western Front*), but he started *The Silk Silvered Skulls* when he arrived at Grandma's. He read every day for hours. He read after dinner and deep into the night, but he never finished the book. His memory of that summer was of delirious hours lost in *Millen Mir*. It seemed as if he was always in the middle, more pages to go, and he loved it. Other books passed too fast until the sad dread of knowing only a few pages remained crept up on him. The dream would soon end.

He'd turn the final page where the text didn't reach the bottom and the facing page was blank. *Lord of the Rings* lasted three days in the 9th grade. He didn't sleep. He faked a cough so he could skip school when he reached *The Return of the King*. Mom left him in his room, Mentholatum rubbed into his chest, vaporizer bubbling, buried in his blankets, deep in Middle Earth. The remaining pages grew fewer and fewer. Sweat poured from him as he lingered over the final paragraphs. The last pages wrinkled in the humid room until he finished, totally drained, sorry the book didn't go on.

But not *The Silk Silvered Skulls of Millen Mir*. How was it possible that he read just that one book all summer? Did he finish, and then lost in the book's spell, turn back to the beginning to start again?

Les put a pillow under his knees. Maybe if he could find just the right position, he would disappear into *A Jungle Crown at Katung Pass* like he did when he was young. He could capture the timelessness again, the dreamy creaminess of pages that vanished, of words that turned into worlds? But the pages remained stubbornly opaque. He tried squinting, turning the light down, relaxing breaths. How did he do it when he was a schoolboy? What was the secret?

After shifting position a dozen times, stretching his back twice, and drinking two cups of strong coffee, Les finished *A Jungle Crown at Katung Pass* after midnight. The story wasn't bad, but he didn't magically transport into it either. He rested the book on his chest and listened to cars on the highway whipping past the motel. The clock on the nightstand ticked loudly, and a through the thin walls, a couple argued.

When he slept, he dreamed of the ruins of Millen Mir, of dread creatures that rose from catacombs at night, of a magnificent barbarian king camped among the moss-covered walls, his back to the fire, holding back black spirits through strength of will.

Miss Rhonim met him at the double doors that lead into the Orne. She wore a brown blazer over a white blouse and mid-calf skirt. In the morning light that bathed the library's front, she looked more like a Valkyrie than a librarian. He wondered if she worked out. Les carried a small backpack. He thought it made him more like a student, albeit an elderly one. The doors closed behind them, shrouding the library's lobby in twilight silence. Real students sat in study carrels, reading by small lights mounted on goosenecks.

"I believe I have a lead on your book, Mr. Bullard. We searched fiction, but what if it was shelved as history or biography? We're going to different sections today."

The stairs to the deeper stacks loomed even darker than they had earlier. Miss Rhonim unlocked the gate and pushed it aside. Lights flicked on as they descended.

"This seems like more stairs than yesterday," said Les. He didn't climb as well as ten years ago, and the trip back become more intimidating the farther they walked.

"That's because it is. History is further down."

Swords in a long line hung from the wall to their right. Spears and shields on the left. Les touched a sword blade, moving the metal against the stone. It rang like a tiny bell. "Why all the armor?"

Miss Rhonim laughed. "Practicality. You never know when you might need a good sword. Besides, I thought you liked heroic fantasy. This should be a dream come true for you."

Like yesterday, the path into the books confused Les. Not only were many of the turns at odd angles, the floor sloped in places so they walked down or up book-lined hills. Lights turned on as they approached and turned off where they'd been. Darkness faced them and followed.

"How deep does the library go?"

"A long way." Miss Rhonim stopped in front of a stack of books that looked indistinguishable from the ones they'd already passed.

None were marked with bar codes or labels. Some were titled on the spine, but many were not. "We're in the right place if your book is in history. Biography is a bit of a walk from here." She climbed a ladder. "You know the routine."

"I brought these." He pulled a pair of gardening kneepads from his backpack. "I have a couple water bottles too if you want one. I didn't notice drinking fountains yesterday. Are we going to the left or right?"

"To the left. If your title is here, it will be within this thirty feet."

Les put the kneepads on over his khakis. His knees wouldn't take the same beating as the day before when he'd spent too much time on the cold cement. He knelt to search the lowest row. Books without titles had to be slid off the shelf. Some didn't have titles on the cover either, so Les fell into a routine of reaching in, slipping the book out, checking the title page, then carefully returning it. He remembered summer days in his library at home when he'd been a boy, sitting on the floor before the books. If his mom didn't expect him home, he would finish one, put it back in its place and then read the next. When he finally stood, he'd realize that he'd skipped lunch, and it would be time to ride his bike home for dinner.

Methodically, Les checked each book. Miss Rhonim showed him where to stop and to start with the higher shelf. He paused with some, marveling at their illustrations, repulsed by others. Hand-written inscriptions in spidery calligraphy marked the inside covers, most dated from the early 1900s to 1940.

A metallic clank sounded from the darkness beyond, distinct, sharp and sudden. Miss Rhonim paused, a book in hand, preternaturally alert.

"What was that?"

"Hush," she said. "I'll check it out. You keep looking."

She climbed down the ladder noiselessly, took off her shoes, put them neatly under the ladder, then moved toward the sound, partly crouched, lithe as a cat. Ceiling lights turned on in front of her until she walked with an island of her own light. She turned down a row a hundred feet away, and suddenly Les felt naked and alone. If she didn't come back, he didn't know the way out, but worse than that was the darkness lurking beyond the fifteen feet of light to his left and right. He could almost see large things standing silently, studying him. Les's knees cracked when he stood.

Cautiously, he walked in the direction opposite of the one Miss Rhonim had taken. A ceiling light flicked on, not revealing monsters, but more books. He laughed to himself. The lights were the secret. They were motion activated, so creatures trying to sneak up on him would trigger a light and show themselves. They were the library's early warning system, but his self-assurances felt hollow. He looked back to where his backpack now sat on the edge of light. Another step or two, and it too would be lost in the dark.

"Miss Rhonim," he called. "Are you okay?" The sound faded without echo or answer. He turned his head to the side, quieted his breath. Somewhere, metal met metal, just on perception's edge. Was that a shout? Was that a roar? He ran past his backpack, following Miss Rhonim, but when he reached an intersection he stopped, gasping for breath and unsure where to go. His heart pounding obscured sounds. "Miss Rhonim! Miss Rhonim!"

Away in the darkness, a ceiling light flicked on. The librarian strode toward him.

"You really shouldn't wander in here," she said when she drew close. "It can be a bit of a maze."

"What was it? I thought I heard something."

"Nothing to worry about. A maintenance issue, really. Why don't we see if we can't find your book now."

She led him back to the shelves they'd been searching.

It wasn't until Miss Rhonim climbed the ladder again that Les noticed a rip in her blazer and blouse, a foot-long cut on her left side angling down from her armpit and ending below her shoulder blade. Les knelt, looking up at her. Not a rip so much as a clean cut like from a knife or sword. Her skin was untouched beneath. He was sure her clothes weren't damaged earlier. What happened to her when she left?

He tried to figure out how to ask her about it, but the next book he pulled from the shelf drove the question from him. Red cover. Black embossed title with a silver vine running through the letters.

"Oh, god," he said, and sat back. *The Silk Silvered Skulls of Millen Mir*, as beautiful as he remembered, by Danny Jan Milton.

"You found it?" Miss Rhonim sounded delighted as she climbed down the ladder. She crouched beside him. "May I?"

She hefted the book in her hand, opened it. "Ah, I see why you thought it was special. Not many like this one."

"What do you mean?"

Miss Rhonim said, "Have you ever gone into an elementary school library?"

Les nodded.

"Most have a sign somewhere, often by the entrance, or a bulletin board. It says, 'Books: Your Ticket to Adventure.'"

Les did remember exactly those words in his childhood library, accompanied with rockets and unicorns and castles. He thought it was true then just as he did now.

Miss Rhonim handed the book back. "Some books don't take you as far, but some, like yours, are infinity passes. I can tell just by holding it. This is a valuable book indeed, exceptionally rare."

Tears burned on Les's cheeks. He'd searched so long. "Can I .. . check it out?"

Miss Rhonim shook her head. Crouched beside him, her face so close, Les noticed her eyes for the first time, sword-metal gray with copper flecks. Startling at this distance, intense but not unkind.

Les pulled the book to his chest. "I can't?"

"Here's why." She held her hand out.

Reluctantly, Les gave it back.

The librarian opened the front cover and showed it to him. "I believe it's your book."

In familiar handwriting, the inscription read, "To Les, my little reader, from Grandma."

"How?"

Miss Rhonim straightened, towering over him. "I told you. Down in the Orne's deep stacks, you and the book you need eventually cross paths. It's one of our best features."

"I can keep it?" He ran his hand over the lettering. The leather felt warm, as if the book had a life of its own. He knew that when he opened it, when he read, it would be as if he was fifteen again. He remembered landscapes that caressed his senses, fogs that chilled his face, forest meadows filled with pine and sweet grass scents, rivers clapping over rounded boulders, the long road and his companions waiting on rampart walls. Not just a ticket, but a key and a pass and a secret handshake into his childhood imagination.

Miss Rhonim turned her gaze from him, peered into the darkness beyond. Her posture alerted Les. He looked back, trying to see what she detected.

"Time to go," she said as she helped him to his feet with one hand and scooped up his backpack with the other.

Beyond the ceiling light's reach, a shuffling sound, a click like bone against stone, or claws.

"We'll be moving smartly here," she said, not flustered, but concentrated and competent. "Looks like I didn't quite solve the problem earlier."

She kept one hand on his elbow, guiding him through the book maze back toward the stairs to the main library.

"If something's following us, why don't the lights turn on?" Les kept checking over his shoulder. There was never more than fifteen feet illuminated behind him. Fifteen feet would only be three or four strides for someone, or something, running, and clearly they were being trailed. If a shape appeared, he would have no time to react.

The librarian turned at a junction, almost jerking him off his feet. "We're visitors. They're denizens. Visitors need light. Denizens don't."

Confused, Les was nearly running to keep up with her. "Do we need to get help? Are they trespassers?" But even as he asked, he thought the question ridiculous. Whatever was going on here didn't feel like a job for the police. It was like he'd stepped into one of his books. If he'd been by himself, he would have been scared, but Miss Rhonim pushed him differently. Not frightened at all. Not out of her element.

The next turn took them to the stairs.

"This is where I leave you," she said. "Just keep going up until you get to the gate." She handed him a large key. "Lock it behind you."

"How will you get out?"

The librarian stepped to the wall, took down a sword and swung it once as if she'd done it thousands of times before. "Oh, there's more ways out than the stairs."

She put her hand on his shoulder. "You're a kindred spirit, Les. I hope you enjoy your book. Now, off you go."

Propelled by her last push, Les climbed several steps. He stopped to watch her stride back into the library, sword tip up and at the ready. She rounded a corner out of sight, and the lights that followed her flicked off. Then, a yell of triumph, the hard clatter of sword on swords, a guttural yell.

Les fled up the stairs, thankful Miss Rhonim took up the battle behind. She felt like she'd stepped from the land of Millen Mir. He'd been in the presence of a hero.

Carefully, after the long, long climb, Les locked the gate as she'd directed. He found a study carrel by the front door, clicked on a reading light, and put the book on the wood desk. He'd read until she returned, not that he doubted she would. No, he didn't doubt that Miss Rhonim the librarian would return.

He settled into the chair, took a deep breath, opened the book to chapter one. The pages welcomed his fingers. He'd come home again. By the end of the first sentence, the letters weren't words on the page; they were a voice in his ear and a picture in his head.

"The swordsman's horse carried the weary warrior down a stony path."

The magic shop story is an old tradition in fantasy. Any story that says just around a corner is a special store or library or gentlemen's club that only a select few know about has joined the tradition. The attraction has to be the idea of a secret place that only the special can visit. It's wish fulfillment, and that's one of fiction's greatest powers: the ability for the writer to create the things they yearn for most. Early in my career, I wrote a series of journal entries I called "Visions in Wish Fulfillment." They were great fun. I identified some of my deepest desires, and it started me thinking about my themes.

The War against non-traditional enemies seems to be a feature of the twenty-first century. It was so much easier to wage battles against an enemy who wore a uniform and met you on the battlefield. Now, the enemy could be driving a taxi during the day or teaching school or selling groceries. Unique enemies require unique strategies to combat. Surely new weapons will be a part of those strategies.

WEAPONIZED GHOSTS OF THE 96TH INFANTRY

U NTIL NOW, VENGEFUL GHOSTS HAVE BEEN DOCUMENT-ed in history but never seen by science," said the General as he led the Secretary of Defense and joint chiefs of staff into the forward bunker. "The army has known about them for years. We've studied the types of persons and the mindset that produces a violent, motivated spirit. Today you will see our first field test of the technology."

The Secretary of Defense, a large and solidly built man despite his age looked out the two-inch thick blast windows that revealed a stretch of desert, bookended by a line of trees on the left and the city on the right. Between them, several hundred yards of heat-baked sand without a hint of cover shimmered in the sun. Bullets and mortars scarred the buildings. Broken windows stared blackly onto the waste. He glanced at the men filling the room, a serious, dour crowd. The war had dragged on for years against what the press had dubbed the "perpetual insurgency," an enemy that ambushed and booby-trapped and melted away in the face of superior force. Impossible to engage. Impossible to defeat.

The General, in his startlingly clean uniform and medals and ribbon-covered chest, took a position at the view port. "Today we will demonstrate how we'll end this war."

The Undersecretary, a young man, said, "I read the release. Do you expect us to believe that not only are ghosts real, but that the army can create them on demand, and that they will fight for us?"

The General nodded. "Yes, inspired by revenge, the oldest of human emotions, our weaponized ghosts hunt down their killers. No walls protect them. No weapons preserve them. Anyone who dares to take American soldiers' lives will face the tireless spirit of the dead."

The Undersecretary thumbed through his papers. "Your information said that the soldiers were hand-picked for the training and medical preparations necessary for them to transition to, um . . ." he looked for a reference among his pages, ". . . postcorporeal status?"

"Our investigations into the technology shows that some soldiers are stronger candidates. Men with families, for example, or ones who are newly engaged, are particularly good. If I would have had my way, the soldiers for this demonstration would be only the ones who recently learned they were to be fathers for the first time."

The Secretary of Defense said, "In other words, a man who has the most to live for is the best subject to become a vengeful spirit."

"Yes. If you'll look into the booklet the lieutenant gave you, you will find a picture and biography of the twenty American heroes who will be our pioneers to take us to peace."

"Brilliant," said the secretary.

The Undersecretary's mouth dropped open in surprise. "Wait, you plan to kill twenty soldiers right now, in front of us, as a proof of concept demonstration?"

The General checked his watch. "This is our Trinity, gentleman. You are about to witness a breakthrough in warfare as world-altering as the first nuclear detonation. Like the atomic bombs that brought Japan to its knees, I believe that our enemies, when they hear of what we do today, may very well put down their arms. What insurgent would fire at an American soldier if he knew that killing him would release an implacable vengeance? We will become their nightmares."

A plume of dust rose from beyond the trees to the left. Visible through the pall, a handful of Humvees opened and spilled soldiers. The Undersecretary checked the shell-damaged buildings to the right. They'd assumed an ominous watchfulness. He hadn't actually seen anything move, but he sensed weapons behind each dark opening.

The soldiers emerged from the behind the trees, spread in loose formation, guns carried in the ready position, walking across the sand.

The Undersecretary, a tinge of horror in his voice, said, "How do you know they will be attacked here?"

The General said, "We leaked intel to the other side."

Now, the rest of the men crowded at the window. "It's about time we had a clear win," said one of them.

The soldiers drew farther and farther from their armored vehicles, heads high, alert, well trained.

"They don't know they are going to die," gasped the Undersecretary.

"Of course not," said the General. "For them to make the jump to the post-corporeal, they have to be on a mission. The men believe they are beginning an assignment that will save the country. They are fighting for their future, for the things they love. We must provide them with sufficient motivation and rage to continue on in death."

The soldier nearest to a building stopped, dropped to his belly, gun pointed at a window. The other soldiers fell also. The bunker glass was too thick to hear their voices, but they were yelling. Several pounded at their weapons. None had fired.

Windows erupted in flame. Despite the insulation, the crackle of small arms penetrated. The soldiers writhed as bullets struck them. Several managed to get to their feet. They staggered toward the buildings, desperate fury on their faces, but they jerked and danced in a lead storm.

"This is where it gets interesting," said the General.

Finally, gunfire quit. Heads appeared in the windows, exulting in the carnage. No movement among the dead at first. Then, a smoke appeared to rise from the bodies, a black haze that eddied to head-height. There was no wind, but the blackness drifted toward the buildings, gained momentum, splashed against the walls like a dark wave, and flowed through the openings.

Suddenly, more gunfire. A man dove from a window, rolled on the sand, and then sprinted away. Smoke followed him, engulfed him, tore him to pieces.

A couple of the Defense Department men cheered, but the Undersecretary wanted to turn away.

The General said, "What our enemy has just discovered is that you can not stop the justice of the dead. You cannot negotiate or run. A ghost's vengeance has no limits. Our ghosts will root out their killers and destroy them."

Finally, the Undersecretary closed his eyes. "You gave our men empty weapons?"

The General cleared his throat impatiently. "Of course. For the demonstration, they couldn't win the battle. They had to die. You must admit, it is a potent display of the technology."

The Undersecretary looked onto the battlefield. Twenty soldiers lay crumpled in the desert. "You took everything from them."

A movement from the buildings caught the Undersecretary's attention. Smoke poured from the windows and doors. It swirled, shifted about as if sniffing or searching.

"Those are our ghosts," said the General. "Our beautiful, deadly, vengeful ghosts."

The smoke paused in its uncertainty.

"Whose ghosts?" said the Undersecretary.

Slowly at first, but then faster and with increasing purpose, the blackness rushed toward the bunker. The Undersecretary wanted to speak, and he would have if the bunker's cement and thick glass had been any barrier at all. He opened his mouth, but in the end all he could do was scream.

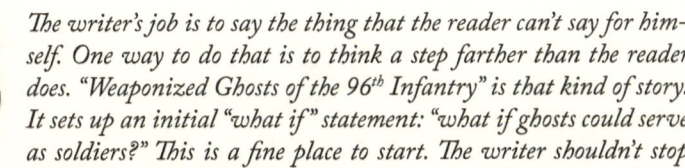

The writer's job is to say the thing that the reader can't say for himself. One way to do that is to think a step farther than the reader does. "Weaponized Ghosts of the 96th Infantry" is that kind of story. It sets up an initial "what if" statement: "what if ghosts could serve as soldiers?" This is a fine place to start. The writer shouldn't stop with the initial "what if," though, because the next step is "if that, then what?" If you're going to write speculative fiction, one of your guiding principles should involve the question of repercussions. If you make a change in the world through either a fantasy idea or a science fiction one, you need to follow the repercussions. Larry Niven is a great example of an author who handles repercussions. If you haven't read "Man of Steel, Woman of Kleenex," or "The Theory and Practice of Teleportation," you should.

When I was young, our minister gave a sermon that stuck with me. He said, "Technology doesn't matter. A man who hates his brother will hate him in exactly the same way whether they are trudging across the country in a horse-drawn wagon or in a spaceship speeding to Mars at thousands of miles per hour. Human nature doesn't change." He may have a point. When humanity goes to the stars, we'll take our weaknesses with us too. Whether you're in the second century or the twenty-second, neurosis, paranoia and obsession are the same.

MAᵥBE IF ONE
PERSON LESS

T HE SPACESHIP *CALLIOPE* BREATHES WITHOUT PAUSE, IN-haling through mouths on the floor and exhaling from mouths overhead. Seaweed streamers on the ceiling vents wave in the continuous sigh. Lying in my bunk, eyes closed, the humming, breathing, great bear of a ship holds me close in warm embrace, its cave spread all around, black and vast and cold.

I miss Earth, how could I not, but I miss Mother too. Her face fades. How did the corners of her eyes wrinkle when she smiled? What color was her favorite blouse? How did she sound when she sang at her table working on what . . . a jigsaw puzzle, a game of solitaire, a paint by numbers picture?

Time robs color from flowers. I can't remember grass under my back when I stared at clouds. Were they really so big? Did the horizon circle me and center me and lift me up, a dot between the plate of sky and earth?

I didn't know to look with fondness at the Earth as the elevator lifted us toward the shuttle to *Calliope.* The shuttle walls vibrated beneath my hand that would never touch beach sand again, that wouldn't brush away a fly, or cup around an ear to hear a night train groaning in the Kansas night.

So *Calliope's* breathing comforts me, a steady suspiration that whispers a long "ah" in my ear.

I hiked the Appalachian Trail on my last outing, starting from Winding Stair Gap at the highway to the Nantahala Gorge and through the Little Tennessee River Valley. The ridges above Fontana Lake offered water glimpses through trees. Twenty-nine miles in three days. Poplar, white and red oak, hemlock, sycamore, basswood, and beech. Tree heaven. Not far from the Joyce Kilmer National Forest. It's true, it's true, there is no poem as lovely as a tree, and there are so many of them they blanketed distant hills with green velvet. I would if I could run my hands over them, pet the planet.

Calliope was the goddess of epic poetry, not a circus pipe organ. The ship is a poem. She would like a forest named after a poet. When she talks, it is always in verse.

But I only hiked in Tennessee for three days, covered less than two percent of the trail. Walked none of the side trails, saw so little of it, one tiny line of footsteps over a tiny portion of an immense globe.

On *Calliope*, the farthest I hike in a straight line is the forty feet up the main corridor. If I walk with my hand touching a wall, turn into every room, never skipping an inch, climbing every ladder, I travel less than two thousand feet. Through any port, the vista is millions of light years deep but less than the distance from one infinitely complicated oak to the completely different one ten strides behind it. I touch a single tree, my fingers sliding over grooves and fiber and fissures, while millions and millions of others remain unseen, untouched but present and weighty. So much life.

Fifteen cabins on *Calliope*. Fourteen long, plastic-wrapped lumps on fourteen bunks. Blankets cover them. Their faces too, are fading. Was the pilot's hair long or short? Did the communications engineer have a pointy chin or was it round? Did the navigator wear yellow on her last day? I resist the urge to look. When I walk their quarters, my fingers tracing along the walls, all two thousand feet of them, I'm careful not to bump their beds. Let them remain still and undisturbed.

The animal world knows murder. Baboons go to war, one tribe against another. Male lions kill cubs that are not their own so females will go into breeding condition sooner. Some animals kill their children if resources are scarce. Earth's a beautiful world, but not a gentle one. People are not so unique in their willingness to kill to protect their interests.

To a human, a forest may seem to teem with life, but to a wolf that cannot find prey, it is a desert. The numbers can be hard to see. Not so on the *Calliope*. The pantry holds a measurable amount of stores, and when we started, for every day, an entire crew consumed from them. Vast distances require time to traverse. Time to watch the food supply dwindle. The mission planners said we would have enough—of course we would—but wouldn't chances improve if only fourteen ate instead of fifteen? Oxygen restores at a calculable rate too, but the buffer for a full crew looks small. Maybe if one person less needed the air, we all would be a little safer.

The Resource Management Officer choked the Electrician to death in their bed. He claimed an argument gone too far, but he knew before anyone else. The Communications Officer slit the Microbiologist's throat. The Nutritionist bludgeoned the Environmental officer. Somehow, the Doctor talked the Physical Therapist into an EVA suit after adjusting the unit to pressurize with carbon dioxide. During breakfast, the Astronomer ate broken glass in her oatmeal. Tore her up inside. No one knew who arranged that. It might have been me; I don't remember. One night, the four killers died in their sleep. An overdose of insulin for each. Already, the ship seemed empty since I and the five remaining crew members stayed in our cabins. Who could be trusted?

The forgetting began. I stared at my cabin wall, a curved, featureless steel surface, and on it I projected from memory the faces. They didn't focus. Not the Astronomer, who'd been my occasional lover, or the Doctor who told jokes. They joined my brothers on Earth who faded away, and cities I'd visited in another lifetime. Only the wall remained. I hummed to it, long, random strings of unharmonious notes. *Calliope* hummed back. She whispered to me when the lights were low. "Check the food lockers," she said. Other times I heard her, but I couldn't make out the words. When I put my head against the metal, her heartbeat ocean pounded waves against invisible cliffs. Throb. Throb. Throb.

Still, the deaths arrived. Someone garroted the Mission Commander with a shoestring. Then the Mechanic grew a screwdriver in her chest. The Historian, a slight man, died with a pillow over his face. We were down to three. That should have been enough. The graph of food stores and oxygen over time looked so much better. But the Morale Officer hung himself, maybe for the greater good, and the Chemist swallowed acid.

I'm rationing myself. If I deny hunger, eat only enough to survive; if I breathe shallowly, sip the air, then I stretch the supplies.

In the meantime, I walk the ship, dragging my fingers against the walls. I've left a stain. When I look at an angle, my skin's mark on *Calliope* is clear. Perhaps I'll wear away the metal, make a groove like those stone steps in Peru where centuries of pedestrians have worn the rock into gentle arcs.

I've broken every mirror on the ship. Given time, I'll forget myself and fade like my mother, like the Tennessee forests, like the fourteen crew members who lie on their bunks in tight plastic cocoons. I talk when *Calliope's* voice is still. I tell her I am happy and all is well. We fly, the two of us, cuddling in deep space, rushing away from what I forgot until we arrive at the unknown, and all that changes are the graphs that slowly creep downward, but oh so slow.

We're feeding just one, after all. We're breathing for one.

Crossing genres is an interesting challenge, and certainly a part of twenty-first century writing. Slipstream, weird westerns, and magical realism are just a few of the possibilities. "Maybe Just One Person Less" looks like a science fiction story, but its DNA shares more with Alfred Hitchcock's Psycho *than traditional space opera.*

There's a Far Side *cartoon that shows two fisherman, sitting in a boat, their lines in the water. In the distance, four mushroom clouds fill the horizon. One fisherman says to the other, "I'll tell you what this means, Norm. No size restrictions and* screw *the limit." Which I always interpreted as each of us would see an apocalypse through our own filters.*

HOUSEKEEPING

SIMON HATED WINTER. HE PEDALED ALL THE TIME, became incredibly fit, and the house still felt cold. He opened a college guide for parents on the reading stand, slipped his feet into the stirrups, and started the session. Last year he'd switched to a recumbent bike. Easier on his back. The pulleys whirred into motion: one connected to a generator and the other to the heater pump. A meter to his left said the batteries were at seventeen percent, not enough to get them through the night unless he pedaled another sixty minutes, and another one said the water in the solar collector lines on the roof had risen to eighty-one degrees, which was plenty warm to pump into the heat retaining wall and run through the radiators. At least the sun was out today, even if the wind blew snow off the trees sideways. The solar cells weren't working, but the water would warm the house and he could take a tepid shower. The tough days were the overcast, cold ones where he had to pedal to keep his system from freezing up.

Phillip stepped into the room. A slender, blond teenager with a broad smile and blue eyes that reminded Simon of the boy's mother, he wore a thick coat and woolen cap. "I thought I'd go over to Trina's house. We have a school project." He tucked a muffler down the front of his coat. "I need another resource for my paper on the Louisiana Purchase. The stupid assignment wants a print source. Don't they know our library burned down forever ago? Where am I going to find a book or journal? Trina says they have some old history books. Maybe we'll find something."

Simon nodded. A bead of sweat ran down the side of his face. At least when he pedaled, he eventually warmed up. "You'll have to invite her to dinner some night."

Phillip blushed. "She's just a study partner."

"Yeah, and its not cold outside either."

"Speaking of cold, her dad and a couple others in the neighborhood are doing a wood scavenging expedition tomorrow. Can I join them?"

Simon thought about it. His was the only house in the area that didn't rely on burning wood for heat. It would look good for the neighbors if Phillip helped them out. "I don't suppose Trina is a part of this expedition?"

"Maybe. Can I go or not?"

"Are they going to try the horse sled again to haul it?"

"I think so, and everyone gets snowshoes this time."

Craig Woolroof, his neighbor on the other side of the street, entered as Phillip went out. Even through the airlock, the wind's howl penetrated. Today might be sunny, but this was the worst winter Simon could remember.

Craig wore only a windbreaker over a couple of sweaters. He clapped his upper arms, and his cheeks were red. "Howdy, Simon. Don't know how you keep so warm in here. My house is freezing."

Simon checked the meter. It hadn't stirred yet. If he biked for a couple hours, he should be able to get it over thirty percent. "My solar panels fritzed out on me. I'll be plenty chilly if I can't chase down the problem. I'm just not keen on working on the roof in this weather, and my skills as an electrician leave a lot to desire."

The ice on Craig's eyebrows melted and ran down his cheeks. "Maybe we can finagle a trade. I wondered if you had a spare car battery? I have a bank on the back wall, but they're too cold, and won't hold a charge. I'm moving them to a warmer spot, but I need something to get through the night. If you help me out, maybe I could track down your panel problem."

Simon pedaled steadily, thinking it over. He did have a spare battery, several of them, but the chance there would be replacements in the spring looked slim, and he had to think about next winter too.

Craig unzipped his jacket. "Look, we're pretty desperate over there. I should have piled more dirt against the house during the summer, like you did, and insulated the roof better. The whole family huddles in the living room. If you've got a battery, it would sure help out."

Simon sighed. "Yeah, no problem. Why don't you go in the kitchen? I've got some hot water on the stove and cocoa in the cabinet. Something warm will do you good."

Craig smiled in relief and pulled a bottle of bourbon from his jacket. "That sounds great. I brought this over to sweeten the deal."

"Pour two. I'll be right back."

Simon opened the door to the hallway and the back of the house. The bedroom doors were closed with rolled up towels against the bottoms to cut down on drafts. He ignored them, reached the bookcase at the hallway's end, double-checked to see that the door to the bike room was closed, then pulled the bookcase away from the wall. A narrow flight of cement stairs led down to his supply shelter. The light at the bottom revealed a deep and broad room with a dirt floor and low ceiling, Phillip's secret project. Boxes crowded the shelves. Canned goods. Cereals. Bins of rice and wheat. Bottled water. Guns. Tools. Clothing. Bolts of canvas. A motorcycle (he had to take the handlebars off to get it down the stairs). Medicine. Liquor. Spare parts for everything he used.

Twenty years of paranoia filled his shelter. Twenty years of reading survivalist literature. He stayed away from the survivalist chat boards on the Internet; someone surely would be monitoring who logged in there. He'd excavated the shelter over the course of a decade. Through Phillip's birth. Through Jennifer's death. Constantly adding on, and then supplying it. He didn't tell the neighbors or his friends.

It's just a hobby, he'd told himself. Being prepared was just a way to fill the time. When Phillip was born, the hobby took on more urgency.

Behind a stack of folded cots and blankets near the back were the spare batteries. He left those alone since he'd have to fill one and charge it. Instead, he disconnected a working one from his battery bank and wrapped it in a towel. Behind the row of interconnected car batteries was his pride and joy, a lithium-ion battery powerwall. State of the art energy storage, if only his solar panels were working. Pedaling power into the batteries was inefficient and time-consuming. Still, as well insulated as his house was, he wouldn't need the electricity he was producing if it wasn't for the farm. A second room, as big as the storage area, smelling moist and fertilizer-earthy, contained low, water-filled tables where he grew their food. Unlike and unknown to his neighbors, Simon didn't depend on canned goods from the summer.

The grow lights, dangling from the ceiling, really sucked up energy. Broccoli was ready for harvest. Tomatoes, cucumbers and peas looked good too. Celery was wilted and yellow, though. He'd have to check the nutrients level. When he'd started the project, the idea was to stock the water with trout. Their waste could feed the plants, and he could have fish for dinner, but balancing water chemistry and temperature proved too daunting. Still, as far as he knew, no one in the neighborhood had fresh produce.

Craig took the battery gratefully. "Thanks, buddy. I'll set this up and come right back. You probably just have an ice block somewhere that's pulling on a connection."

"I'll meet you on the roof. I have to sweep off the snow anyway."

Simon wore ski goggles, a heavy coat, and good gloves as he walked up the snow-covered slope to the top of his house, which was mostly underground now. He'd sealed the siding with tar and layers of heavy plastic before he'd bulldozed the soil against it, but he still worried about seepage and termites. Wood frame houses were not designed to be buried. What he had wanted was a cement geodesic dome house that was built for dirt insulation, but he didn't have the resources. Besides, the housing covenants would have never gone for it at the time.

From the roof, he looked out on the neighborhood. Last week's storm had dumped a couple feet and then cleared out, leaving high winds and sub-zero temperatures, turning the landscape into a uniform white of snow drifts. Streets and sidewalks were covered. Lumps with a fender sticking out or a part of a window visible showed where cars that no one drove anymore were parked. Three out of every four homes that had stood ten years ago were now gone, leveled for their wood when the families fled south, or whatever they did. Families disappeared over the course of the last few winters when delivery trucks quit supplying the stores regularly, before the stores closed permanently. The scene would be attractive as a Christmas card if it weren't so cold.

Craig came out of his house across the street, wearing a better coat. He carried a tool box in one hand and a shovel in the other. He trudged through the trail he'd made going back and forth earlier. The wind had nearly erased Phillip's track toward Trina's house.

"Point me to where your lines go into the house, and I'll start there," said Craig through a yellow muffler he'd wrapped over the lower part of his face. He shielded his eyes against the reflected sunlight.

Simon swept snow from the solar cells and the long water line boxes that striped his roof. The water boxes were efficiently insulated on the sides, glassed in along the top for the sunlight to enter, and mirrored inside to focus the sun onto the black pipes. Most of his house's heat came from the arrangement. The lines wove through rock heat retention walls he'd built. The rooms were smaller, of course, but even bitter days like this didn't bother them much inside.

Craig dug into the snow, revealing a metal box and electrical lines. "How's your boy doing?"

"Heading to college next summer, I think. He wants to go to UNM in Albuquerque. He's got one of those 'Northern Climes' scholarships."

Craig grunted. "Remember your college years? Those were good times." He cleared away more snow, and tested the main line for power. "Your break is farther up."

Simon thought about the University of Colorado. Boulder felt like a dim memory now, before things really started to get cold. He suspected no one lived there now. Too close to the mountains. Pretty in late July, when the ground cleared and plants had a chance to spring up, but the foothills' glaciers would be glistening only a few miles away and hundreds of feet closer than they'd been the year before.

"How about your oldest? She still with the Merchant Marines?"

Craig dug a trench beneath the power cable, then shoveled away enough snow to get himself under it. "Here's your problem I'll bet. You've got ice built up on this juncture. Maybe a leak from your water lines. It's putting pressure on the joint. Sweet Jesus, it's cold up here." He stabbed at the ice with a screwdriver until a big chunk broke free. "Vickie's working with the costal civil engineers in the Gulf of Mexico. Too many critical infrastructures are in the tidal flood zones. It's good work. Plenty of job security and a solid health plan."

Although the sky was clear, the wind picked up snow and blew it past them. Simon wiped at his goggles. The little bit of his face exposed to the elements stung.

"It's the coming industry they say. When's the last time you saw her?" Simon finished the sweeping. The next storm wasn't supposed to come in until the end of the week. He wouldn't mind the break from clearing his system, and if Craig was right and he fixed the connection, a couple cloudless days would fully charge his batteries.

"Travel's been iffy. She came back the summer before last for a couple days. I heard they might close I-70 altogether. They do that and we're stuck with what comes through the airport. We'll have to clear out. Nothing I've read about housing down south makes me eager to head that way."

"What are you going to do?"

Craig tested for power. "I think we solved it." He levered himself from the snow and brushed himself off. "Have to take care of the family. If we can get to northern Africa, they seem to be doing well. Tunis is supposed to be welcoming, or Algiers or Oran. Well, at least as welcoming as any place is right now. The key is to go in on a work visa, not a refugee one."

"Tough to find room when seven billion people want to live there."

"It's not seven billion any more," said Craig.

"Good point."

Despite the gloves, Simon's fingers tingled, but the snow looked heavier than he liked. The roof could only take so much weight. "Help me clear this off, then we can sample that bottle you brought over again. You can keep the battery too. I should be fine." He felt only a twinge of guilt at the lie.

"Deal!" Craig shoveled enthusiastically, taking pounds off with each shovelful.

When they went inside a half hour later, the gauges showed a steady rise. The men hung their snow-soaked coats, and within minutes, the rhythmic drip provided a pleasant backdrop. "How about Irish coffee this time?"

"Spiked and hot is good for me. Don't care what you call it."

Simon poured the drinks. He didn't know Craig well. The man worked for the Bureau of Land Management and was often gone, touring the wastelands, Simon assumed. His wife was pleasant enough. He waved at her from across the street in the summer. Sometimes their kids played in the yard, a little girl who was eight and her ten-year-old brother. "How's schooling going at your house?"

Craig took a long swig from the steaming mug. "I'm not much of a teacher. Between Eloise's patience and the LearnTime program, they seem to be doing well. Does your boy use LearnTime?"

The coffee tasted good with an alcoholic bite. "We did Learn-Time early, then switched to CollegeStart. It's stronger in math and science they say. Another six weeks and spring semester will be over."

Craig snorted. "Spring semester. We've got the shit end of climate change here."

"It could be worse. We survived the plagues." He smoothed the placemat, a long ago wedding present. "Most of us."

"I'll be happy to make it through March. They're predicting another big storm heading our way."

Last year Simon planted his early vegetables in late April. This year he might have to wait until May the way snow was piling up. Since first frost could hit in September, getting a whole crop in might be tough. With luck, Phillip would be away at school, and Simon would only be planting for one. He added another dollop of bourbon to Craig's coffee.

"That's going to be mostly booze by the time I'm done. Thanks."

"It's all about the children, isn't it?"

"As long as the Internet is up, we can keep schooling them."

"That and the wolves don't come."

Craig chuckled. "Truer than you think, buddy." He guzzled his drink. "I'd better get back home."

"You going to be all right?"

"Yeah. We scavenged another solar panel system yesterday. Remember the Fredrickson's, the old couple on Rose and 5th Street? He used to teach social studies at DU. Found them frozen to death in their bedroom, but they had new solar on the roof. I won the drawing for one of the panels. I'll get it hooked up and take advantage of the sunny days. With better insulation around my battery bank and the new juice, we'll have plenty of buffer." He pulled his coat off the hook and put it on. "I really can't get over how warm your house is. You've done a great job here."

After Craig left, Simon checked the gauges again. With the solar panels operating, the electric pump whirred on its own, pulling sun-warmed water off the roof and storing the heat in the stone walls. Batteries were charging. He wouldn't have to pedal unless he decided to bank extra juice for the coming storm.

In the meantime, he had an errand to run. Simon donned his coat, gloves, muffler and heavy hat with earmuffs. Cross-country skis waited in the airlock. His goggles went on before he pushed the outside door open against the wind. The glare blinded him at first, and the wind peppered sharp-sharded ice crystals that hissed and bounced off his coat and face.

Unfortunately, the wind was to his back as he skied down the street. A following wind could tempt a man into believing the weather wasn't as bad as it was. Every foot with the wind behind him would be a foot that was twice as hard with the wind fighting him on the return.

He remembered when the neighborhood had been green, when houses stood next to houses and everyone played golf or tennis or belonged to the PTA at the elementary school. It seemed a long time ago. Many of the homes were gone. Some that remained were collapsed shells, the roofs long ago losing the battle to snow's weight and inevitable destruction from leaks and ice.

The road rose in front of him, a gentle white hill unmarked by tracks. Only his familiarity with the area kept him moving in the right direction. This used to be Pinewood Ave. He was coming up on the intersection with 1st Street. From the crest of the hill at 3rd, the town spread below him. Wind pushed ghostly shadows of snow across the fields. Simon pressed on, taking advantage of the slope down and the wind behind him. The effort felt good, and he generated heat from the exercise. At 5th, he turned right and went a block to Rose Street. Half of the Fredrickson's house still stood, but the other side slumped beneath its collapsed roof. He didn't bother with the front door, but went through a rift in the wall beside it. Sheltered now from the unrelenting wind's whine, he moved from room to room until he found a long bookcase in their living room. The light was poor. He wished he'd brought a flashlight, but with his goggles off and some close up squinting, he could just make out the titles.

Simon took three heavy textbooks from the shelves, wrapped them in plastic, and prepared to go outside again. He smiled. Fredrickson had been a social studies teacher. It was only natural that he would have U.S. history textbooks in the house.

He was right about the wind in his face on the way home. It cut cruelly, made every move forward a struggle, but Simon was happy. Standing on the hill again at 3rd Street, he rested. A movement a block to his left caught his attention: five wolves in single file trotted through the snow going the other direction. They moved silently, nearly gliding. One looked his way, but they didn't vary their course.

Simon didn't worry much. He hadn't heard of wolves attacking a person yet with elk so plentiful. Besides, a few apex predators couldn't take the bloom off his day. The solar panels were working, there'd be fresh vegetables on the table tonight, and surely one of the books under his arm would have information about the Louisiana Purchase. Phillip could complete his paper with a print resource.

Taking care of his kid, that's what mattered. Support him through school. Help him get a start on life. What dad would behave differently?

A oft repeated truism in government is "All politics is local." The similar saying can be applied to the big picture ideas behind many science fiction stories: "All science fiction is local." No matter what change to the world the story posits, the most effective stories are the ones about how an individual or very small group are affected. One of the best stories that illustrates this is Fritz Leiber's "A Pail of Air." The future for humanity he creates is bleak and horrifying, but the story is about a ten-year-old boy and his efforts to stay alive. It's important to remember when writing fiction that history may be about nations and movements and the tidal forces that impact nations, but history is lived by individuals.

Some people give in to an urge to get away from it all. The reasons can be external. Perhaps the world is too noisy or too confusing or too superficial, or the reasons are internal. They feel empty inside or they want to confront their inner selves. They seek enlightenment. One should be careful of such journeys. The old maps said of the unexplored areas, "Here there be dragons." Joseph Conrad wrote about such a journey. He called it Heart of Darkness.

NO ONE IS SO FIERCE

'M FORTY-NINE, JAMIE THOUGHT, AND LIVE WITH AN ocean view. She paused on the quarter-mile long causeway to the Kingsmark Reef Lighthouse, shifting the heavy book bag from one shoulder to the other. Waves slid by on each side of the strip of rock and cement that connected the lighthouse property to the mainland. Nice day. A manageably cool breeze off the Pacific instead of the steady coat-cutter that kept all but the hardiest tourists from visiting. She'd heard Mark Twain said the coldest winter he'd ever spent was a summer in San Francisco, which was three hundred and seventy miles south. Clearly he'd never visited Kingsmark Reef in early September.

The tide would cover the causeway in an hour. Already, higher waves lapped over, sending long ripples down the sidewalk. Water trickled off the rocks. Crabs scuttled away. A seagull hopped aside to let her pass, and the wind smelled like seaweed and icebergs. Wet shoes were a small inconvenience to not living in a sterile, urban studio apartment with noisy neighbors and drive-by shootings. Much better than stepping over trash spilled from broken bags in the alley. Better than Friday nights sitting at the Slap and Tickle, fending off married realtors whose wives didn't know when their husbands got off work.

Jamie mounted the steps to the lighthouse door beneath a biblical verse inscribed in a corroded brass plaque. Predictions said the waves would rise tonight. An unseasonal Labor Day storm hundreds of miles away churned the ocean already and was coming this way. By morning, they'd close the beaches. Too early to be a true winter tempest, but a harbinger of the season to come.

The heavy metal door creaked open into the blockhouse the light tower rose from. She turned back. If she could have seen over the bluff, only her car covered with a tarp remained in the parking lot. She'd pulled the shutters over the visitor center and gift shop windows, giving the place a huddled and deserted look.

The lighthouse clung to a spit of land fifteen feet above sea level. Too dangerous for a boat to moor, the land bridge was her only route in and out, and was wet so often that algae slickened it. From a rock farther from shore, seals barked. A cormorant streaked low, skimming the water. If the storm lasted, she might be stuck inside for a week or more since waves would splash over the walkway even at low tide. She hoped for a big one, a long, violent, pounding storm that dumped rain so fast she could wade into the sea and not notice the difference, one that kicked waves into a froth and rattled the lighthouse's foundation. The kind of storm primitive people would have attributed to vengeful gods. That's what Jamie wanted. Give me a storm to raise leviathans, she thought.

The door creaked open. At one time, it might have been waterproof, but now during a storm the ground floor filled with water that slammed against the door and pushed through the cracks. The room drained slowly and smelled like a fishy vegetable tray gone bad.

Still, I've won the lottery, she thought. Most people never run away to the circus, despite their hopes. They don't become firemen or astronauts or surgeons. They don't get to raise the dream family, or their kids turn out bad. Not many fairy tale endings in the real world, but here she lived the fantasy. Jamie clanged the door shut, threw down the heavy bolt that held the ocean at bay, and hung up her raincoat. She breathed easily for the first time all day. Sitting in the gift shop stressed her more than it should. Most people came to the lighthouse looking for someplace else, like St. George Reef Lighthouse, twenty miles down the coast, a much more scenic attraction, although it took a helicopter to get to it. Fussy parents with whiny children. College kids on a lark. Foreign tourists collecting post cards and those little silver spoons with tiny cameos of the site. Kingsmark Reef Lighthouse stood impressively above the water, but the park trail to it was poorly marked and there were no photogenic overlooks from the road to set it off. Steep stairs in six long flights led to the shore, and all those steps had to be climbed to bring a tourist back to the visitor center. The wind, too, sweeping off the frigid Pacific, made it uninviting. Rocky spurs around the lighthouse shattered waves, creating a near constant salt-water mist that soaked coats and ruined cameras. It was a singularly uninviting place. Jamie loved it.

The only feature of the lighthouse's main floor was a large, round wooden trapdoor to one side. A long metal bar that ran between two iron brackets anchored in stone held it shut. Jamie had opened it her first week on the job to reveal a well. The dark and silent water swirled slowly and rose and fell with the ocean swell. During a storm, water pounded against the trapdoor from below, like a monster's fist, and squirted from the edges all around.

She mounted the spiral staircase. Since 1881 when the lighthouse was put into service, every metal surface, like the stairs and central stair pole had been scrubbed of corrosion, primed and repainted many times, but now the paint covered pits and ridges and other imperfections. Nothing in Kingsmark was smooth, not the metal nor the wood nor the stone. Even the heavy glass in the lantern room had grown wavy with time. In the hundred and forty years the lighthouse had stood, three keepers had died, two from waves crashing through the lantern room glass. If anyone doubted the sea's power, they only had to look at the first death: a seventy-pound rock cannonballed through the glass, catching the light-house keeper in the chest.

Jamie had not seen a storm where the waves crashed that high, but Park Service Superintendent Tacket warned her about them. "In the old days, when the light had to be tended, the worse the weather, the more we needed a manned lighthouse. But now the whole operation is automated, and ships have GPS positioning. There's no need to put anyone's life in danger. Even the lighthouse keeper's cottage is miserable in the winter. We have a deal with the Holiday Inn Express off the highway to put our keeper up. You don't need to stay here during storms. I don't want you to stay here." He looked solemn and serious in his park ranger uniform. Some-times he'd drop by the gift shop for a coffee. Tacket had worked for the park service for forty-five years, and they all showed on him. When he took off his hat, his wispy gray hair looked like an afterthought.

Jamie read everything she could find on lighthouses before she took the job. She told him, "The beacon is still an active guide to navigation, sir. GPS can fail. A ship in trouble needs visible mark-ers." She thought about Kingsmark Reef's reputation. In 1871, a coastal steamer named the *Sister Hibiscus* tore out its bottom during a fall storm. Only eight people (and a pair of goats) survived of the one hundred and sixty-one on board. "I don't mind the weather. Have you seen this poster?" She held a framed image they sold in the gift shop of a man standing at the blockhouse door of a lighthouse, a huge wave crashing against and enveloping the tower above him. It seemed impossible that the wave wouldn't engulf him and sweep him away. "My life was sort of like this before I got here. I'm staying."

He'd given her a puzzled look.

Jamie mounted the circular stairs, keeping a hand on the center pole. In an hour, she wouldn't be able to leave. When the storm hit, the waves would burst around the blockhouse base and overwhelm anything standing. Now, though, middle of the day, light streamed through the tower windows, tall gun slits filled with twelve-inch thick glass bricks. She didn't need to turn on the lights. The second floor room held food, water, furnace and the kitchen. The third floor were the keeper's living quarters, while the fourth floor contained electrical equipment to run the beacon and the radio. Eighty-nine feet from base to top, Kingsmark Reef was the second tallest lighthouse on the Oregon coast.

She checked her phone. No reception, which filled her with joy. No television in the lighthouse, no Internet. Only the radio. She dropped the book bag on her bed before rushing to the lantern room, a untraditionally large space, lantern in the middle, a circular bench against the wall facing in surrounded it, which was an addition in the late 1990s when the lighthouse became a tourist attraction. A mannequin dressed in a navy-blue wool, traditional double-breasted sack coat stood beside the lamp looking out to sea, his cap at a jaunty angle. When Jamie brought tour groups up, the lantern room could accommodate about a dozen. With the doors to the catwalk open, there was room for more, but for now, the lantern room was hers. Standing at the catwalk, she felt like a queen, like Thalassa, the Greek goddess who was the progenitor of fish, older than Poseidon even. She arched her back, pressed her belly against the rail and let the sun bathe her despite the cold breeze.

Last week, on a particularly clear and calm night, she'd stood in the same spot with a full moon heading toward the horizon. She gazed into the gleaming sea, awash with silver and bright glitters. A couple miles out, a freighter glided by, its deck lights flashing. She'd looked fruitlessly for mermaids, because the night was too perfect for them not to exist. Selkies too or Jonah's whale or Melville's. Anything could come to reality on a night such as that. Werewolves on the shore, perhaps, or Valkyrie descending from Valhalla.

The next day, she called her sister in Portland. "Give my renters notice and sell my house," Jamie said. "Put a price on it that will move it in a hurry. Deposit the money in my account. I've filled out all the paperwork for you to do it, and I put it on my desk in my office. Take anything you want. Estate sell the rest."

"What's going on, Jamie. Are you in trouble?"

"Never been better." Jamie hung up.

Was it being forty-nine? When she'd turned thirty, she wondered where her twenties had gone. Her diploma brought her a middle-management position, and her portfolio grew. Portland provided plenty of entertainment. She'd joined a book club, made friends, moved out of the apartment and bought a house, but when she looked back, her twenties felt too short and wasted.

The thirties looked the same with a little more body fat. Three affairs, all short-lived. Moved back to the city. Leased the house out as a real-estate investment. Saw a therapist for insomnia that turned out to be depression, and somehow limped into her forties. She commuted on the bus. One day last year, a teenager sat next to her, her hair done in green and purple spikes, a nose peg, a skull tattoo on her neck. Jamie balanced a briefcase on her lap wearing a light green pantsuit and beige jacket. Her shoes pinched, but they matched the belt. She'd spent the morning in a budget meeting and the afternoon at a values, vision and mission seminar. Tomorrow was her performance review with her manager, a pimply man fifteen years younger who she'd trained a decade ago. The spiky haired girl faced her and said, "Did you see yourself like this when you were my age?"

Wind pressed relentlessly from the west, snapping tops off waves, sapping the sun's heat, but clouds covered the horizon, growing as she watched, pushing a storm swell. Translucent gray-green ridges, rich with seaweed shadows and fantastic shapes swept towards shore, shattered against the rocks. She couldn't feel it yet in the guardrail, but when the tide rose, when the waves grew, they'd shake the tower.

Eight hours later, after the sun set, the wind's muted caterwaul echoed in the living quarters. Jamie sat on the bed, quilt wrapped around her shoulders, reading a book. This is what she missed in her old life, the unrestricted indulgence in her senses, in her imagination, in the world shuddering and alive around her. She tried, oh she had tried. Hiking when she could get away. Vacations. Meditation. Prayer. But people surrounded her. Certainly not all bad. Jamie volunteered at the soup kitchen. She joined charities where she found the selfless who devoted their lives to helping others. People who were spiritual and inspirational, but they didn't overwhelm the mundane work, the debts and taxes and indelicacies that came her way every day. The distractions and indiginities. She'd memorized Hamlet's "to be or not to be speech" because Shakespeare captured the essence.

A solid boom echoed from below. Jamie laughed, dropped her book, then ran down the spiral stairs barefoot, the metal cold and sharp. She carried a lamp because the ground floor had no electrical lights—they'd short out when the sea invaded. The top stair overlooked the trapdoor in the floor. Ten feet across. Water dampened the dark stone, and a sucking sound came from the trapdoor's circumference as the water retreated. A moment's pause, as the air reversed, whistling before a solid water column rushing upward. Then a whump she felt in her chest. Water sprayed from the trapdoor's edges. It leaked from the metal door that was her only exit. The ocean had come. If she loosened the trapdoor's bar, the water would slam into the ceiling in a powerful spout. It wasn't just the sea, though, trying to batter its way in. Denizens lived below, she was sure, which was the hope she couldn't share with her workers, with her neighbors, with the spiky-haired teenager who had no idea who Jamie was. Wonders and monsters lurked in the world, Jamie was sure. They lived in the blank spaces people ignored, in the terrain they could not tolerate, in severe weather. As sure as she was sure of anything, Jamie knew terror and beauty in the leviathan, in hidden nature, multiplied and made grand.

An inch of water caressed the floor like oil, then flowed back toward the trapdoor. The powerful entrance demand would come again. A "let me in" that could not be denied. Jamie didn't feel forty-nine while sitting on the stairs, shivering in the stone ocean cold broadcasting from the brick walls. Back she went, to when she was seven, laying in bed on a turbulent night, as tree shadows waved on the wall, where the open closet door hid horrors, when her hands and feet retreated under the cover, pulled tight in, like a child-sized armadillo, locking out the claws, teeth, tentacles and spines. Scary, yes, but also huge and glorious and limitless.

The sea, now, would be churning and wild. Jamie mounted the stairs toward the lantern room, like an acolyte or penitent, lamp in one hand. If she'd been the keeper a hundred years earlier, she would have spent the afternoon buffing the reflector, cleaning smoke residue from the lamp lens, trimming the wick, checking the whale oil or kerosene or carbide supply. She would have adjusted the vents to provide a steady draw for the flame, and wound the clockwork to rotate the beam through the night. Now, though, the lamp was electric. It still flashed forth as a beam, three quick rotations followed by three slow ones, the lighthouse's signature pattern, not only warning of the rocks, but also telling ships where they were. This was her first ocean storm, the reason Kingsmark Reef Lighthouse existed, a beacon sending light into the darkness, warning mariners of rocks that poked up like massive megalodon teeth waiting to rip the flimsy hulls asunder. She shielded her eyes. No rain in the storm yet, only wind. Jamie put a raincoat over her nightshirt. She needed more clothes, but she wanted to see, she needed to see what was out there.

The wind pulled the door hard against her grip, and now the full throated roar of the provoked ocean pummeled her, dampened her face and soaked her hair. The light swept by, throwing her shadow out to sea, then moving on like a vast, foggy sword. This wasn't a January storm, not the kind of waves that knocked down lighthouses or picked up rocks to throw through the lantern room, but it was her first one. The *Sister Hibiscus* sank during a September storm, maybe no worse than this one. There could be ghosts, she thought, and for a second she heard voices calling for help in the ocean's cacophony before losing them in the grinding clash between waves and reef. The mist dancing light stabbed toward the sea again.

She wasn't a middle-management drone, clinging to her desk and employees, serving her bosses' whims. Companies couldn't reach her here with targeted advertising, nor could politicians chart her leanings. Standing at the rail, she reveled in the cold baptism of salt spray, of the heady gusts that tugged at her coat. When the light went round again, two bright spots reflected back to her from far at sea, and by the next light, they were closer and larger and twice of a height of the lantern room. Jamie leaned toward the shape coming toward her, vast, cyclopean, leather-winged, a face filled with tentacles dipping from the clouds and then hidden within them, and then another behind it just as big, waves breaking harmlessly against them. The first one reached out; its hand grasped the lighthouse just below her feet, shaking the structure. Revealed in the light, its skin was obscenely lumpy, and then the lumps were not lumps, but clinging man-sized creatures, water and seaweed streaming from them. Hysterical with joy, Jamie remembered the inscription above the lighthouse door, "No one is so fierce that dare stir him up: who then is able to stand before me?" She'd thought it meant the sea.

I've seen the leviathan, she thought. I'm not that poor woman who'd sat in her apartment night after night, afraid that an empty wine class, a torn pay stub, a lifeless daily commute were all the world offered. She felt the ocean's cold in her feet, on her bare legs that seemed as solid now and as slick as marble. Ocean trickled on her face. She licked at its salt on her lips. If the tentacled creature looked down at her, even noticed her, she knew she would go mad—she was nearly mad now—but it would not be Jamie who would be lost. That sad person died long ago.

Its skin was so close, she could mount the rail, leap onto it, but the beings who already had attached themselves looked hungry. In the arcing brightness and acetylene shadows, they stared at her, ready to render her to her bones, and she felt kinship.

Then the hand moved on. The giant turned to walk along the shore. Light shone on it, slid away, and when the light returned, it revealed only an ocean at war with the wind and shore. The woman who had been Jamie laughed at the fullness of the world.

I am the keeper, she thought. I tend the light at night, and all beings who visit are welcome. I am ageless.

 *Plot is a metaphor. How you think about the metaphor determines what kind of stories you write. If you think of plot as war, you make stories with clearly identifiable opponents whose success requires their opponent to fail. Every James Bond film is based on this plot metaphor. But that's not the only way to go. A plot can be a journey. A plot can be a birth. A plot can be an awakening. For most of us, the story of our lives is not war. We don't have enemies to defeat, and no one is trying to crush us (and if that is the case, I'm sorry for you). This story is a birth. The character who says at the end, "I am ageless," is not the same one at the beginning who was just happy to get away from the city.*

Famous swords speckle history and literature. Excalibur is perhaps the most recognized. Other weapons have their background and legends too, like Balmung, which belonged to Siegfried, or Sikanda from The Never Ending Story *that would leap from it sheath when needed, or Graywand that Fafhrd wielded in Fritz Leiber's stories. Even little kids, playing in the back yard with anything long enough to serve as a sword know that when you give your weapon a name it is somehow cooler and more powerful.*

THE SWORD IMPERIAL

A S HE HAD FOR THE LAST YEAR, HNDRED CHOPPED WOOD and built fences and cleaned the stables for old Bakken the innskeeper for a month before he'd earned enough credit for one night in the The Broken Beast. He had left his field at sunset, walked an hour on the darkening road to the inn so that he could put in the work by moonlight or starlight. The month finished, Bakken, a short, burly figure whose dark, curly hair receded at his forehead, tallied Hndred's time, checking his figures twice, then said, "You have been helpful once again. My inn is open to you when you return. It's a good thing your appetite does not match your size, or two months labor wouldn't be enough to feed you."

The next day, Hndred laid out the guardsman tunic that had been his father's prize possession from his days when he was young, and the fine pants of brushed wool. He quit the field early, washed, dressed, his father's jacket tight across his shoulders—for the son had outgrown the father—and then set out for the Broken Beast, a hand barrow before him, filled with fresh produce for the inn's kitchen, and hiding a leather-wrapped parcel beneath. Hndred walked despite rumor of raiding parties from the north, the Bandihai, who waylaid travelers on the road. They had grown much worse of late, men who wore green leathers and carried double-edged knives and cruel curved swords. Hndred heard they'd sacked Tayfer on the Yent, a village a half-day's walk up the harbor road, where they'd emptied its treasury and burned down the mill.

Hndred arrived before the evening trade, took a stool and table near the fire, ate the dinner Bakken's kitchen had prepared, which, no matter what, tasted better than any meal Hndred prepared for himself. Tonight Bakken filled him with roasted hare, pepper seasoned and covered with savory gravy. Hndred mopped his plate clean with a hunk of rough bread, then ordered a mug of Bakken's mead. He drank slowly while waiting for the inn to fill.

The Broken Beast sat near the junction of three roads, one which led to the harbor on the distant sea, one from the forests and fields of the western plain, and the third, which was the long road that traders and travellers from the south used. They met at the Broken Beast and fed into the King's Road, a hard day's travel to King's Keep and the royal city. Wondrous wanderers came to the Broken Beast, nobles and merchants, mercenaries and knights errant. They took their meals and rest in Bakken's place, bringing tales of their journeys and tales of the heroic past. Hndred sat on his stool to listen, to ask questions when invited, to join in the singing when song broke out. But mostly Hndred thought about his secret parcel and wished to hear about swords.

Two years ago, a week after his father died, leaving him the farm, Hnrdred plowed the field, readying it for the spring planting. He plodded thoughtlessly behind the ox, holding the plow steady, stopping only to toss aside the rocks he turned up. Grief filled his head like a fog. Only Hndred and father survived the sickness in the winter that killed his mother, sister and two brothers. Now, Hndred was alone. The plow bumped over another obstruction. Hndred lay the plow down, dug out the rock half as big as his head, and cast it off the field. He didn't know it, but other farmers talked about him, about his size and strength. The rock flew much farther than anyone else could have flung it, if they would have attempted as unlikely a feat.

Why bother planting? he thought. If there is no rain, the crop will fail and I will die. If there is rain, insects could come and eat the grain before I harvest, and I will die. Or marauders might burn the fields, or a flood, or, worse, the crops might thrive, and I will gather them, live through the winter just so I can plant again in the next spring. He could see nothing in the future that wasn't gray and without hope.

The ox needed little direction. Dirt turned away from the plow, leaving the groove for him to plant, then it fetched against another rock, nearly tearing the handles from his hands. The ox stopped on its own. Hndred dropped to his knees and dug with his bare hands, but the obstruction was dirt-clotted cloth, not a stone, and much larger than a rock. He dug the shape free and laid it across his legs. It was long. Rotted leather strings held the package closed but broke when he tugged them. He unwrapped the heavy fabric, an oiled canvas. The top layers shredded under his hands, but the deeper ones were whole. Whatever was within had been well protected. Then the last layer fell away. Sun glinted off metal and multiplied into a thousand shards from the single jewel embedded in its hilt. Hndred looked upon it dumbly, and then drew the sword from its unmarred sheath. When he touched the blade, it hummed like a living thing. He took his hand back. The ox turned to look at him, as if he wondered why they were not continuing. Hndred had only plowed half the field so to his left the dirt was dark and fertile, ready for seed, and to the right the stubble covered land showed how much work was left. The field was quiet, but it had given up a secret. He touched the blade again. This time, it was cool and smooth, without imperfection, totally out of place. How was it possible that a sword was buried in his field?

*

A lone man came through the door first, a satchel slung over his shoulder, perhaps a messenger. Next, three soldiers. The two who held pikes looked no older than Hndred, but their captain, who wore a sword in a fine-tooled scabbard, carried himself like a man of many campaigns. Soldiers often told the best stories. Hndred saluted with his mug when they sat near him. Night had fallen without. A fire at each end of the hall and oil lamps hung from the rafters provided a smoky light. Four waiters served the tables, three women and a young man. The women attracted attention, but woe to the traveller who bothered them. The threat of banishment from the Broken Beast kept the servants safe.

"I defended the east gate during the Pretender's siege," said the captain. His companions leaned in. "Only two in my command beside myself had seen battle before that day. It was close work on the causeway. A knife served better than a sword. The Pretender brought three times our force to bear. I tell you, more than one of my men cried in their sleep after seeing their fires on the mountain the night before."

"Weren't you afraid?" asked one of the soldiers. "How could you stand against such a force?"

The captain took a long drink. "The King's Keep was built for defense, boy. I could hold the walls against an army with a handful of milkmaids and a dozen stable boys. The Pretender's head swung above the main gate the next day, ah, but there was labor befitting a soldier on the causeway. I got this there." He touched a thick red scar along his neck.

"One of the Pretender's followers? Did you kill him?"

The captain laughed. "Not so brave as that. This is from one of my green young men who swung an axe too wide."

Hndred couldn't restrain himself. "Does your sword have a lineage, sire? Is it storied?"

The captain turned to him. "Are you a historian, perhaps?" He laughed. "You look more like a farmer."

Hndred stood, embarrassed. "I didn't mean to offend." More than once he'd been rebuffed when he asked questions.

The captain leaned back in his chair. "A very big farmer. No, no offense. Ah, perhaps I am mistaken. Your coat is castle-cut—not a farmer—but I don't know you."

"You are right about my profession. The coat was my father's. He once served."

The captain nodded. "You are looking for a tale then, something to dream about as you toil among quiet grains and attentive livestock?"

His men laughed at that, but with good humor. Hndred thought that this would be an interesting night.

"I do like a fine story about swords when I hear it if you have one to share."

The captain drew his sword and placed it on the table. "Are you superstitious, farmer? Have you heard that a sword holds the soul of every man it kills? Do you know of the swords that betray their masters, breaking when most needed and proving faithless in the end?"

Hndred pulled his stool close. "I would listen to such stories."

"Would you be disappointed if I told you that a sword is just a tool, no more special than a hammer to a carpenter or a brush to a painter?"

Hndred sagged on the stool.

"I see you would." The captain twisted the hilt, flipping the blade over. "So I have two portraits for you. The first is about the sword as a common tool. Through much practice, a man can learn to use this tool to defend himself and to kill if needed. Wars are won by men who wield them well. Kingdoms are gained or lost when the metal sings, but the sword itself means much less than the man. Champions make stories with swords, not the other way around. But, there are rare swords, contrary tools that seem sometime bigger than the metal the smithy pounded them from. Give a man a choice of five swords that are the same, one will speak to him when he grasps it. One will leap out in battle faster than it should. It will not break when the club strikes it. It holds its edge. Such swords are passed on. They become legendary. They earn names."

"Can you tell me about such?" asked Hndred.

Men at nearby tables stopped their conversations. Soldiers told the best stories. The captain settled in and spoke.

The Bramble Knight fought in the mêlée at seven major festival, winning every battle and standing alone as the defeated tended their injuries and bandaged their pride. They say he fought like a coyote who baits a puppy into leaving the safety of its yard, only to carry the animal off for a meal. He retired before the onslaught, seeming to keep himself unscathed as much by accident as by plan. A practiced eye, though, saw that he never backed into a wall. His feet and wrist were a wonder.

He talked while he fought. "I'm sorry, sire," he'd say, "that I have not fallen yet. Your swordsmanship is a marvel. Oh, that was good. I don't know how I am so lucky."

And then his opponent would be on the ground, wondering how he got there, and he'd hear the Bramble Knight talking to someone else. "Please accept my apologies. I don't know how I was allowed in this year. I've been injured. See how my shoulder sags. Nice thrust, sire," and then the other man would suddenly be without his weapon and have to yield.

They say the Bramble Knight's sword glinted gold in the sun, that by torchlight it flamed red, and that when struck it rang like a bell.

So the Bramble Knight rose in the king's service and became the prince's personal guard. One day, when the young prince was hunting, assassins surrounded them in the wood, three seasoned killers who hoped to make short work of the prince and his single companion.

"We are no match for you," said the Bramble Knight. He had not even drawn his sword.

One man wielded an axe, another a spear, and the third a sword in one hand and a fisherman's hook in the other. Surely they planned an easy conquest.

The spearman thrust at the Bramble Knight whose sword had somehow cleared the scabbard, clipping the spear point and disappearing into the man's side. "I was only trying to scare him," the Bramble Knight said to the prince, who had drawn his own sword.

The other two moved to flank the Bramble Knight, ignoring the young prince. They were not careless or inexperienced. Like wolves, they knew how to kill. This was no joust, no polite melee with padded weapons and codes of behavior.

"Maybe we can talk," said the Bramble Knight. His sword pointed down as if he wasn't sure how to handle it. "You gentlemen can hardly be blamed for mistaking us for important people, but we can not be worth your trouble."

The axe man feinted as if to swing. The Bramble Knight flinched away. He appeared to stumble. The assassins grinned and moved as if on a signal.

Then the axe man staggered back, looking puzzled, a rose blossoming in his chest, and the other swordsman had lost a hand. He had no time to scream before the Bramble Knight pivoted and the blade blurred into a neck-high scythe.

The prince said later that the Bramble Knight's sword whispered when it dealt death. It slipped through enemies like a fish in a river. The knight held the sword in front of him, looking at it as if he'd not seen it before. No blood stained the metal. "We make a good couple, this blade and I."

So the sword became known as Bramble's Bride. When the Bramble Knight died in his old age many years later, the prince who had become king held a great tournament with Bramble's Bride as the trophy, and the sword has passed on the same ever since.

Hndred took the sword from the field, leaving the ox and plow unattended. No one saw him, but he held the treasure close. Any sword, the plainest of construction, was valuable at market, the making of them taking rare knowledge and skill. This weapon, though, looked to be worth a thousand such ordinary swords. In his low-roofed house, he grasped the hilt with both hands, pointing it in front of him. The tip vanished into sharpness. Touching its edge drew blood. He swung the blade in a wide arc. It was much lighter than it looked and didn't pull at his wrists. Hndred struck a pose like a knight he'd seen at a tournament, his hands close to his waist, the sword up and tilted so it passed the side of his face, then the farmer lunged forward with it. He stepped and swung as if defending an attack from behind. Hndred smelled the battlefield, the clash of arms, the screams of triumph and moans of the defeated. He saw himself, sword at his side, standing before the king and royal court, presented as a hero. The balladiers rushed to write songs about him. Reluctantly, he returned the sword to its sheath and put it under his mattress.

He might be a champion in his imagination, but the ox and field needed tending.

That night, though, by the cooking fire's low light, he brought the sword out again and watched the smoldering reflection in the metal. Once again, he heard horse's hooves thudding, the rip of banners in the wind, and the joy of battles unfought.

A wealthy trader bought the captain and his men a round. "For another story," he said.

The captain thanked the trader for the drink, and seeing that the crowd had turned their attention to him, sighed. "Facing a man with a sword is not so glorious as you seem to think." He caught Hndred's eye, as if he was for the moment addressing him only. "It is a fearsome weapon that leaves terrible wounds. A man can be split from crown to crotch. The blade makes a sound when it hits bone that you will not forget, and the vibration weds itself to a man's hands. I have felt a fighter's last second flee through my sword. The lost man never laughs again. He never raises his mug at an inn to spin a tale." The grizzled fighter lifted his mug to the men around him.

"So I'll tell you a story about the Ungallent, a sword that served no men but led to their ruin. The worst weapon in a kingdom facing defeat from an enemy who seemed unstoppable.

"It was not a pretty sword. No artist's attention went into its hilt, an unadorned, functional spot for a man to grasp, and it would look as any other sword, but the metal had taken a taint at the smithy, a blue-gray streak that ran partly down the blade. A squire, handing it up to his master on a platform died first. The knight claimed he never touched the weapon, that his unaneled squire held the naked blade above his head and then it slipped, while others said the knight brushed his fingers against the metal and drew back, as if the sword had warned him away. The squire, though, died instantly as the weapon's weight drove the point home."

"That was a stupid way to handle a sword," said one of the soldiers.

"Indeed," the captain agreed.

Hndred swallowed hard. Stories of the supernatural disturbed him. He'd spent too many nights in the dark of the family home, laying awake, wondering if he heard the murmur of his father in the wind outside.

"The knight threw the sword away, but a stable hand retrieved it. War went badly, and every weapon might be of use. A soldier, though, saw the stable boy with it on the street and took it from him, his own sword being bent and dull. The soldier bragged to his friends about his new sword. None of them knew that it had been discarded. During a drill, the soldier's training partner struck at his neck, a blow that soldiers block hundreds of times in practice, but the Ungallent caught on the soldier's leg leaving him open for a killing stroke.

"The blade passed from soldier to soldier, giving each one bad luck or maiming or killing him. Soon, all misfortune of any kind was blamed on the blade. Meanwhile, battles were lost. The opposing army marched into the kingdom's fields and burned them. The soldiers put the Ungallent in a closet to never be used, but stories, being what they are, go on and are told again and again. The king's grandmaster, commander of all the armies, came to the soldiers' quarters. An imposing man, a veteran of hundreds of campaigns, feted for his victories in his youth, but now a beaten general, he called the men to him. 'Let me see this sword, the one you call Ungallent. Bring it to me.'

"Reluctantly, they obeyed. Surely such a sword would not be the one to give the grandmaster when his hour was so dire. The sword lay on a table in the common room, while the man who brought it rubbed his hands hard against his pants, sorry that he'd touched the evil blade. The grandmaster called his servant to him who carried in a magnificent scabbard, the pinnacle of an artist's efforts, inlaid with gold and silver filigree. Gems glittered on it. Gold cords dangled. The soldiers' eyes grew wide. The wealth of a mighty house would be broken to pay for a scabbard such as this.

"The grandmaster held the Ungallent and inspected it. 'It is indeed an ordinary-looking article. This is the one of so many tragedies?'

"The soldiers nodded.

"Satisfied, the grandmaster put the Ungallent into the beautiful scabbard. Such a joining of the beautiful and demonic had never been seen before. Angels must have cried out as that marked blade slid into its holy home.

"The grandmaster instructed his servant. 'Take this as a present to the enemy's camp with this scroll. Tell him it is from the king, and that he asks mercy. The sword is our gift, a family heirloom passed from father to son through the generations. It is our dearest possession."

"On the battlefield the next day, the enemy's armies stood at the castle gates. The enemy king rode with his army on this last battle, intent on making the victory his. On his waist, the jeweled scabbard glittered and shone, a shining symbol of the castle's defeat. Surely the kingdom's ruin awaited, but the enemy king's horse shied when crossing the moat bridge, a horse that by all accounts had been the most steady of steeds. It shied, and the king fell into the water. The weight of his armor and his treacherous sword pulled him under. He could not be saved. During the loss and confusion, the castle guard rushed from within. The army without its king fled, and the grandmaster lead his troops in pursuit, slaughtering them who would not surrender and disarming the rest."

Hndred asked, "What became of the sword?"

The captain finished his mead. "I am dry after such a story." Someone hurried to replace it. After a long drink, he said, "The Ungallent was taken to sea and dropped in a deep place. You can be sure that no boat's crew was as nervous as the sailors who transported that cursed sword."

Bathed by the inn's firelight, the crowd facing him, the captain appeared to Hndred to be the sagest of men. He was one to be trusted, one who could lead men in battle, one whose wisdom penetrated the mysteries. Or it could be the mead had worked its way upon the young farmer's mind as is its wont to do, so that the most ordinary of women walked like princesses, the most dullard of men became savants, and inane pronouncements of the unlearned rang profound.

A trader from the south began a ballad, drawing attention away from the captain and his men, but Hndred had no interest in poetry tonight. He felt a kinship with the captain gained through the many evenings Hndred had spent practicing with the sword, mimicking knight's moves from tournaments. He imagined himself bringing enemies to their knees, presenting his sword to the king, taking a place in the king's guard as his father once had. His wrist, already grown strong through farm labor, no longer tired, no matter how long he swung the sword. The magnificent sword must have chosen him. No accident would bring such a boon.

So, with confidence in his heart, Hndred approached the captain as his men laughed at a ribald part of the trader's ballad.

"Captain, if I may, I need your opinion on a sword that I have found. No man other than myself has seen it since it came from my field. It had been buried." Even as the words left his lips, Hndred regretted speaking. What would he appear to be to a captain in the king's service other than an unschooled farmer? A fool. How could he dare bother a man who'd fought real battles, gave orders that were followed not because of his rank but because of the respect earned through real accomplishment. At best, the captain would dismiss him, maybe mock him before the crowd.

The captain gazed thoughtfully upon Hndred, his hands cupping his mug. "You ask about swords not from idle curiosity then?"

"My presumption, sir."

"Let's see this discovery of yours then. I have been sitting on this stool forever."

Hndred led the captain through the hall. Many tables were empty now. Only the carousers listening to stories remained at one end by the fire. Bakken's staff cleaned dishes and pots as the two men passed through the kitchen.

The captain liberated a lamp that cast a buttery light at their feet. Outside, the warm and windless evening welcomed them with silence. Hndred uncovered the long shape in his barrow, then carefully undid the cloth he'd used as a shroud until the scabbarded blade lay revealed. Lamplight caught the jewel set in the hilt, and in the softer light, the metal shifted from well-polished bronze to silver and back.

The captain sucked in a breath, ran his hand down the unadorned sheath. "May I draw the sword, boy?" He sounded reverent.

The captain paused before touching the hilt. "My hands are unclean. If this is truly a great sword, I hope it forgives me."

The sword revealed itself in a smooth motion, then the captain held the lamp close to inspect it. Hndred wished he'd kept the prize hidden. No farmer deserved to own a weapon such as this. Only a great fighter or the most noble of knights could be worthy. The captain would take it from him.

"You say that it was wrapped in oilcloth and buried in your field?"

Hndred nodded.

The captain turned the blade over in his hand, thoughtfully. "So it must have been stolen and then hidden; or perhaps someone pursued, knowing he could not save it, used your field to keep it from passing into bad hands. I know many stories about swords, including ones that were lost or secreted, but I don't know of this one." He swung the sword once, sheathed it, and handed it to Hndred. "Swords seek their owners, though. I know that. There must be a powerful reason it made its way to your field and that you found it. Whoever the smith was who formed that sword was a master, but it's not a battle blade. The jewel in the hilt speaks to ceremony or a gift. No nicks, no wear, I doubt your sword has seen true use."

Hndred held the sword's weight in his hands. He had fought a hundred battles with it in his mind. As he fell asleep, he heard the sharp metal slice the air. Dust from men's feet pounding the tourney grounds filled his nose. He had wondered if the dreams were really the sword's memories relived within him. In the dreams, he saw a familiar hand holding the hilt, a familiar arm flexing and bulging and wielding the sword with glorious skill. "A champion owned the sword, I know."

The captain opened his mouth to speak, then cocked his head.

In the distance, horse hooves thudded against the road.

"Strange that a party would ride so late," said Hndred.

The horses stopped at the inn. Hndred started toward the building's corner to see who they were. The captain held him back.

Shouts came from inside. Metal clashed on metal. A man cried out. Two cooks burst through the back door. "Bandihai!" one shouted as he fled into the dark.

Hndred would have rushed into the inn, the beautiful sword in hand, but the captain, whose own weapon now caught the lamp light, said, "There will be too many of them. Only my soldiers and myself are trained to fight, and I will bet my men had no time to arm themselves. The Bandihai are robbers and cowards. They will take our valuables, and, if the mood strikes them, kill some or all. If the women did not escape, they will suffer their own fates, and the Bandihai may burn the inn. We have one play, if you are willing to take part, farmer."

He explained his plan to Hndred.

The captain stepped into the smoky dining hall. Hndred stayed back, in the shadows. Against the far wall, the merchants and tradesmen stood, facing a half-dozen leather-clad Bandihai whose curved swords threatened them. On the floor, clutching his bleeding arm, a soldier glared defiantly.

The Bandihai leader, a tall man whose blond hair caught the ceiling light, gave orders. "Your money purses into the bag, and do it smartly. I'd rather not search for them among your corpses."

Kicking plates to the floor, the captain mounted a table. The Bandihai and their leader turned to face the intrusion.

"You have made a mistake coming here," announced the captain. "It is time for you to leave."

The leader, whose scarred face showed he'd survived many encounters, laughed. "You are bold to face us, old man, but you must see how you are outnumbered. Only this boy soldier among your friends attempted to fight, and look at the wound he suffered. So be quick about it and join the rest. We'll liberate you of your coin, and if you're lucky, we'll spare you despite your impertinence."

"You may try," said the captain, "but I do not think you want to fight. You shall surrender immediately."

The Bandihai leader laughed even harder until his face turned dark with it. When he regained his breath, he gestured to two of his men. "Kill him now."

The captain put up his hand. "Fighting me would be a mistake."

"Why?" said the leader, profoundly amused.

"You do not think I have been a warrior for so long and grown this old by accident, do you? If so, send your men, but you misunderstand my mission."

The leader raised a hand to hold his men back. "What is your mission?"

"I am an old campaigner as you have pointed out," said the captain. "I led men at Torshein Gap against the Lendilian horde until we prevailed when nine out every ten of our troops fell. I protected the infant king at the liege lord's court against his treacherous cabinet. I have trained with tournament victors and been victorious myself, but now I fulfill my greatest calling. If you value your life, you will not ask me to reveal it. Put down your arms. Save yourselves while you can."

The Bandihai leader did not appear nervous. "I will risk it. What is your calling, old man?"

The captain gave Hndred the signal behind his back. Hndred walked into the light, his treasure revealed. Polished as a mirror, the blade gathered the room's light, and quivered in Hndred's grip. He moved aside a heavy table with one hand and stood still while the captain spoke.

"I am now foot servant to the champion of the Sword Imperial, bane of a thousand armies, protector of the great kingdom, the blade that was never forged but has been forever and will forever be. The bearer of the sword, my master, can not be defeated."

The leader of the Bandihai looked up at Hndred who stared

back. The captain's directions had been clear: "Look him in the eyes. Do not waver. Consider him as you would a pig before slaughter, and when the moment is ripe, step toward him boldly."

Hndred had said as they stood behind the inn. "What if I am not brave?"

"When you heard the Bandihai attack, you ran toward the noise. Your instinct is to fight. I believe you would make your father whose jacket you wear proud." He reached up to clap Hndred upon the shoulder. "Plus, you hold a sword like they have never seen."

The Bandihai leader did not move, but Hndred imagined what he must see: the captain, standing aside for a giant bearing a sword that was brighter than any of legend. As the captain said, it was the Sword Imperial.

For the moment, Hndred felt like a myth made real. It was the sword, of course, the pull of it in his hand, like an extension of his arm, glowing and warm. Hndred had said, "But what if they attack? I have no training."

"You are the biggest man I have ever met, which means you have the longest reach. Fell them like trees. No style needed for that, and if they attack, you will be fighting for your life anyway."

Hndred believed he had become a man whose enemies would melt before him. It must have shown on his face, in the strength of his arm. A tableau of frozen expressions stared at him, the Bandihai and their leader, the merchants and tradesman, the wounded soldier on the floor. Standing as he was, one arrayed against the many, put him in the hero's place. If men were to write songs, they might remember the night that Hndred bore the Sword Imperial.

The Bandihai leader blinked. Hndred stepped forward. The men with their curved swords broke for the door, tripping over each other in their rush to exit. The leader retreated a step, glanced back at his fleeing men, then turned and rushed after them.

For a moment, glory filled the farmer like heady drink. Hoofbeats echoed on the highway. Then the men crowded round him, cheering and yelling like boys.

*

Later, the captain talked to Hndred in front of the inn. His men busied themselves in the stable, packing their horses.

"For a moment, I was convinced you were the champion I said you were. You didn't hold the weapon like a farmer, nor did you appear frightened."

Hndred didn't know what to say.

"You could come with us," said the captain. "A soldier's life is hard, but it has its advantages. It is not a choice to make quickly, though. You will need training, and many start much younger than you. Still, think about it. We will come this way again in a week. Tell me your answer then."

The captain's men brought the horses around the inn, both dressed for the road. "All is ready, sir," said the wounded one, his bandaged arm secured to his chest. Soon, the three were mounted.

"Our duties call," said the captain.

They trotted in the direction the Bandihai had fled.

Hndred watched until they were out of sight. Before their dust had settled, he knew he didn't need a week. Nothing he'd left at the farm seemed important. His oxen could fend for itself. Perhaps his neighbors would plant the fields. It did not matter.

The young man took the package from his barrow, unwrapped it and strapped the Sword Imperial to his back. Was the blade a legend or not? Was he the kind of man who they'd make songs about? Hndred didn't know, but if he started walking now, he could catch up to the captain and his men where they made camp.

His legs were long, his stride mighty, and he bet they'd find for him a place by the fire.

Messing with time can be a great deal of fun for the writer, but it can be a morass for the reader if it's not handled well. In "The Sword Imperial" the captain breaks Hndred's narrative with his stories of other famous swords. For the interruptions to work, they have to add to Hndred's story in some way and build suspense. I wish I could tell you what the formula is for how long a break from the story's timeline you can take before the reader gets lost. There isn't one. All you can do is make sure there's a logical reason for going away from the story, that the stuff you tell the reader when you aren't telling the main story is worth reading, and that the breaks create a stronger story than if they didn't happen.

AFTERWORD

O N MARCH 3, 2015, I DECIDED TO TAKE UP RAY Brad-bury's challenge to young writers to write a story for a week for a year. He said that you couldn't possibly write 52 bad stories in a row. I wasn't a "young" writer at that point. My first story sale came twenty-five years earlier, and I've been writing and sell-ing stories steadily since. Writing, however, is not an activity where you can say, "I've arrived." My friend, the prolific Jay Lake, said that a writer's career consists of trading up for a better set of problems. At first, you're happy that you finished a story. Then, you get up the nerve to submit it to a market. Maybe the next milestone is a per-sonal rejection. Finally, the first story sale. You've arrived: you're a published author. But it doesn't take long before you want to sell to better markets or sell more often or be nominated for awards, and even win awards. It doesn't matter where you are in your writing career. There's always something more that you want; there's always something that leaves you dissatisfied.

That same dynamic works on how well you write. Writing is (or ought to be) a continuous growth pursuit. That's why I took on the Bradbury challenge. The stories in this collection came out of my year of writing a story a week. I learned a lot about myself, about crafting sentences, and the act of creativity. Most weeks I finished the first draft on Sunday. When Monday came, I had to come up with something new. Almost every story started feeling small, stupid or insignificant. Even the ones that didn't feel that way were simple, single-noted or slight. However, after two or three days, my interest in the story grew. What seemed trivial at the beginning took on more significance. Through working on the story, my engagement with the story increased. By the end of the week, I sometimes found I'd tied myself into a much larger and layered story than I thought when I began. A couple times the story turned out to be more than a one-week effort. I learned to trust that the story would become more interesting than it started. No matter what I thought at the beginning, the story would deepen. Here's a way to try this on your own: use a writing prompt from someone else. All you have then is the merest kernel, but you still grow a story.

I've come to believe that writing is an almost entirely self-taught endeavor. That sounds funny coming from someone who has taught writing for years, but I think it's true. There are plenty of books and teachers and articles and workshops where you can learn, but you as an individual will never know what you'll get from them. The real learning comes from sitting down and trying to write your stories. That's why I tackled the 52-story challenge. Even though I've been writing for a long time, I have plenty to learn. That's why I think writing is so exciting. I hope that if you are reading this as someone who writes or would like to write that you find the journey you are on to improve yourself to be equally exciting.

If you are reading this as a writing teacher, I don't mean to discourage you by saying all writers are self-taught. Of course the teachers make a difference. Sadly enough, though, we can never tell what that difference is. Whatever you say to your students in the classroom will affect them unevenly if at all. Some of what you say will impact them tangentially. Some they push away from. And some will soak in like osmosis and never be a part of their conscious thought but still will make a change. That's why I teach. I have no idea what I'm saying that adds to my students' knowledge, but I'm confident that some of it works some of the time for some of my students. That's much, much better than nothing.

Because I often think about teachers, I've created a resource for educators who might like to teach any of these stories. If you point your browser at jamesvanpelt.com, then click on "The Experience Arcade," you'll find suggestions and resources for presenting the stories to literature or writing students. I welcome feedback and sharing, so I hope the site will be a place filled with discussion and anecdotes about your students and their time with these pieces.

ABOUT THE AUTHOR

James Van Pelt, a high school English
teacher, is also a full-time science fiction,
fantasy and horror writer (among other
things). His short stories have appeared
in numerous magazines and anthologies,
including *Asimov's, Analog, Talebones, Realms
of Fantasy, Weird Tales* and others. His books
include five short story collections—*Strangers
and Beggars, The Last of the O-Forms, The Radio*

Magician, Flying in the Heart of the Lafayette Escadrille, and *The
Experience Arcade*—and two novels, *Summer of the Apocalypse* and
Pandora's Gun.

He has been a Nebula finalist, a John W. Campbell Award
finalist, and has been nominated for Pushcart prizes. His first
collection was named a Best Book for Young Adults by the
American Library Association, and his last collection won the
Colorado Book Award. Many of his short stories have appeared in
various Year's Best collections.

PUBLICATION CREDITS

"In Memoriam" originally appeared in *Abyss & Apex*, 2016 | "The Continuing Saga of Tom Corbett: Space Cadet" originally appeared in *Analog*, 2016 | "The Lawn Fairy War" originally appeared in *Metaphysical Circus: Love and War in the Slipstream*, 2016 | "Experience Arcade" originally appeared in *Daily Science Fiction*, 2015 | "Death of a Starship Poet" originally appeared in *Analog*, 2016 | "Ghost Ship" originally appeared in *Worlds of Science Fiction, Fantasy and Horror*, 2015 | "Mars, Aphids, and Your Cheating Heart" originally appeared in *Interzone*, 2016 | "Three Paintings" originally appeared in *Asimov's*, 2016 | "We Have Always Lived in the Hamlet" originally appeared in *Lightships and Sabers*, 2016 | "ProLong" originally appeared in *Perihelion*, 2017 | "Orphaned" originally appeared in *Orson Scott Card's Intergalactic Medicine Show*, 2016 | "The Lies" originally appeared in *Daily Science Fiction*, 2016 | "Falling Out of Downey" originally appeared in *Grand Valley Magazine*, 2016 | "Apprentice" originally appeared in *Fantasy Scroll Magazine*, 2016 | "Titan Descansos" originally appeared in *Alien Artifacts*, 2016 | "The Children's Collection" originally appeared in *Tales from the Miskatonic Library*, 2017 | "Writing Advice" originally appeared in *Daily Science Fiction*, 2016 | "The Golden Daffodils" originally appeared in *Abyss & Apex*, 2017 | "The Silk Silvered Skulls of Millen Mir" originally appeared in *Triangulation: Beneath the Surface*, 2016 | "Weaponized Ghosts of the 96th Infantry" originally appeared in *Daily Science Fiction*, 2016 | "Maybe if One Person Less" originally appeared in *Daily Science Fiction*, 2016 | "Housekeeping" originally appeared in *Enter the Apocalypse*, 2016 | "No One is So Fierce" originally appeared in *Worlds of Science Fiction, Fantasy and Horror*, 2016 | "The Sword Imperial" originally appeared in *Sword and Sorcery Magazine*, 2017

OTHER TITLES FROM FAIRWOOD PRESS

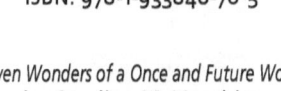

www.ingramcontent.com/pod-product-compliance
Lightning Source LLC
Chambersburg PA
CBHW060611030726
47498CB00005B/1629